THE ORACLE *of* MARACOOR

THE ORACLE *of*
MARACOOR

A Novel

GREGORY
MAGUIRE

WILLIAM MORROW
An Imprint of HarperCollins*Publishers*

HarperCollins books may be purchased for educational, business, or sales promotional use. For information, please email the Special Markets Department at SPsales@harpercollins.com.

FIRST EDITION

Designed by Bonni Leon-Berman
Illustrations by Scott McKowen

Library of Congress Cataloging-in-Publication Data has been applied for.

ISBN 978-0-06-309401-7

22 23 24 25 26 LSC 10 9 8 7 6 5 4 3 2 1

For Patricia McMahon and Joseph McCarthy

Castle remembered how . . . he had asked his father whether there were really fairies. . . . His father had been a sentimental man; he wished to reassure his small son at any cost that living was worthwhile. It would have been unfair to accuse him of dishonesty: a fairy, he might well have argued, was a symbol which represented something which was at least approximately true. There were still fathers around even today who told their children that God existed.

—Graham Greene, *The Human Factor*

"Have you ever known a magician, Uncle Stephen?"

"I have known people—unpleasant people—
who tried experiments in magic."

. . . "Did you help them—in the experiments?"

"Yes."

"And were they unpleasant too?"

"Not at the beginning—only foolish; but in the end—yes."

—Forrest Reid, *Uncle Stephen*

Rain, Rain, go away.

Come again another day.

—trad.

CONTENTS

PART·ONE

A STORY IS A ROOM

1

Sidestep the hangman's noose, don't show up for your own execution, and where has it got you?

A hurtling between warehouses. Alleys overhung with laundry heavied by sudden rain. Stink of tannery—ammonia and piss. Goat blood leaching from some dodgy abattoir.

Yet turn a corner: the wind off the harbor, the freshness of sea-salted air. Now the sun of late afternoon, look at it. Casual as a holiday. Stems of ivory glass tilting among thunderheads.

Troubled weather benefits the jailbreak. Ambition in every thudded footprint. A cramp in the calf, a barked shin. Go go go.

The clockwork of organic life all but seizes up with greed. Biology may be little more than a fuel grab, but hold your heart, what biology dares to make of such a hoist.

Sidle. Dart. Stop drop-dead still—a marble bust in a niche doesn't do it better. Breathe out. Breathe in. Naked, unapologetic rapture at the whole setup.

Though a busybody god murmurs, *Well done; come home,* the world sometimes replies, *not so fast.*

2

The skies over Maracoor Crown echoing with populations of the alarmed. Pigeons, rattled mourning doves, gusts of grasshoppers. Armies on the approach unsettle an entire city.

Some denizens of Maracoor Crown had caught sight of winged monkeys upon the roofs of municipal offices. A few crones swore they could pick up on the nervous energy of a flying horse nearby. Couldn't you just about smell it?

Hush, you, elder-crank, you're putting sweet vapors in our children's minds, who must keep up, must build the barricade, have to collect stones for the catapult. The Skedian army is nearly upon us. If you can't help, shut up and sit down. No, over there. Out of the way.

3

The two prison escapees needed crowds. Comes a mêlée, comes opportunity.

Cossy, a scrappy kid about ten years old. Dashing ahead. Followed by a figure in her late teens, an adult by comparison to Cossy but truly only a girl herself—if well traveled for her years.

Lucky, that the impending assault on the capital distracted its citizens from flinching at the sight of a girl with green skin in their midst. She could slip by in the frenzy. A girl, a young woman, a figure with childhood still itchy in her limbs but a rich, adult sorrow on her brow.

Her name was Rain. If no one in Maracoor knew her, so what; she hardly knew herself. Having survived a plunge into the sea from a great height, she'd awakened to a life only partly remembered— a faded etching glimpsed through a cloudy broth. Moods and inclinations. Memory loss—amnesia, they called it. The old person's ailment in a girl with fresh breath still. Here and there she clutched a scrap of her life with a name attached, but nothing distinct.

She had words for solid things—she knew a spoon from a stone, a duck from a donkey. She could speak and even argue. If her friend Iskinaary told her something about the past, she could remember it the next day. And the next. But she couldn't yet go back into her closed mind of her own accord. Her past seemed a padlocked box hidden in a black velvet sack—she could imagine putting her hands inside the sack and trying to work open the lock by mere feel—but she had no skill at this yet. At least she could remember what a velvet sack *was*. But so much of her brief life remained sealed in darkness. She was merely a creature running for her life.

With Rain, and the young Cossy, flapped the brown-grey Goose called Iskinaary. Also four flying monkeys who had flown in across the eastern ocean from some unknown why-hello-there place called Oz.

They were fleeing, these two female humans. Fleeing jail (the child) and probably worse than that (the older girl). Final details of their crimes and sentences hadn't yet been established by the court. In its brazen manner, however, fate had afforded the convicts an escape route by way of a wind-snapped tree trunk. Guards otherwise occupied. Neither Rain nor Cossy had asked permission to skive off. Something in the world wanted them to survive a little while longer.

Watch out. Here comes the rain again. A burst at first, enough to darken stone walls. A perfume of damp—that arresting trick, how dirt can seem full of potential when newly wet. The cobbles slickened. The Goose and the flying monkeys lifted aloft a few feet at a time, but thumped to earth, to keep close to the girls.

"Should we hide someplace till the hunt for us dies down?" asked Cossy.

"Don't be self-important. No one's looking for *you* yet," huffed the Goose. "This city's got other menace on its mind. According to our simian friends, who've been circling the skies searching for Rain, an army's advancing from the south. No, if we're going to skedaddle before the city buttons up entirely, we have to hurry. We'll head west, or north."

"Won't that take us through the city centre?" asked Rain.

"No time to be timid. We'll snatch a shawl from somewhere and you can pull it over your face. Find something, Tiotro, if you can?"

Tiotro seemed the most reliable of the flying monkeys. Diving under a spice merchant's awning, he returned trailing a length of burlap. Rain twisted it around her head—it smelled of cumin and kumquat—riding it low upon her forehead and draping it above her nostrils. It would have to do.

So she could remember *disguise*. Another tiny thrill, to realize this. But every new clarity seemed packed with potential for harm. What is disguise when it is used against you—when your mind is disguising you from yourself?

They were moving all the while, in patches of downpour followed by spells of wet rainless wind.

"No point in trying to go by sea?" asked Rain.

"No pleasure excursions heading out today. Check for yourself—we're right here."

Sure enough, clearing the warrens of light industry, they'd arrived at the harborside. To their left, the palisades of legislative and orthodox Maracoor Crown. Marble columns streaked with cloudburst, pox on copper domes. To their right, the black waters of Maracoor Harbor, where the few vessels that had weathered the naval invasion some weeks earlier were trying, and failing, to string themselves into a cordon.

The waterfront desolate but for seagulls and blown trash. Then Rain said, "Cossy . . . Cossy."

Cossy looked where Rain was pointing.

Huddled on the quay, in a bit of a dilemma—the four stranded brides of Maracoor Spot. Cossy's only people. Until her arrest for murder the girl had been one of that rare sect: the brides of Maracoor. But no ship strained at tie-up, ready to carry the brides back to their island cloister. In their clutched veils and wind-snapped skirts they looked a study of bleak expectation. They didn't see their former companion. Their eyes trained seaward.

"Cossy," hissed Rain again, and grabbed her by the shoulder.

"Cossy. There they are. This is your chance to rejoin your life with theirs, if you want. You may never get this moment again. They came here to be your family, after all."

Cossy paused. She glanced at them. "I hate all of them. Are you trying to dump me already?"

Rain grabbed the child's hand and squeezed it. "Don't be a fool. I just don't want you to tell yourself later that you were kidnapped. Leave or stay, it's your decision. I won't stop you. But these brides can take proper care of you. They know you."

"Am I better off with you?" said Cossy, as if asking herself. Then she shrugged and turned her shoulder on her past, turned toward the thoroughfare opposite the corniche. Between slatternly, cross-eyed sphinxes it advanced past a palace, perhaps the home roost of that avatar of the Great Mara, the Bvasil of Maracoor himself.

"Are you sure, Cossy?" But Rain guessed that no child at ten could see how today's decision determined tomorrow's sorrow. Could she have been any wiser at Cossy's age? Velvet sack blackout again: she didn't remember.

Cossy said nothing more. The small group—the green teen-ager, the ten-year-old girl, the Goose, the winged monkeys—made a run for it. The wind and rain came about again, this time from the east, across the harbor. The fugitives ducked their heads. They didn't turn to catch a last glimpse of the four brides of Maracoor waiting quayside for some rescue that might never arrive.

4

I n the streets beyond the palace, oh, such panic. Soldiers in incomplete uniform clattered by with their spears. Pedestrians flattened themselves against shop fronts, hoping not to be run through. The hammering of shutters over windows, the boarding up of doorways.

The human mess of it all. Couples, families. Packs of youths screaming with laughter. Merchants with heaps of wares, artisans spilling from their guildhalls. A few single women trying to look less ravishing than their profession ordinarily called for. The hubbub of a market day, a festival day, thought Rain. But the tone was wrong.

The crowd had to be straining toward the nearest gate for escape. The fugitives joined them, funneling onto a stone bridge spanning a canal cut between close-set buildings. The girls and the monkeys and the Goose were stuck, as a pinch-point between buildings at the far end slowed everyone's passage.

"Lookit." Cossy pointed upstream. Another bridge. A sound of brass and drum over there had cleared the way. Marching six feet apart, men in sharp uniform hoisted aloft a long canopy of saffron-colored fabric. Underneath it, at the bridge's arch, a quartet of lackeys labored with the handrails of a gilded palanquin.

"The Bvasil!" cried people from every side. "Hail the Bvasil of Maracoor!"

"He's fleeing too, the bastard," muttered some smart-mouth kid.

"We'll be lucky to get through," said Rain. "Everyone's got the same idea."

The Goose flapped his wings. "I should peel off. Likewise, these monkeys. They won't be allowed just to slip by. They'll be thought enemy agents. Or anyway, bad omens. We'll wing it. But how to get you two out?"

Debouching into a plaza, they came upon the western gates. Stout wooden wings, bound with iron, looming but still ajar. Soldiers in cuirasses and greaves were allowing certain groups and individuals through. Women and children, the elderly. No single men. The throng quieted, cowed by the military protocols. The selection seemed arbitrary—mere chance whether you would be deemed old, or young, or infirm, or female enough to get an exit visa.

The Goose said, "Someone might recognize you. You don't exactly disappear into a crowd, not with your, um, complexion of pale avocado."

"We'll try," replied Rain. "Cossy, you up for whatever happens?"

"Anything's better than prison." The girl looked sideways at Rain. A snarl of contradictions, this child Cossy. Sullen. Not trustworthy. But who was trustworthy these days? "I don't care, whatever," said the girl. "Suit yourself."

"Okay," said Iskinaary. "We'll perch on the city wall over that way and keep guard. If the Bvasil's minions try to arrest you, we'll dive into their faces, and you make a dash for it. Again. After that, we improvise. Let's go."

Without a *goodbye, good-luck, it's been swell,* the Goose and the winged monkeys diverted into a side street and took off in the air.

As the crowd began to murmur, heads swiveled in the opposite direction. Along a parapet at the top of a slight hill—some pleasure garden up there, or memorial grove—the saffron serpent on its tilting verticals came into view again. "What *is* that all about?" asked Cossy.

"The Bvasil himself in his veiled sedan chair. No one else merits such magnificence," said a straw-hatted farmer standing a few feet away. His tone might have been ironic; Rain couldn't tell. "The Great Mara showing his solidarity with his panicked subjects." He ran his fingers through the ends of his lank, shoulder-length grey hair and whistled some uncertain editorial opinion.

Rain pulled the sackcloth even lower on her forehead, the way she'd seen the brides of Maracoor wearing theirs. What showed of her green nose and cheeks—and hands—would give her away if anyone were looking for her. But her face was in shadow and she could tuck her hands under the yardage. "You'll have to hold on to my skirt as if you're scared," she murmured to Cossy. "Can you do the talking? If anyone asks, you're my sister. I'll play mute—my accent might be suspicious. We're going to Auntie's house in the hills. You don't know any more because you've never been there before, and I can't speak. Ready?"

"I'll do you one better than that," said the farmer, who'd begun to inch along beside them. "I've been watching the guards. You'll increase your chances of slipping through if you're pregnant. Here, can you rearrange that shawl to take a parcel underneath it? My satchel can play the part of an infant in your belly. The soldiers respect motherhood more than anything. Happy to oblige."

A middle-aged man by the sound of his voice, in a pair of rural trousers. His straw hat sloped unraveling latticework over his eyes. He addressed a younger companion at his side. "Tycheron, this is perfect. We'll be a family unit. I'll be the papa, you my son, and these two can be your wife and her little sister. You, you young newlywed, here's your first baby on its way. Hold still."

"I don't want a baby," protested Rain.

"That's what all women say till they have one," said the farmer. His companion, rabbity with alertness, pushed Rain into a recessed doorway. Rain didn't dare start screaming or she'd just draw attention to herself. "You're taking liberties, fellows," she said in a low, throttled voice as the older man reached under her shawl to tie a leather keep-sack around her waist. When he'd pulled the cords tight, he shifted the sack from her strong hip to her front. It pulled her down, the weight of it; it made her months pregnant in one go.

"Train your fingers on the hems of your cloth to keep the veil closed," he said. "You're a natural. So you're mute: that's good. Tycheron, this is your wife. You can call her Pet."

"No, he can't," said Rain.

"It's a charade. Act the part, Pet. As if you're in the troupe of players that annually mounts the mystery cycle in the cypress grove. Easy and slow. Your role will be over when we get through the gate. We're helping you, honey, and your little sister. Let her carry the broom—you're playing beleaguered, remember? Be reticent. Be mute. What could be easier."

"Rain?" said Cossy warningly.

"Not yet," said the older man, glancing skyward. "It'll pour again before long but let's push through while they're still letting people leave." He spied a bucket of sand and ash for putting out street fires. He scooped up a handful. "Tycheron, your outfit needs the soil of honest labor. There, that's more convincing." He smeared grit on his own elbows and knees. Glancing at Rain and Cossy, he said, "You've already got this look mastered, I see. Let's go."

There was nothing for it but to join the throng. They waited in turn, jostling elbows. "Tycheron," practiced Cossy. "Tycheron. What's your name, you other guy?"

"Uncle will do for you," said the bossy man.

The weight of the satchel dragged Rain's belly toward the pavement. It wasn't hard to act ungainly. "Are you smuggling gold bullion out of the capital?" she murmured. "What have you got in here?"

"Your future, so shut up. If you can't manage your own infant, think of it as a sack of pomegranates—the richest pomegranates in the country. What's our future without eating, what's our regional cuisine without pomegranates? Here we go."

They'd been absorbed into the last bunch to be interviewed and were summoned forward. It was nearly too late. Even now the home guard was angling the western gates to close them, readying the crossbeams for sliding into place.

"Who are you and why are you leaving?" asked a man with eyebrows like carded wool.

"I'm an old fool," garbled the straw-hatted mastermind of this pantomime. "I live at the mercy of my son Tycheron. We're rushing his young sister-in-law and his wife to safety before her time comes. She's with child. As you see."

Under her shawl Rain's hands cradled the sack, which was starting to slip. It would be shame to give birth to a scatter of overweight pomegranates right here in the public square.

"Tycheron and father," said the guardsman to an assistant making notes. "And wife. Who are you, ma'am?"

"We call her Pet," said the older man. "She was born with a weak tongue and she can't complain. Can you, Pet? Sweet Pet."

"What's *her* name?" demanded the guardsman, pointing at the child.

"I'm nobody," said Cossy. "Nobody calls me nothing. She's Pet, I'm wild."

"All right then. The family Tycheron. And rural patriarch. You're awfully hale to be fleeing for your life, young Kerr." He was addressing the slighter fellow.

"I'll settle them safely and come back."

The guardsman snorted. "Oh, sure. Sure you will. What house are you from?"

Tycheron sniffed. "We're hill people. We don't count ourselves as houses, but as laborers. I'm a miller and this is the miller's family. That's it."

"Awfully clean hands for a miller," said the guardsman, looking over Rain's shoulder to see who was next.

"Shows what you know. A *successful* miller," said Tycheron, growing into his role, "is one who can hire other laborers to do the heavy work."

"I should impound you for insolence, but a newborn benefits from a father, however cocky. Anyway, we're out of time. Get through fast, there's the gates rolling forward. Back, you lot, we're done here!"

The old man and Tycheron, and Rain and Cossy too, lurched forward. Rain's artificial pregnancy slowed her progress—what a bitch, this heavyweight. The older man's grandfatherly gimp, patently false. But the quality of their performance didn't matter now. The crowd of twenty or so remaining citizens behind them broke through the ranks of soldiers and swarmed out the closing gate, hurrying the band of four along with them.

5

Rain felt that the Goose, who'd been at her side since she'd awakened from her coma, was still nearby. She turned and looked. Yes, as he'd promised. He was strutting the top of the city walls to the south, keeping an eye on her. The flying monkeys must have found someplace less public to take cover.

That the Goose was attentive to her, when she couldn't quite say who she was—there was something sweet about it. The Goose knew the trajectory of her life better than she did. She hadn't wanted to interview Iskinaary for her own past for fear she would buy wholesale his interpretation of her experiences. She wanted to discover what she could about herself, to weigh it on her own scales, with her own calipers and loupe to address its substance, however mealy or corrupt.

Still—whatever might a Goose remember about the past? Was it any more reliable than what an addle-pated teenage girl could manage? Perhaps, more than his human companions, he lived in the here and now of the natural world, and less in his head.

Anyway, who could ever know what to anticipate? A matter curious to a girl bereft of the benefit of hindsight.

Iskinaary, after all, had been born a sentient and articulate Goose—not a goose. One of the fragments of Rain's secret childhood she did recall was this: Murthy, some fragrant governess at Mockbeggar Hall, explaining it to her. "The difference in pronunciation, Rainary, is simply a matter of emphasis. 'Look, Mama, what is that bird? Can it talk?' 'Oh, yes, my dear, it can; I believe that's not a goose, darling, but a *Goose*.' Watch me. The eyebrows lift, the chin inches forward; the speaking Animal is indicated by gesture and inflection in human speech. Rain, are you listening? You'll grow up quite the fool if you're not alert."

Any Goose with language must be able to make predictions. Of the flying monkeys, though, it was harder for Rain to say. These monkeys, and all their kin, were a downstream generation of what had amounted to genetic engineering by Rain's grandmother, the famous Wicked Witch of the West. Elphaba herself. If only a so-so magician, she'd been a more competent biologist, botanist, and expert in the Life sciences. That's Life, not just life.

Rain remembered hearing that it had been Elphaba who'd conjured up the wings on the first flying monkey—her aide-de-mischief, Chistery—and on his kin. Likely she'd been the only sorceress ever to teach a creature born animal to talk as an Animal. But the acquisition of language hadn't evenly vested. Downstream generations of the fabricated species could talk, after a fashion, some more eloquently than others. But many didn't have much to say. If they spoke, it was usually in the service of some chore—say, gathering firewood, or slaughtering a pineapple.

Rain hadn't yet taken the measure of the winged monkeys who accompanied Iskinaary. Those creatures could follow orders, they could communicate. According to the Goose, they'd come from far away to find Rain and rescue her. But their language seemed weak, so their capacity for foretelling the future would remain a dusty uncertainty to her, she supposed. As would their grasp of the past. Without language, crucial coordinates might vanish.

While incarcerated, she'd been trying to assemble pieces of her own past. They appeared to her as frozen images rather than episodes of drama—portraits, not pantomimes. Her father, Liir, the only offspring of Elphaba Thropp. And Glinda, who had taken Rain in when she was young, to protect her. Mockbeggar Hall, Glinda's country pile. Then Rain reuniting with Liir and with Candle, her mother, for a while.

Rain's accidental crossing of paths with a boy named Tip. Tip, her fellow. A lad not yet filled out with the packed certainty of adult maleness. In her mind he wobbled within the margins; a glowing smile, and those caresses, the avowals of affection. Love, call it that. The force of the whole memory was of being cherished, but Tip—it was as if the sun was always in her eyes as she looked up from the black sack of memory; the silhouette of Tip was indistinct. She couldn't bring him into registration. What had happened to him? Had he died, and was that why she had fled—fled from Oz?

Her ability to sequence recent memories began somewhat after the disappearance of Tip, which seemed the central darkness in her mind. Rain had only recently remembered digging up the Grimmerie, that old dangerous tome of high magic. She'd revived a flitch of Elphaba's enchanted broomstick. In a state of foul and glassy conviction she'd flown out over the little-known Nonestic Sea to the west of Oz. Iskinaary, sent by Rain's father to protect her, had accompanied her. Before Rain was too bone-exhausted to lose sight of her mission, she had pawed the Grimmerie out of her satchel and let it drop into the open ocean. How the Grimmerie had offended her she couldn't yet recall, but she had taken her revenge upon it, for good.

Collapse into the sea; amnesia; exile. Now she was awake. She had escaped prison. Her memories were struggling to return. The furnace of her mind was beginning to roar, at least quietly, between her own ears. She was walking with energy despite the heaviness at her belly.

They'd slipped through the gates. She gripped Cossy's hand a little more tightly and winced a smile sideways at her, hoping to be encouraging.

Of Cossy, hardly more could be said than what was posited of the flying monkeys or of the Goose. But it wasn't Cossy's fault. Raised remotely, the child had been scarcely more than a specimen in a controlled experiment. She seemed about ten, more or less. Old enough, no? But ignorant as clay. She'd had almost no exposure to human society. Scant weeks ago, she'd known only six females until Rain had appeared, a green and sodden castaway on island sands. Until evacuation, Cossy had seen and met only one man ever. Literally. A civil servant from the mainland called Lucikles. And Cossy had come in contact with a single boy—the son of Lucikles, a lad three years older than Cossy. His name was Leorix. And Cossy had never encountered a talking Animal until Iskinaary opened his beak and began to quawk.

Cossy, convicted of murder only that morning, was giving nothing away. She matched her pace to Rain's. Amoral, or merely betrayed by circumstance, she stalked on, fleeing the invading army, lunging toward whatever future it was that not one of the party could possibly predict.

Almost under her breath, Cossy was muttering a spell.

> *Swift our feet*
> *Along the street*
> *And steer us clear*
> *Away from here.*

Of Tycheron and his uncle or boss, Rain couldn't say. They were glancing at each other, scheming in semaphore.

6

The lucky ones who'd made it out were still scrabbling and clawing up the slope when a noise bellied out behind them, a sound of human alarm. Pivoting, they saw the scarf of saffron thrown off the wall. The wind caught it and drifted it above the palanquin, which had been jettisoned onto the rocks below the walls.

"They've turned on the Bvasil," said the older man. "I can't believe it."

"Surely—" began Tycheron, but he didn't seem so sure, and stopped speaking.

"This can't be good. The citizens of Maracoor Crown have blocked the Bvasil's royal progress and ambushed his carriage. He was only trying to boost their morale in fighting the Skedes. Look what they've done."

"There's nothing more to be seen here, Uncle," said Tycheron. "Turn away. We'll hide our faces from what we knew. Press on."

At the ridge, the crowd of forty or fifty paused. Rain and her fake family listened to arguments about which route to take.

The juncture afforded several choices, Rain learned. One northern road led to trackless marshes. Fine for smugglers but total shit for the uninitiated. Other roads turning back to the sea were out of the question, frying-pan-into-the-fire options. The Skedian navy must be landing more forces along the coast.

Of the remaining tracks making for the western uplands, one was rumored to be a remote passage through the Thalassic Wood, risky at best. The more popular route seemed to be a high road, a ribbon of pitted grey marble slabs lined with tilting milestones. A track of switchbacks upon spare terrain. Easy picking for any predator: beasts, armies, spirits, or highway robbers. No traveler walked anonymously upon this road. Still, enemies could be spotted at a distance, too. Were pilgrims numerous enough, they might protect one another. Maybe.

"What do you propose?" asked Tycheron, looking not at Uncle but at Rain.

"*Me*? I'm a stranger here," said Rain. She waved at Iskinaary to come nearer. "I don't know where we're headed, except out of danger. While there's time."

"Well, as we're going west," said Tycheron, "we'll stay with the group on the high road. Join us or not."

"Not," said Cossy.

"Hang on to the pregnancy, Pet," said the older fellow with a generous wave. "It helped you get clearance to leave. It might provide you with protection further along. Even the more savage among us won't attack a pregnant woman."

"It's as heavy as sin," said Rain. "No thank you." She began to unclasp the buckle under her burlap shawl.

"You may never get this chance again." With a tone of cunning. "Salvation of the nation?"

"A child of mine? I doubt it," said Rain. "And if you mean Maracoor, all I say is: Not my nation." The satchel was hard to unclasp; the weight seemed to fit to her belly with a magnetized seal. The burlap snood slipped off her head as she wrestled with the cincture.

The younger man stifled a gasp. "In the name of the Great Mara, has the parcel poisoned you?"

"You mean my green skin tones? No, I come by this naturally. You've only just noticed? You fellows don't pay attention much to people helping you out, do you. So whichever way you're going, we're going the other. Who are you, anyway?"

"I'm a job, not a person," said the older peasant. "Some are called Smith, some Miller, some Archer. It's what they do. I'm Burden, that'll do for me. As long as you're rejecting my gift." With a look of resignation if not loathing he retrieved the belted satchel at last and hoisted it on his shoulders. "For helping you trick your way out of the city I might have expected a little gratitude."

"You used me and I used you; I guess we're even."

"You're the creature who flew in from the east," said Burden. "I've heard tell of you. And that thing is the self-same broom, isn't it? Looks like it couldn't snag a cobweb from a stag's antlers."

"Flattery hasn't gotten you far so far, so why start now? Where are you headed?"

"We're making a pilgrimage in the hour of our nation's need. We're heading to High Chora, hoping to locate an obscurity known as the Oracle of Maracoor."

As Iskinaary swooped down to rejoin them, Rain felt a shiver run along her shoulder blades. She put it down to her body re-adjusting from the weight of the leathern pregnancy, but it also seemed—portentous, maybe? Something scratched her nerves into antsy alignment, paying attention.

The title—the Oracle of Maracoor—maybe pompous—maybe holy. An Oracle sounded like a figurehead, as Glinda had seemed to Rain, or the Wizard of Oz had once been in Glinda's own youth. Like impossible legend. But what was impossible these days? The seams of this nation's folklore seemed to be splitting, with rumors of manticores and dyanis and whatnot spotted in every cave and countinghouse. Maybe the Oracle of Maracoor was another fusty old idea breathed back into life by the crack in the universe that had also brought Rain and Iskinaary to Maracoor. "Is soothsaying even true?" she asked, despite wanting to be on her way. "Or some fairy story folderol? And what do you want to find some old fortune-teller for?"

"Who knows what's true until you stub your toe against it in the dark?" replied Burden. "Finding the Oracle will take some travel, and we have time to work out our agenda on the road. Come—Pet—Rain, is it, do I remember hearing?—shall we take the high road together? You're a figure of some notoriety. If the Oracle is still alive, he'll want to meet you, and make of you what he will. And tell you something, too. The few pilgrims who claim to have met such an Oracle speak of a pious simplicity in his countenance and counsel. They could be lying, of course."

"You know a lot about it for a beast of burden," said Rain.

"I babble a lot but I keep my ears open. That's how I heard of you. And you could borrow back your pregnancy when it suited you."

"Come on, Cossy," said Rain, "Burden is right in this. I'd stick out like a gangrenous thumb on the open road. Let's take our chances elsewhere."

The Goose snapped, "Indeed we do have other plans. *Pet*. Good day to you, kind sir." He nodded at Burden but his tone was off-putting.

"If we're going, we should go now," said Tycheron to Burden. He pointed to the evacuees moving ahead on the high road. "We don't want to be alone when darkness falls. And this is getting us nowhere."

The Goose said, "Let's get outta here, Rain." He scowled at Burden and Tycheron. "We'll hunker down in the forest for a day or two till the dust settles, and then we'll circle back to the coast to plan our evacuation from this hellhole."

Rain raised her eyebrow but chose not to argue about their itinerary in front of the strangers.

"I vote for the forest, too," said Cossy.

7

W hy didn't you want us to travel together?" asked Rain of Cossy.

"He's a man, and I don't know yet if I like men. And he lied to save his own skin."

Rain laughed. "You lied too. You said I was called Pet."

"Anyway, you didn't feel like going with him. I could tell."

"I hate to break up a bonding moment among the sisterhood," said Iskinaary, "but may I point out that a battle for the capital city of this country is about to begin? And you have both just escaped from jail? And one of you is an immigrant who can't pass for anything else? Perhaps we should get the hell out of here? Survive first, strategize later? Look, here come the monkeys. We're intact. Let's scram."

They were now scrabbling along the track that veered toward the margin of a great woods. Rain turned to glance back at Tycheron and Burden. She marked them easily; they stood out against chalk bluffs glaring like salt in the sunlight. Dark green cypress trees, scattered about the slope, seemed to pin the rare day down to a map of the earth. The men had made up some time on the paving stones. The older one was pacing with his head lowered, his satchel like a hunch grown into the nape of his neck. Tycheron was craning to watch Rain's party as it veered through burdocky meadows toward the cover of forest. He waved. Rain didn't wave back.

The woods closed in around Rain and her companions. Only then did they pause for breath.

"The winged monkeys," said Iskinaary. "If we're going to be traveling together, you should get to know their names anyway. This is Tiotro. These two are Faro and Finistro. The smaller one is called Thilma."

Tiotro and Thilma, the largest and smallest, nodded at their names. Faro and Finistro plodded on ahead. Hard of hearing, or maybe just not interested in niceties.

"I'm Rain," said Rain to these winged monkeys, "and this is Cossy."

"Thilma speaks some," said the Goose, "but Faro, Finistro, and Tiotro are prone to silence. They're all males."

"Except Thilma," said Thilma.

"Oh, slight mistake. Apologies," said the Goose. "No offense."

"Offense taken," said Thilma, "stored for Thilma to chew on later, when bored."

The sense of calamity died down, thanks to the screening woods. More common needs reasserted themselves. Supper, water. Shelter from the rainstorm, which would break again, eventually.

Iskinaary sent the flying monkeys scavenging for food. He and the girls hunted for a place to hunker down for the night. Before long they found a lean-to whose sloping roof needed only a bit of replacement thatching. Cossy and Rain, being the ones equipped with opposable thumbs, dragged fallen cedar boughs to hitch onto the roof-frame. And just in time. The woods lost definition behind a thrum of downpour.

Rain and Cossy tucked themselves in as far as they could get. They bent their heads over their knees and watched Iskinaary standing in the rain. "What are you doing out there?" called Rain.

"Getting wet," he replied. "You, too. Come here."

Rain pulled her shawl thing over her head and joined him in the rain. He quawked in as soft a voice as he had—which wasn't very. "We need to devise an exit strategy," he said. "Out of Maracoor. Back to Oz."

"But the girl."

"She's not your charge. Lose her," said the Goose. "She had her chance at the quay."

"She's a child."

"So are you, and I came with you to flap some sense into your head when you need it. Like now. We have to turn back. Back to Oz."

"Give it a break, Iskinaary. First things first. We're not abandoning a child in the woods."

"I can hear you both perfectly well, you know," said Cossy, "and you're stuck with me. You couldn't lose me if you tried. I'm not losable."

THE MONKEYS HAD NO TROUBLE finding the lean-to. Tiotro brought fistfuls of nuts, quite a few of them wormy as it turned out, and berries that had gotten crushed in the pockets of his vest. Faro and Finistro offered a decomposing squirrel and the foot of a rabbit that looked as if it had been removed from an iron trap. Thilma had a capful of wild cherries and tart orange olives. It wasn't a balanced meal. The rotten meat was inedible. But the rest was enough.

"Shall I tell you a story?" asked Rain as night fell.

"Something ordinary," said Cossy. "Nothing about monsters or magicks."

"Nothing ordinary is without magic," said Rain.

"Well, try," said Cossy, who wasn't about to put up with existential philosophy at this point in her day. The child had been convicted of murder hardly six hours earlier. There was a limit to how much you could tolerate between dawn and dusk. "Something ordinary to you is still a story to me. Start with: Do you have a mother and do you have a father?"

"Everyone has a father and mother."

That was so patently false to Cossy, who'd been raised not by wolves but by unmarried religious women, that she rolled her eyes. Rain took pity. "I'll tell you an old story that doesn't have to do with me or you."

"What's the point then?"

"I don't know. It passes the time."

"I don't even really know what a story is," said Cossy in a tone that said, And I don't know why I should be bothered to learn.

"A story," said Rain, "is like a room. You enter it through a door, like 'Once upon a time' or 'Once there was a little girl' or something like that. You stay in the room and things happen there to the little girl. Then you find a door that says something like, 'And they lived happily ever after,' or 'So that's all there is, there isn't anything else.' And you walk out of the room and the story is all done. It's only one thing that happened, and nothing else that ever happened can be in it."

"And that," said Iskinaary from his place in the downpour, "is why Geese don't tell stories."

"Why?" asked Rain, despite herself, because the Goose could be such a kick in the knickers.

"Because we don't go in rooms if we can help it," said the Goose. "Too many doors can slam shut, and without hands we are helpless to turn the knobs. The world to us is one thing; everything that happens is simultaneous and diffuse. A story seems to me to be a very small box in which to find meaning. But that's humans for you, and why they need us Geese. To see a little farther."

"Thilma likes the story," piped up Thilma, and gave a tortured expression that, just in time, Rain interpreted as a smile.

"Well, thank you. But it wasn't really a story," said Rain.

"That's what Thilma likes about it," said Thilma.

The roof leaked only a little. The silent monkeys—Faro and—Rain was trying to remember their names, Faro and Finistro, that was it—spread their wings over Rain and Cossy like blankets. The wings were more or less waterproof, though there was an animal odor that Rain swore she could never sleep through.

But escaping from prison and from a city about to be besieged, both on the same afternoon, it takes the bounce out of you. Rain was only half aware that Cossy was asleep in a scatter of mangy wings before Thilma had finished the simple monkey lullaby she was crooning. Maybe it comprised a story to Thilma, at least all the story she could need to tell. It went:

"Fly, fly, fly, fly, fly, fly, fly."

As Rain closed her eyes, she thought how odd that she couldn't say the story of her own life, really; but she could describe what a story was to Cossy. A situation; a challenge; a struggle of some sort; an outcome. The shape of story must be an undergirding element of perception, a structure that outlasted all the dissolving details. Even the very elderly, lost to language, would lean forward if someone said, "Shall I tell you a story about the time Maracoor Crown was besieged by an invading army . . . ?"

A few moments later, in the swimmy obscurities of pre-sleep, she caught a sense of menace. For a moment she thought: a wolf in these woods, and he's stalking me. The rank aroma of danger. Then she thought: Or is the wolf just the story of my own life that I can't yet reassemble? Pacing with me? She floated laterally into the black sack of dreamlessness, curled up like a nameless pet inside it, with nothing in her head, nothing graspable to exhume in tomorrow's light.

FARMSTEAD

1

Within a few days of their arrival, the little girls had settled into the routine of household chores and private games. Their grandmother's farm was a known thing to them, beloved and safe. When the first attack by those bad guys happened last month, while Papa was away at sea, Mama had brought her children to stay with their grandmother. The repeat flight from the capital this week had been less alarming than the earlier exodus. This time the family had command of a donkey cart, the one they'd borrowed from the barn last time. That was fun. Though the fear of wolves on the open road had sort of ruined it. Especially for their brother, Leorix. He'd been attacked last time, and fended them off. Even now his wounds oozed at night as he tossed in bad dreams. He didn't describe them when he woke up. Though the girls wheedled, really, they were secretly glad. It was funner to imagine than to know for sure.

The girls were Poena and Star. Ages eight and five. They pattered into and out of the kitchen, paying little mind to the discussions their parents and their grandmother were having. They wanted a sip of water. There was an ouchy needing a kiss. Shhh, go play now, Mama's busy.

The farm wasn't situated on a trunk road. No such item existed across High Chora, this tableland rising west of Maracoor Crown. Branching tracks linked farmsteads and villages, but without an urban hub, all destinations were equally incidental.

Therefore, as fugitives from the capital city breasted the highland, they fanned out. Some sought distant family members. Others posed as victims of history. The grandmother worried. "We locals are pinched between an instinct of charity and the common sense to husband our resources. I hear the Speziou brothers have taken to sleeping in their barns to avert cattle theft. Roosters cry themselves hoarse, hearing fricassee at every footfall."

Who cared. The children were safe.

Leorix and his father, Lucikles, had tried to help with the cows. They weren't good with cows. Father and son got shooed away by inbred cousins whose backbones and forearms helped keep Mia Zephana on her own homestead this late in her life. So father and son merely gathered brush for kitchen fires instead. They didn't talk much, though they stuck close together in the dales—now bucolic, now doomy. It was all in the light. Sometimes they came home with mushrooms.

"*We* found two baby chicks who are eating dirt," said Poena, darting through the kitchen door at a clip. Star followed, panting too hard to chime in. "Mamanoo, can I have an apple for their supper?"

"Birds don't eat apples," said their grandmother, but she nodded anyway and continued cleaning the next fleece. Her daughter worked the other end. "I don't like the thought of setting a binding spell upon this home, Oena. I've never stooped to that. When neighbors have done so, it leaves a nasty stink after it wears away."

"An actual stench of deteriorating magic, or just a bad impression?" said Oena.

"These apples are kind of yucky so can I have three of them?" asked Poena.

The grandmother said, "The Tonneros family, a little downslope of the falls? They put a binding spell on their establishment last year because they thought someone was going to abduct the teenage girl. Who, to be honest, didn't shy away from being attractive.

But she wasn't old enough yet to manage her appeal. You never had that problem, Oena."

"The binding spell," said Oena drily, who was a handsome woman by all accounts but had seen some hardships in her day. "Can we keep to the matter at hand?"

"Another family group approaching on the road from the Springs of Cynerra," reported Lucikles, coming in through the cold storage room. "Shall I greet them and offer them yesterday's bread?" So mingy a gesture could encourage the hungry into passing by in the hopes for richer fare up the road.

"Set Leorix at the gate," said his wife. "They won't browbeat a beardless lad, and it'll make him feel as if he's contributing."

Lucikles picked his moments of disagreement carefully. "I'll give him a sack of hard rolls, but I'll linger in the shrubbery in case things get out of hand."

"But do call in the girls." Oena didn't like them running around carefree while hard-up families were passing by. She could imagine the resentment. "See what I mean?" she continued to her mother. "A binding spell would do the job for us. Deflect these uninvited callers."

"You asked about the stink," replied Mia Zephana. "Our neighbors would know if we decided to shirk our duty during this crisis. And what would happen to the needy if everyone in High Chora were to do the same?"

"What happened to the Tonneros family?" pushed Oena.

Her mother said, "They kept to themselves. But on market days, folks looked the other way when they came through. And then their sheep shed caught fire."

"Malice? Revenge? Surely not."

"You think maybe the sheep were smoking in bed? No, I don't think it was malice. Would have been hard to manage, though the binding spell was eroding at its usual rate. My point is that the neighbors didn't bestir themselves to help save the flock until they were good and ready. So the family upped and left. Though perhaps they've come back now, too. No, Oena, a binding spell is a last-ditch measure. Listen, I've lived here on my own since your father died. And I haven't needed a binding spell so far. I don't want to become wary in my final years."

The girls pushed in again, huffing and teary. "Why do we have to come back every time someone walks on the road, it's not fair," cried Poena. "The chicks said they liked the red apples but would rather a green one."

"What are you singing about," said their grandmother. "Never knew a chick to order off a menu. These are the last of the autumn apples—deal with it. Oena, the night is about to fall. Those passersby ask for a roof, we'll tell them to go find the Tonneros farmstead. If the place is still abandoned, they can harbor there until they collect their wits and press on to somewhere else."

"Maybe they'll pass by of their own accord. Let's hold the Tonneros home in reserve for a more pressing moment." Oena moved to the window and shifted a curtain. "They look harmless enough. A substantial woman wearing heavy jewelry. No wonder she's exhausted. Her man must be a merchant or a court appointment. But the bedazzle won't do her any good in these parts."

"Poor thing. She meant to impress." Mia Zephana kept to her task. "A family group? Children?" She looked wary; children in wartime deserve dispensations.

"Hardly. A dicey brood of young men in the down of their first whisker."

"Then they ought to have stayed to defend the Bvasil and his city. We shouldn't offer them old dishwater to drink."

"By that reckoning, I should have stayed behind, too," said Lucikles, coming back in.

"You have three children, a wife, and a mother-in-law. It was your duty to evacuate," said Mia Zephana, seeing no contradiction in her assertions. "Children, you're driving me mad. If you won't climb up in the loft, you'll have to go back outside, but stay behind the house till the strangers pass by."

"I'll go with the girls," said Oena.

"Leorix is doing a fine job, holding his own," said his father. "He's learned a lot from his adventures this year, my dear. But I'll keep an eye out anyway."

My dear was a splinter under Oena's fingernail, a hot twinge in her eyeball. She hadn't wanted the boy to leave the farm with his father on that sudden mission to the city, let alone to sail off to the island of Maracoor Spot. She hadn't forgiven Lucikles for allowing the boy to join him at sea. Still, the appearance of normalcy was better for everyone. Indeed, probably for her. For half a day at a time she could forget her resentment, a lingering offshoot of her terror at the time. (The throb of outrage never failed to return sooner or later.)

Despite all that, there was much to love about being back at the farmstead. Oena had grown up here with her parents and a few brothers who had married and settled nearby, or near enough. The holding wasn't a showpiece, but it wasn't shabby. The thatch was fresh, the shutters retouched from time to time, the fences in good repair. The grange appealed to the kids, as it was home to the cozier farm animals. Also the standard sort of country rodents: mice, rats, stoats. Meadows for crops; pastures for grazing; paddocks for animal husbandry. A barn in better nick than the house. A hen coop, a few scattered sheds. A pond more ornamental than useful.

In this pink and gold late-afternoon light the trees nodded like ancestral presences. Here all at once Oena was a child and a young woman in love and a mother of three and, for all she knew, a widow in the making. She breathed deeply, trying to block out the chatter of her daughters, those small me-but-not-mes.

"Have they gone yet, can we go back to our chickies?" asked

Poena. Her mother wondered how any child could determine, unerringly, which register of plangency to employ for maximum persuasion. A human mystery no sage or scholar had yet plumbed.

"Bossy birds," endorsed Star, putting her hands behind her back the way her father sometimes did when contemplative.

"Where are your little friends? Do they have a nest in a hedge? I'd like to come see."

"I think the birds don't want company," said Poena.

Oena thought, I've taken the kids on this gallop from town to farm twice in the past few weeks. They're feeling unmoored. They need something of their own to serve as an anchor. Who knows how long we'll be here this time. If the capital falls to the barbarian—if the nation falls—how do we live then? Let them have their secret childhood while they can. As I had mine.

"Very well," she said. "I can hear your brother in the house now. The wanderers must have passed by. Tell me where you're going so I know where to look if it gets dark."

"Over by the Throne Tree," said Poena, pointing across a stone wall to a meadow that cupped the pond. Oena knew the reference. A flat-topped elm stump with a rising backboard left over from where the trunk had split as it fell. It had been there in her childhood too, and she had played Queen of the Forest from that seat, even though Oena's brothers had rarely kowtowed to her supreme authority.

How marvelous that Poena and Star had each other.

"Don't pester your birds," said the mother. "It's spring, they might be guarding their eggs. They'll come at you if you get too close."

"We're not stupid," said Poena.

"Stupid," whispered Star, which seemed neither argument nor agreement, but such was the vagary of a five-year-old's editorial stance that it couldn't be challenged.

2

L eorix didn't know he was both a hero and a monster to his
sisters.

The boy, now thirteen years of age, was neither sensitive
nor doltish. He was a lad's lad. Inquisitive if not yet rational. Im-
pulsive, though still cautious.

He was glad his parents and grandmother trusted him to deal
with the rabble-de-roy on the path. They'd been easy enough to
deflect, that fat woman with her baubles, her shuffling sons who
slid their eyes to the ground, avoiding Leorix's direct gaze. He offered water in clay cups and the bread his father had supplied before slipping away. One of the travelers cursed, but another made a
gesture of blessing. The woman accepted two refills of water. When
it was clear Leorix wasn't going to mention lodging, her stamina
gave up and the party shuffled away. "We're shafted, aren't we,"
muttered one of the sons. "Not yet," replied his mother in society
tones, "that's on the schedule for tomorrow, if it can be arranged."

About his parents, the boy entertained the usual apprehensions.
He wanted their approval but not too openly, their love only if
given drily. With the luck of the stars, he intended to be as unlike
his father as he could manage. Leorix found the paterfamilias,
Lucikles, to be overly accommodating. Open to persuasion, guilty
of rumination. The boy considered these weaknesses of character.
A boy wants, in a father, either a pirate or a minor deity. Not someone good at finding a legal work-around for pesky import duties.
That type of papa was, by definition, a loser.

In the past few weeks Leorix had shadowed his father to the remote island of Maracoor Spot, and then into the courtrooms at the House of Balances. He'd witnessed the trial for murder of that girl called Cossy. He'd found appalling his father's acquiescence at the girl's arraignment and conviction. How could Lucikles fail to take any responsibility for it, when he'd kidnapped the child and brought her to "justice"? So weak in moral muscle, so wet, so—*uggh*—as to make everyday chatter nearly impossible. His papa would say, "Hey there, chief; how'd you sleep?" and Leorix's jaw muscles would clench. It took all he had to hold his tongue for four or five seconds and then let a monotonic "Fine" slip out between his teeth. To add, "And you?" would have been to become a collaborator in his father's failings. He didn't care if his father ever slept well again. The old bastard didn't deserve to.

So Leorix largely kept out of Lucikles's way.

His mother, his quiet, sober, upright, capable mother—well, he had to stand at a distance from her, too, but for a different reason. Given the slightest threat to him, she lost her sense of propriety and treated him like an infant. His chums in the agora said that at home they all suffered the same thing. Mothers were, apparently, insane. Incapable of growing up. But this hardly made the condition easier to bear.

Now he loitered for long, lazy periods by the gate, waiting for life to show up. Betwixt and between, a dangerous way station for a boy hankering to become something else, something next.

Not long ago, when he'd been feverish with wolf-scratch and recovering in his grandmother's loft, he'd looked out the window and been startled by an apparition. He'd imagined he was seeing a figure sitting on the tree-stump seat in stark and magnificent nudity, a male figure of regal bearing who shimmered in and out of focus. A god of some sort. He wore an ornamental collar and nothing else. Leorix was too bewildered to bring the matter up to his parents or grandmother, but he was pretty sure the character was one of the deities honored by statues in the temples of Maracoor Crown. Leorix didn't know which personage his callow mind was conjuring up. He couldn't figure out how to ask a parent about which god or demi-god was a handsome male youth wearing only a neck ornament. It would have sounded iffy. So he'd let it go.

3

Lucikles and Oena had tucked their children up in their blankets, taken a last sip of cherry ale, and bid Mia Zephana good night. They lay for a while unspeaking in the dark, letting the issues of the day try to unknot themselves separately in their two separate hearts.

They weren't at peace with each other, but what husband and wife could manage to be when the nation was being invaded? What near or distant future danger lurked for their children? And so in their soft cooling sweat they lay in parallel prisons of resentment about insignificant matters. So tired that nonsense irritants were all that they could manage to consider.

She thought: He shouldn't have given the girls two extra biscuits for their chickies; the children were conniving him, and the sweet will jump the girls awake all night. (The girls were already sleeping soundly.)

He thought: She oughtn't send Leorix to the gate to fend off the grasping homeless; it will overwhelm him. Leorix needs a duty cut to the size of his competence. Guarding the family was a father's job, and as the father, tomorrow he would insist.

Each one thought: My spouse takes too much responsibility, and upon such tired shoulders; I should do more. I will do more. Still, I wish I could get some help at this, or that, or the other. I'm alone in my worry; mine is the deeper capacity for dread.

Eventually a hand reached out and another hand met it. It didn't matter whose was first. Their marital relations began as a performance of tenderness that neither one of them felt. But then the human apparatus of mood did its old trick of not being able to read two texts at once: The text of the skin took precedence over the text of the uncertain heart. The familiar fiction of erotic theater. In which both spouses pretended to be less aggrieved and more aroused than was true. And in the time they took for it, such pretense at romance once again had the power to convince them love was near. The catharsis enacted upon the stage of the mattress proved to imitate true feeling so well that neither partner could fully return to the attitude of offense in which they'd begun.

Oena fell asleep first. Lucikles gathered lengths of her hair and moved them off his pillow because they were tickling his jaw. He might have slept, but if so he awoke again soon enough. The light had shifted in the room; the moon was crawling about the clouds.

The last time they'd been here together, a month ago or so, he'd sensed a quickening of the world outside. An assembly of energies, like the coiling power of a cat's haunches as the creature prepares to spring. He had thought he'd heard creatures on the roof. Not the usual rats in the thatch. Something larger, investigative. Something foreign.

The morning had cleared that sensation away so well that he hadn't thought about it again until tonight.

He tried to relax. He prayed to the family deity. A different sort of letting go than that of sex. The loneliness of the mid-level civil servant. Reading nuances of atmosphere wasn't his métier; he tried nonetheless. With three children and a wife and mother-in-law in the house, it was his job to do his crude best in the protection of them all.

Eventually he caught a sound in the kitchen or larder. A normal noise, the sound of human agency. He got up to make sure it wasn't one of the children filching apples or getting into other mischief.

His mother-in-law was rolling out a round of pastry. "Couldn't sleep either?" she said.

"Not with the racket you're making." He grinned and sat down.

She worked in silence for a while, though she gestured toward the flagon of wine and nodded for him to help himself if he wanted. He didn't.

After she'd finished with the brisk work and stored the disc of dough in the tin box slotted in the cold outside wall, she sat down opposite Lucikles. She began to scrape the peels off apples. He offered to help but she said, "Stretching out a job gives me more time to think."

"What are you having to think about?"

"Other than how old I'm getting, and just as our nation is under attack?"

She was right; in this light he saw something aged in her that he'd never observed before. As if there was a second skin upon this vigorous farmwoman, an invisible skin but it had weight; and it was exhaustion.

He said evenly, "Can't do anything about the former, I'm afraid. And you and I can do precious little about the latter, either."

"True. We can't stop a military threat against us. But how we behave while it happens is still up to us," she said, congenial in disagreement. "However old we are."

"You sound as if you have a campaign in mind."

"Oena is asking me to get someone to lay in a binding spell around the place. She was spooked a month ago, Lucikles, by having to flee with the children when the vandal Skedes first came into the harbor of Maracoor Crown. She hasn't recovered yet—you being away when it happened. The rushed evacuation on the road. Leorix attacked by that wolf."

He didn't need to be reminded. "I wasn't malingering on some holiday island. I was at work at my job. As usual. And the boy has recovered just fine."

"That's a reasonable response, but reason isn't always useful against alarm. Oena is just so *jittery* about unknown people wandering this pastoral outback."

"What do you have against a binding spell, then? Assuming such a thing even works?"

"Oh, they work, but often against one's best interests. I know an old fellow over to Kloixou Stables who might do it well enough, and he'd only charge twice what he's worth instead of eight times. But I'm thinking it's the wrong thing to do. In fact, I'm inclined to take the opposite approach. Which would drive my daughter crazy. And that's why I'm peeling apples. Because worrying about her is driving *me* crazy."

"The opposite approach? What do you mean?"

"It's not good for the children to see us bar the door just when someone else's need is so obvious. We ought to take someone in. Then anyone who follows could see that we've already opened our doors to the refugee. Besides—I'm not a fool—nothing stops us from applying a binding spell later if it becomes necessary."

"And you'd put your own family in danger by admitting a stranger?"

"There are many legends of how it's the stranger who brings the blessing."

"Or the curse at the child's naming, or the scrap of pox, or the evil eye."

Mia Zephana waved her hand distractedly in the air, as if brushing off invisible flies. "You don't like it, you can take yourselves elsewhere and then watch and see who opens their gate to *you*. It's my house, sonny."

"Always admired you for your winning ways. I'll put myself on sentry duty tomorrow and choose a safe candidate for inviting in." He went back to bed.

4

The morning had turned clearer. The blue overhead seemed to throb. Sipping peligrasse tea, he realized that his mother-in-law's midnight argument had changed his mind. As his family wandered in for rusks of bread and jam—all but Mia Zephana, who was already out watering the sheep—he rubbed his jaw, as if it had been dislocated in a lumpy sort of sleep. "Leorix," he told the boy, "I've decided to lurk around the roadside today. Give you a day off."

"You don't think I've been doing a good job? You have any complaints?"

"You need some rest. All the excitement of the past month—the wolf attack, the ocean voyage, the trial, the invasion. You ought to go off with your sisters and play."

"I don't *play*," he said. "I'm not an adult yet but I am a *student*, Papa. I haven't played since I started at the lyceum."

"Your lyceum is overrun with Skedes and we're in the hinterlands anyway. You're spared. If you don't want to play, take the girls and go exploring. There are stands of trees beyond the pond that we've never ventured into. I doubt you can get lost—the woods will fetch up on some other farm's backfield. But see if you can keep within hollering distance of the house here."

"You talk as if I'm going to do what you tell me."

"Oh, do I? Well, you are. Take a break from this worry, my boy. We've got things covered here, your mother and grandmother and I."

"The three of you will hold off the invaders by yourselves? Right."

"I'll yell for you if we need backup."

"You mock me," he said. "I hate that."

"We don't *want* him to play with us," said Poena, finishing her apple.

With her usual dazzling incoherence, little Star said, "Me too."

Lucikles yawned and ran a hand through his hair. "Well, I'm off for a morning constitutional. I'll keep on the lane so I'll be able to see if anyone is coming along. I'll handle them. I *mean* it, Leorix. Do as I say."

As Lucikles stumped out the door, Leorix swiveled toward his sisters. He was in so foul a temper that he was nearly enjoying himself. "You can take care of yourselves or go drown in the pond. It doesn't matter to me."

"I love how you're learning to be a jerk," said Poena. "You're so good at it, but you should practice some more." She fled his uplifted hand. He wouldn't have hit her, but it was fun to raise his fist sometimes.

The girls got dressed and put together a sack of crusts and carrots. Every time their mother turned her head, they squirreled away more scraps. Leorix returned to the loft room where he had recuperated from the wolf attack. From here he could lean down and peer through the low-slung window, out under the eaves, across the meadow. He waited to watch his sisters make their trudging way, lugging the sack between them. He would find out where they went and then go to spy on them. What could be more annoying than that?

They reached the pond, hugged the margin of the water, and headed toward the Throne Tree. Then they diverted into the tall grasses.

He lay there, feeling as much wolf as boy. He didn't know for how long. His breath was hot upon his own clavicle. A mood of election stole over him, as if the world had centered its ambitions in his own hollowed-out soul. It was tough to hover between duty and delinquency. He supposed anyone who had ever been mauled by a wolf might be intrigued to know what the wolf had actually wanted with him. More than, say, his liver.

Time inched in patterns of leaf-shadow cast on the whitewash. Hints and hunches. Leorix stole down the stairs on bare feet. He was a shadow of himself, now being a kid again, now trying out his new, older self. Wolf-boy.

He achieved the blind of a clump of thick holly and paused there, listening. The sound of his sisters' voices came to him from over the water and the stone wall, indistinct but fluting with excitement. Behind him, his grandmother called something to his mother. In the farmhouse, a tin pail dropped noisily to the stone floor. He trained his eyes on the light that trembled around the Throne Tree. A peculiar wind stirred the leaves there with precision while the rest of the slope lay stupefied, languid.

Over the wall, along the pond. He moved with stealthy movements to keep as silent as possible but he didn't crouch. He guessed that whatever the girls were doing, they weren't paying attention to the perimeters of their game. Lupine?—as if the scars left by boss wolf a month ago had infected him? But he shook the panic off and lowered his nose and slunk forward, listening, listening. He would never hurt his sisters. Them and their stupid idiocies.

"I don't think the little chicks like apples anymore," Poena was saying. "They aren't eating a bite."

He was at the Throne Tree and he still couldn't see them. They were somewhere close by. Maybe he should pretend-roar to flush them out, and chase them and tickle them. Or act more like a wolf-prince and really growl, to scare them. He practiced.

He put one foot and then the other on the flat trunk of the Throne Tree, squatting, and then slowly he stood up on the seat, steadying himself on the high backboard of the chair. The feeling was fierce, from the soles of his feet to his jutted jaw. Leorix of the House of Korayus, age thirteen, firstborn son of a miserable if reliable public servant. A family boy at home, but in flashier self-disguise, a rogue, an outlier.

"What's the matter, chickie?" Poena's voice had taken on a change of tone. "You don't like Papa's pipe tobacco?"

Something flushed through Leorix then, an unnerving jolt, like a bad tooth biting on tin. A shooting awareness. He sensed *wolf* nearby. Something not pretend, realer than he was, maybe centering in on his sisters without their knowledge. Or were they *talking* to a baby wolf? He was humiliated, jealous, terrified, all at once.

Leorix tensed his thigh muscles and bent his knees, preparing to leap. Before he launched, though, the reeds and grasses rustled. A head lifted up and glared at him. It wasn't Poena or Star, nor was it a wolf before whom he was ready to die or pledge troth. A face of a vicious little demon sorceress of some sort.

Star and Poena rose to their feet too, and stared at their brother.

"Get away from that thing before I kill it." Leorix's menacing wolf voice came out in a squeak. "Don't run, just move away."

"Chickie, I said no. Now *you behave*," said Star. "Go home, Lorry."

"You shouldn't have come here, we told you," added Poena in a voice of sorrow.

"Who is this nuisance?" said the bird-thing, its humanesque face flashing a hostile bronze.

The girls stood up and turned to their brother. The creature's expression was frightened and menacing at once. She roared, her little point-teeth flashing at Leorix.

"I don't know who your imaginary friend is," was all Leorix could say. "But there's a wolf nearby. This game is over. Star. Poena. Let's go back. Now." He held out his paws. They came to take his hands; reluctantly; but he was the big brother, after all.

5

Lucikles lounging against the gatepost. Drawing on his pipe, watching the smoke unfurl. He had already refused one old couple who had hobbled along with a nasty mutt on a rope. "I'm afraid we have a fierce guard dog who doesn't take kindly to visitors," Lucikles had ventured. The little critter, Cur, came sprigging up from nowhere and greeted the new arrivals with wagging tail and attempted sniffing of nethers. "That's not the pup I'm talking about," said Lucikles. "Cur, get back here."

"We'll lose our hound if you like," said the old woman. "We'll take Old Pretty out in that field and brain him with a big stone. Balls, but I'm knackered, I need a break."

"You take Old Pretty out in any field and I'll brain *you,* for that idea," said her tatterdemalion husband, spitting.

"You'll have better luck just a little way along," said Lucikles, hoping it was so. Old Pretty snarled, as if he understood human mendacity. The couple left. Cur followed them until Old Pretty lunged at him. Cur suffered a change of heart and came whimpering home at a clip.

"You don't know when you have it good," said Lucikles. He was fond of the dog, perhaps because although Cur was old enough to know better, he remained one of those happy creatures who didn't learn from experience. In that regard Lucikles felt that he and Cur were soul mates.

When his pipe was done and Lucikles was ready to head for a midmorning ale, along came another pair, traveling from the direction that Old Pretty and his people had headed. An older man and a younger. A hunched fellow with a farmer's hat and a satchel dragging from his shoulders. The younger one, carrying a larger rucksack, was limping and rubbing his left calf.

"Did that wretched fool dog break the skin?" asked Lucikles.

"Yes," said the younger man. "Apparently he passed this way. You're familiar with the creature?"

"Old Pretty. Glad it was you and not me. Let me see the damage."

The fellow cocked his knee to show the gash and the running blood. The wound needed cleaning and binding. "You'd better come in," said Lucikles. "The women do the mending around here."

"Call of nature first," said the older man, indicating the latrine. "Obliged if you'll see to my nephew."

The kitchen swam with a smell of fruit soaking in cold spring water. Mia Zephana looked up from the pastry board. "What have we here?" she asked. Oena was entering through the opposite door, the one to the herb garden. She carried an armful of lavender that looked like buds of cloud-shadow. She paused in the doorway, light welling around her, silhouetted and fragrant. Lucikles could tell by her locked shoulders that she was alert for trouble.

"This passerby has been pestered by a dog in the neighborhood," he said.

"Not our Cur?" asked Oena, amazed, almost proud.

Lucikles didn't answer. Let her conclude what she would. He continued, "Can we offer this pilgrim a soapy rinse and a dressing of the wound?"

Mia Zephana said to her daughter, "I have to finish this pastry before it collapses. The salve is in the ointment box." She didn't look at Oena. "You might as well sit down, stranger, you're blocking the light."

The other man stumped in. Oena glanced at her husband, but Lucikles merely said, "Let me take those cuttings." Oena had no authority to disobey her mother, whose place this was, so she did as she was bade and she went for the bandage strips.

"You're not local, from your accent," said Lucikles, acting the man of the house.

"Nor are you," said the younger man. "From the city, you and me both." The uncle didn't remove his hat, but pulled it lower upon his forehead and closed his eyes and descended into an immediate sleep.

"This is the family home," said Lucikles, taking privileges. Mia Zephana, skeptical of urban courtliness, kept her eyes to her work—though her nostrils flared just a bit. Lucikles went on. "Are you headed to a friend's for shelter?"

"We have no friends." The traveler winced, because Oena had come back with a bowl of water warmed at the hearth, and was beginning to clean the wound.

"Well, you have family, then."

"No. Not here. We are new to High Chora. I suppose we're petitioners for asylum. At least until we regain our strength to continue on."

"But on to where, if you have no connections in this region?"

"We're searching for a certain fortune-teller," replied the younger man. "May we take our rest here until we recover? My uncle isn't the strong man he appears."

"Such a pity," blurted in Oena, "but we have children in the house, and they are—"

Lucikles corrected her. "They're accommodating enough. They could manage—"

"They are ill with an unknown contagion. We couldn't risk exposing you," continued Oena over him. "A harsh sort of charity requires us to send you onward, where you will be safer."

"Oena," said her mother in a level tone.

"Allow us to stay till the old man has taken some rest," pleaded the younger. "Damn steep hike up the main road from Maracoor Crown. Uncle isn't accustomed to such exertions. His pack is heavy, and we've been hiding in foxholes and woodsheds for several days. We had a night in the open last night. Most uncomfortable. And the howling of wolves—who could sleep through that? We can't go on without a rest."

"Have you news of the invasion?" asked Lucikles, to change the subject. "Has the city fallen? Has the Bvasil capitulated? You must have left later than we did. We had the farm cart and we made good time, so we've been installed here for a few days now."

"Can you reach me the two smaller copper pots, please; I need to strain the fruit and begin to thicken the compote," said Mia Zephana. Lucikles gathered the items from the low shelf under the window.

"We saw the Bvasil's portable chair tossed over the side of city walls," said the younger man. "My, that is much better. You have a gentle touch, woman." He smiled at Oena with a look of tender appreciation that irked Lucikles.

"The Bvasil is fallen?" Lucikles stood up in a flush of instinct toward ceremony. "The Great Mara in person? We are lost."

"We are not lost," said the man in the straw hat, speaking for the first time. He didn't open his eyes. Lucikles clutched the wooden rim of the washing-up bucket. "We simply aren't yet found."

"Your Magnificence—" said Lucikles. He dropped the two pans he'd been carrying; they clattered on the flagstones.

"Uncle, you're delusional again," stammered the younger man. "We talked about this—"

The uncle pulled his hat off his head and lifted his chin. The stubble was real but the fringe of grey hair was theater, sewn to the rim of his hat. "I know your voice, you, you Kerr Middleman, it's a grating voice. You delivered a report unto me not all that long ago. It's all right," he said to his troubled companion. "He'd have recognized me sooner or later. You, I remember why you were called in. Remind me of your name. I tell you, the headaches I've suffered in service to the nation."

Oena stayed on her knees, where she'd been tending to the companion's leg. Mia Zephana slapped her pastry crust into a clay bowl and said, "Sorry, this can't wait if you want something to eat eventually," and began to drain and press the soaking fruit.

Lucikles, in a state of cold horror, said, "Mia Zephana, this is the Bvasil of Maracoor himself."

"And this is my house, not yours," replied his mother-in-law.

"It rhymes with *keys*, doesn't it," said the man. "Parocles? Mitropoles? That's all I remember. I meet so many people and usually my secretary whispers the names to me as they come forward in humble obeisance. I never minded humble obeisance. Well, one gets used to it, doesn't one? Don't pretend otherwise, Kerr Minor Adjutant. We talked about that matter of Maracoor Spot. I bade you fetch the green-skinned stranger who had dropped in, and that other business beside. You're the functionary for that outpost of the empire. What is your name? Do you even remember it, or are you too tongue-tied by the honor of my visit?"

Lucikles could imagine about five reasons to lie, but he couldn't summon a lie quickly enough to serve. "Lucikles, of the House of Korayus," he mumbled.

"Yes, that's it," said the peasant—the uncle—the Bvasil of Maracoor himself—avatar of the Great Mara, spirit of the land of Maracoor Abiding. "Lucikles. Well, thank you for your offer of hospitality, Lucikles. We shall be delighted to accept—"

Before there could be objection mounted or further fealty paid, a sound came, of children pelting across the herb garden and the tomato patches out back. Leorix was first through the door, with

Star in his arms. Though she was sobbing, she appeared unhurt. Poena with a face of molten iron came next. "This is *so* not the time—" began Lucikles.

"What, what is it?" said his wife, talking over him.

"Something in the grass," said Leorix, wheezing. "Some idiot talky bird-lady."

"She's our *pet*," screamed Star, and beat her fists against her brother's neck.

"See, I told you the children were ill, and it takes such a form," said Oena to the room, improvising desperately—to no avail.

But the Bvasil, and yes it was truly he, now Lucikles could recognize him through the disguise, merely laughed. "Well, this kind of thing is bound to happen when the Great Mara comes to stay for supper. *Will* you stop that squalling, child, you sound like the Prime Protectress of Melody when she feels fortified enough to favor me with a concert of ancient hymnody. Tycheron, do something about that child."

The Bvasil sat back and put his left ankle upon his right knee and pressed down to stretch his thigh muscles. "So we've fetched up at the very home of a Minor Adjutant," he said, and whistled. "That's a second coincidence, Tycheron. One too many to be dumb luck. Must be destiny. Next thing you know, my old mother will walk in the door looking to borrow a cup of ground sugar."

"I thought she was dead," said Tycheron.

"She is, so that would really prove my point, eh?" He was relaxed, the potentate of Maracoor. "Were our steps guided here or is this really bizarre accident?"

"That dog bit me," said Tycheron. "That was the accident part."

"Ah yes. Must have been my mother in disguise. Sounds just like her. Always looking out for her son, and pretty vicious about it. You can close your mouth and stop gaping," he said to Lucikles. "You, too, boy," to Leorix. "We're being hammered into place by the Fist of Mara. Look sharp and get me something eat."

"Lunch is ready when it's ready," said Mia Zephana.

"You're not listening," cried Leorix, beside himself, "it's a damn *wolf*. I can feel it." The boy began to cry in front of the Bvasil, which was the most tragic thing that had happened to him in his life so far, worse even than being wolf-bait.

6

She's our chickie," said Poena. "And so is her sister. They have names but I forget them. They told us when they came out of the eggs."

"She's dreadful," said Leorix. "A human bird-toy. Lit up like she's swallowed a candle."

"Did you actually see a wolf?" asked Lucikles. "No. You just imagined one, I bet. It's not uncommon after what you've been through, son. I'll take a look, shall I?" He'd be glad for a moment's breather. He was still trying to accommodate the thought of a king paying a call at his mother-in-law's hearth.

"I'm coming back with you," said Leorix. "Now that I've rescued my sisters."

"No," said Lucikles. "*Now* you are needed to fend off other beggars. If they pass by, say we've taken in all the needy travelers that we can manage. Which is more than true. Keep at the gate and warn people away."

"Do as your father tells you," said Oena. "Wait for me, Lucikles. I need to see this bright fancy, too. Mamanoo, you're all right with this?"

"Don't dawdle, I'd join you, but this finicky pastry still wants tending and the oven is nearly the right amount of hot."

The girls screamed at having their secret friends co-opted by the grown-ups. "Don't step on them!" cried Poena. "Or I'll kill you! I'll hate you more than I already do. Which is totally."

Husband and wife set off across the yard. It was as if merely going to see a barn on fire. Nothing to say till they got there, till they saw what the situation required. They did not hold hands these days.

The meadow gave way to the scrub, the incidental woods. Lucikles and Oena approached the lateral thrust of ledge rock beyond the pond. It was like the protruding top of a table, and the cave-like area beneath exhaled a cold and iron atmosphere. "I never noticed that slot of space before, did you?" said Lucikles, ashamed that he was whispering. Not a bad lair for a wolf, actually.

"It wasn't like that when I was a child," said Oena. "But the ground shifts and stirs. One spring the wheat-growing people, that family over toward Mileaus, well they went out to plow, and what next? They found six ancient swords poking out of their field like a new sort of bramble."

Lucikles, stooping, called into the low cave. "Is someone in there?" He didn't know quite how to address a rogue wolf or a talking bird for that matter, even if such a thing existed outside of stories. Still, he'd never have believed in a green girl, either. So go figure.

At first nothing, but then two brushes of golden featheriness scraped out of the cave and flew before them, heading for the top of the Throne Tree like a pair of sentinels. Luminous energy given off like sparks from an anvil. But when the creatures landed and folded their wings at their sides, they seemed no more than a natural element of spring woods. A sort of mossy brown; no gold about them. Not chickadees, as the girls had called them. More solid, more like fat falcons. Lethal claws. Feather leggings and shaggy ruff. Crests of lapis lazuli—improbable ornamentation for dun-colored birds of provincial origins. But, neither beaked nor chinless, their faces were, if this could be said, more human than anything else. Set upright into the front plate of the skull the same way a woman's face appears when bounded by tight veils and cowl.

Applied. On a smaller scale, however. Perhaps a hand-span wide, and seven or eight inches high.

"Mara abounding, will you save us from sights of frightful nonsense," hissed Oena, making a pious gesture upon her eyelids.

"We might ask the same." The larger bird figure looked balefully at the humans.

"Do you think we should?" fussed the other. "Very well. I'll do it. 'Mara abounding, save us from'—how did it go?"

"The ungluing of reality," said Lucikles. He was almost relieved. The worst of earlier exposures to abnormality had happened while he was alone. Quietly he'd questioned the soundness of his mind. But there was no doubt that these aberrations were visible to Oena, too. She was cringing, revolted.

The one on the left said, "You're bold to come calling without an invitation. Don't you think they're bold, Asparine? I think they're bold. At least from what I can tell so far. Then again I don't have much experience with this kind of—"

"Moey," said the one called Asparine, "bite your own tongue for a moment."

"Yes, dear," said Moey, and did it, and then said, "Ow," and then, "Sorry," and then said, "*Shhh!*" to herself.

Asparine was the bigger of the two—the two whatever-they-were—and apparently the senior of them. She moved her claws back and forth on the ragged back of the Throne Tree, looking at the humans from a height twice theirs. "I don't know what you're doing here. You're not what we need. He said you'd be green. I think you should go away. We'll wait here for the right one to come along."

"Who said we'd be green?" asked the Minor Adjutant.

"That's all for now. Goodbye," said the more acerbic of the two.

But the pair of anomalies didn't fly off. So Lucikles took a step forward. "Is someone else in there? In the pocket cave under the ledge? We don't have time to play games. Too much is going on. Tell it to come out. Is it a him? Is he a wolf? Whoever it is."

"We're not answerable to you," said Asparine.

Moey asked, "Shall I fly at them and peck their eyes out?" She sounded dubious, as if she hoped Asparine wouldn't say yes. In any case, Asparine didn't need to reply. A rustle in the weeds behind the Throne Tree, and up popped a garden-variety hoopoe. Unimpressed by human company, it gave out a signature call and took off with its flash of rust wings. The consolation of the ordinary.

"I thought it would never leave," said Moey, and winked at the humans in a way that seemed almost flirtatious.

"You're harpies?" said Oena, in delight but also wary. "Harpies! Imagine."

Moey inched nearer. She smelled of hay and vanilla and burned cayenne. "Don't go making friends, Moey, stay on agenda here," snapped Asparine. "They're not green."

"Look, when someone comes to call," replied Moey, "it doesn't do to be rude." To Oena: "I suppose you're the one who laid the eggs that those great galumphing girl-children hatched out of? Are there more of you at home?"

"Well," said Oena, "the house is full, and getting fuller."

"Oh, all right," said Asparine. "As long as we're flushed out already. We were told to expect a green girl, but we can't sit here until we molt. Maybe someone in your nest knows where she is. Let's go."

They launched off the Throne Tree and flashed above the pond, flares that sizzled more in the back of the eyes than against the morning paleness of a spring sky. The effect was thrilling.

So, thought Lucikles. Relexis Kee shows himself a month ago, and now these venomous little busybodies? And they mention a green girl—that Greenie from Maracoor Spot, probably—at best, a stranglehold of coincidences, or a conspiracy of the half-light world. And just as the Bvasil rolls himself up to our door.

Lucikles turned away from the pond, crossing over the meadow and beyond the stone wall and through the herb garden. His wife at his side quickly grabbed his hands. The two harpies, if that's what they were, made flourishes in the air. The Minor Adjutant found that his sight was suddenly glossy. From hope, or a suspicion of imminent loss, he didn't know which.

7

Nearing the house, the Minor Adjutant swept off his cap. A middle-aged human man with a natural tonsure. The harpies managed a clumsy landing upon the lip of a laundry bucket in the yard. "We won't come inside," said Asparine. "We're not household items."

"It's a dog door; it divides at the waist. You can come to the lip if you want," said Lucikles, as if being a Minor Adjutant gave him authority over creatures from the halfway realm. He and Oena pushed into the kitchen. Tycheron was wringing his hands, but looked with gratitude at them, at Oena especially. Leorix must have fled in shame to his cot in the loft. Burden—the Bvasil of Maracoor himself—was amusing the little girls by swinging some sort of golden pendant hung on a chain around his neck. They tried to clap their hands upon it, but he was deft. Those born to power know how to keep it.

"So tell us all," said Mia Zephana, turning from the kettle, "shall I set a place for a wolf? Oh—I see." The others looked up. The harpies had pricked their talons upon the edge of the lower door. In settling, their light diminished. Their female faces looked oaken, of a piece with the farmhouse timbers.

The girls saw their friends and came running to them, but the harpies were in no mood and Asparine raised a talon in warning. "Oh, great, you're all grown-up now, already." Poena turned her grief upon her father. "I knew you'd ruin it."

"Time goes by in a rush, nobody says it doesn't," said Asparine. "Leave us be. We now have work to do."

"What manner of aberration is this, to punish us in our time of trial?" asked Burden.

Mia Zephana dug a crust from the breadcrumb pot and put it to soak in some milk and honey. "You call yourself harpies?" asked Mia Zephana of Moey and Asparine. "You two, you busy-body feather dusters, what do you say for yourselves? I thought harpies were snatchers of babies. You look more like disgruntled farmwives whose pickles took last place at the harvest festival."

"Condescension, a bad look for you," said Asparine. She sniffed. "We come as we are. I'm not interested in snatching babies myself. Have no idea what to do with one."

"They called you chickadees. I wouldn't quite say you were chickadees," said Oena.

"I'm Asparine, she's Moey, we're eager to get going. What's the delay here?"

"Where are you off to?" asked Lucikles.

"Nowhere, yet. We're not all here. We've been told there's a verdant young woman joining us."

The Bvasil put his fingertips together and spoke to the harpies and to the humans. "We repaired to the highland to collect our strength. We didn't expect to uncover allies and abettors. But if figures of myth are joining us, maybe we should change our plans about finding a soothsayer, and instead turn back to the city. A Bvasil presumed to have died but returning with figures of legend—well, that would polish my brass buttons, but good. I don't suppose we could scare up a centaur or two?"

"If you're going to liberate Maracoor Crown," said Leorix, descending the ladder, "I am with you. My Lord." He glared at his father preemptively.

"Oh please," said Lucikles. "Spare us the theatrics, honey. Not to mention the insolence—addressing His Magnificence when you've not even been formally introduced."

"We already met, remember?" said the boy. "I was there in the chamber when we had the appointment before going to the island to nab the green stranger."

"Ah, a green stranger?" said Asparine. "Moey, pay attention."

"You can help, lad," said Burden equably enough. "Before we decide about whether or not to return to the capital, we have to learn what's going on there. Will you find out what the news is today from anyone passing by?"

Leorix nearly fainted with pride. "I will." He raised his elbow to shoulder height and advanced his chin, an old-fashioned military salute he'd probably learned doing student theatricals. The boy then spirited himself out the doorway in a move as much like a caper as anything else. Lucikles rolled his eyes.

"But about this green stranger," said Moey. "She's the one we've been told to watch out for. You know where she is?"

"She's in custody in the capital," said Lucikles. "Detained. Some women's prison."

"She's not," said Tycheron. "She liberated herself. We saw her on the road. We asked her to join us but she and her companion chose to take the forest road."

"Under these circumstances the forest isn't safe," said Lucikles. "You oughtn't have let her make that choice."

"It wasn't a question of permissions," said Tycheron. "The Bvasil was in disguise. And as a peasant farmer he has no authority over civilians."

Moey and Asparine glanced at each other. "The forest *isn't* safe," agreed Asparine. "The sooner she emerges the better. Shall we go find her, Moey?"

Without another word of discussion, nor did she seek permission of the potentate in residence, Moey took to the wing, galloped brightly up the breeze, and disappeared.

"Hot-headed gadabout," muttered Asparine. "Should have canvassed the place first. Wait for me, girl."

"Before you go," said Mia Zephana, "tell us how you came to be hunkering down here. It's my farm, after all, even if I can't light myself up like some festival decoration."

"All the obvious questions. But you can't help it," replied the harpy. "It only looks as if Moey and I were born yesterday out of eggs. We're emollients of the natural world, we creatures of human story, no less than you are, come to that. But we live in a different fretwork of time and of constancy. Get it? That's all I've got for you."

"Are you fairy tale, or something else?" asked Mia Zephana. Lucikles admired the frank way his mother-in-law addressed a creature of myth. He supposed farm life did that to a woman. You learned to face things squarely.

"It's safer to say that story is made around us, because we do exist, than that we exist because of story. That about covers it."

"You're part human and part hawk, is that it?" asked Tycheron.

"I know what I know, and I am ignorant of everything else. Like every creature that blinks awake. Put aside these questions; you won't find answers to comfort you. And you'll need to sleep, too. Tonight is a time for rest. The campaigns of untold tomorrows will take everything that we have. Now might I go join Moey before she forgets where she's headed?"

"But how do you even know about a green girl from away?" Lucikles asked Asparine.

"We have our sources of information. Enough said about *that*. In any case, that girl's foolhardiness brought us forward. Us, and the Skedes, too. She has a lot to answer for. Let me take a look around." She spiraled out the doorway.

8

The Bvasil—no, he must now be thought of as Burden, for his own security, thought Lucikles—finally arose and said, "I'm going for a stroll to clear my head." Tycheron made as if to accompany him, but with a slice of his hand, Burden forbade it.

The others fell silent. The girls were already resigned. Their precious chickadees were flown. Life had reverted to its proper arrangement, where, like any children, they belonged at the bottom of the heap. "Let's go make a mud pie," said Poena. They skipped out the side entrance, because the dirt in that dooryard was a better grade for pastry-making.

Mia Zephana put up a pot of tea. Tycheron, Lucikles, and Oena accepted cups. The four of them hunched with their elbows on the table. A rare occasion, when a busy farm pauses its operations midmorning. Visiting crowned heads and emerging creatures of the mythic history or not, the cows still wanted moving to the lower pasture, the curd its sieving through cloth. But that would have to wait.

The question in Lucikles's mind was about destiny.

Consider a character in an old tale—say the story of Relexis Kee, the son of the Great Mara herself. There may be variants in his story, but he can't step beyond the most outlying of the versions and do something entirely different. Lucikles felt himself to be cast, in this aberration of history, as if in a theatrical role. The honor of being, for the moment, near the center of something that involved both the ruler of the nation and the phantasms of mythic history—it almost but didn't eclipse the suspicion he was being conned. Even gods can have agendas, he supposed, wearily.

But, if conned, by whom? By what? Neither the harpies nor the Bvasil seemed in control of history. So perhaps it was only the roiling of circumstance after all.

"Did you and—and Burden—come here on purpose, looking for me?" Lucikles asked Tycheron.

"I never heard of you before," said the younger man.

"I mean, did you flee the city to look for the man who had brought the green girl and the amulet to Maracoor Crown?"

"We were looking for the chance to get as far away from the teaming crowds as possible. We will command an audience with a renowned but secret fortune-teller if we can find him. That a dog bit my leg and we then crossed your path, just dumb luck."

"It's hard to credit, when I'm nominally in the employ of the Bvasil."

"He's just Burden now," said Tycheron wryly. "I guess you're not in *his* employ."

Lucikles turned to Mia Zephana. "And here you are, Mamanoo, on this nap of land tucked on the near side of nothing. How is it that the very place the great ruler of Maracoor stops for succor is the place where children unearth creatures of myth?"

"Well, why shouldn't it be?" Mia Zephana took the honey spool and dribbled a golden strand into her cup. "I pay my taxes. I keep a tidy barn. I suppose the point of a miracle is that it can happen anyplace."

"Have you had inklings of these presences upon your property and you never remembered to mention them?"

Her laconic expression, that raised eyebrow. "You get to a certain age," she said drily, "nothing much surprises you. I suppose, to be fair, I've always felt this holding was a little special. But what farmer doesn't? We see life come and go here with pace, with merciless efficiency. Death and pain and reward, and chickadees under foot every now and then. No, I've never seen harpies before, if that's what you're asking. I've never seen harpies or a centaur or a talking centipede or a dancing rat anywhere in High Chora. But I have seen the sun in the trees, and the mist hovering over the meadow, and the wind sculpting shapes in a snow squall, and I've wondered what is hidden in what I can see, and felt the allure of what I don't know. So excuse me, please, if I'm not overwhelmed and falling on the floor, slack-jawed like a holy fool."

She was annoyed at him. She'd never made such a long speech in her life. As with many upland people, her taciturnity wasn't so much a virtue as a necessity. She stood and put aside the unfinished portion of tea in her cup. "I'd better see to those cows. That grass isn't going to eat itself." She stumped over the threshold.

Oena pursed her lips at her husband. "You might have asked me your question about presences. After all, I was born here."

"What's that supposed to mean?"

"Well, doesn't childhood really only amount to a sorting out between what is magic and what isn't—what is possible, what is likely, what is impossible? Where a childhood takes place provides the testing ground for those experiments in—in perception. So my answer to your question might have been different from my mother's."

He stared at her, rolled his hand, *Go on*. Tycheron watched her with interest.

It was Oena's turn to stand and move around the room. "Yes, I suppose I did. Piskies, baby basilisks, who were perhaps iguanas—who knows? But I bet you did, too, before you came of age in the city. You saw mice and thought they were little people. You heard birds cry and thought you understood. Only when you got older did you decide it hadn't really happened. Mice weren't people, birds couldn't talk, or not to us. I'm not saying that what I perceived had much basis in reality. But what I perceived when I was a child, it was real to *me*. So when the girls come in and say they've found some chickadees and they turn out to be harpies, I'm not as surprised as you are. That's all."

"It's the farmer's instinct for life in all its mystery," intoned Tycheron.

"Oh, put a bung in that hole, and give it a rest," said Lucikles.

He was kept from saying more by the arrival of Leorix at the door. "Papa. People are stopping and insisting on being given safe harbor. I've told them we can't, but these ones are pushy." He then muttered, "I think you'd better come," and looked disgusted with himself at having to utter those words.

Lucikles followed his son with relief, eager to leave behind the blather in the room. Tycheron stayed where he was, sipping the tea and reaching for a scone, and favoring his bandaged calf.

The group of travelers were five men. At least Lucikles assumed they were men. Smoke-smudged, their clothes in tatters. Maybe one or two were women camouflaged for their own safety. But oh, Leorix was canny. This group had a look of desperation about it.

"What did you tell them?" he muttered to his son as they approached the gate. One of the men had an iron crowbar over his shoulder.

"That we couldn't have them to stay. I didn't give a reason."

"Friends," said Lucikles, with all the false charm that a life in civil service had taught him. "I bid you peace but I'm afraid you'll have to pass by. This can't be the place for you."

"You don't know where we're from or what we're fleeing," said crowbar man. "You'd have mercy if you knew."

"We're all up against it. It's mortal grief, these days. What news do you bring?"

"The Bvasil was thrown to his death by an angry mob. The city has fallen."

"We've heard."

"The bloodthirsty Skedes scaled the walls like spiders or lizards."

"But what mayhem?" He realized he should send Leorix away, but his eagerness to know was too strong. "Have they razed the city with fire?"

"No. They rolled through the palace and spent several nights taking apart the treasury. But they left behind most of the jewelry, and gold, and precious books and muck. I mean, there was likely some looting, but it wasn't the point. And although they rounded up what they could of the home guard, they merely locked them in the city's stadia. They aren't killing them, much, or even starving them. The invaders aren't raping or kidnapping the women. Mostly. They're leaving children alone. But they are taking animals and food and they are—" The man shook his head as if in disbelief. "They're fanning out. Heading this way."

"Whatever for?"

"They didn't find what they came to find. Whatever that is. But new legions are pouring in for reinforcement. The populace is penned in. Last we heard, the barbarians are dividing into smaller bands. Some are heading out on the main thoroughfare to High Chora. Other details are combing the Thalassic Wood and monitoring the forest road to the south. Word of some mighty strange doings, though whether of alien marauders or minor homeland demi-urges, who the hell knows. As the Skedes move, they've got to be thinning out in number. But they're scaling the palisades behind us. We're desperate for water, food, for a safe place to rest before we move on." His grip on the crowbar tightened. "You can't deny us. I think you won't deny us."

"You're in your rights to expect safe harbor," said Lucikles, "but you won't find it here. We're in the grip of a terrible wasting illness. The symptoms are horrible and we don't yet know whether they are fatal. Honor requires that we bid you pass us by, for your own sakes."

"That's a crock of shit," said the leader, beginning to push against the wooden gate. "You're a fat, self-satisfied rump of beef. Let us in. We need food and a floor to doss down on. We've been on the road all night. The wolves. You hear about the wolves?"

"Oh, we know about wolves," said Leorix, a darkness in his voice that sent chills down his father's spine. "They're closer than you think."

"Boy," said Lucikles, "go inside and tend your mother and your sisters. That's a command." For a moment Lucikles thought Leorix was going to refuse to go. But with an evil look at his father, the lad did as he was told. For once.

"I do know about the wolves," said Lucikles. "Several months ago, a pack attacked my family, and grazed that son you met. He isn't quite right even now. But you'll be smarter to move along, and the sooner the better. I can't answer for what may befall you if you linger. Really."

"That's the shabbiest lie I ever heard told," said one of the others, and Lucikles was right: it was a woman's voice emitting from the hooded garb of a young man.

"I haven't the time to lie," said Lucikles sharply, hoping his ruse was strong enough to protect them. "Get away, get your filthy hands off that gate! I'm warning you." They were beginning to shove through, an angry mob of five, enough to overwhelm him. He pushed back, ready to go down in defense of his family and the unspecified needs of the nation, when an unearthly, guttural howl came from somewhere above his shoulders, from the thatched eaves of the farmhouse. A wolf's anger. For an unholy instant he imagined it was Leorix in extremis. Cruel, hollow. And effective.

"I have no more time for you! Move along, or be stricken," he roared at the travelers, and turned his back on them. Though he heard their crowbar come down upon the gate, he also heard them leave. With a lively pace. What do you know—the stop had rejuvenated them after all.

Asparine ruffled her feathers. "Little party trick," she called down. "Now I'm off to find Moey before she thinks I got eaten by a wolf. You kidnapped the green girl but you let her escape. We'll bring her in."

"You'll stay right here," said Lucikles. "You're a better guard-dog than our Cur could ever be. While the Bvasil of Maracoor is in residence, you're the honor guard. That's an order."

Hardly expecting her to obey, he went back into the farmhouse. The wolf-howl from the roof was criticism or warning. Also a bit show-offy, he concluded. Even though he knew it was a kind of ventriloquism, his blood still ran cold at the sound. And poor Leorix? He'd be out of his wits with the thought of a wolf on the premises, this one at the very door. He hurried to his son.

HAUNTS *of the*
THALASSIC WOOD

1

fter the clenched streets of the stone city, Rain found the Thalassic Wood an impossible riddle. Nature—what a rebuke of orderliness it could be. Great oaks downed like army generals fallen in battle. Thornweed ivy, poison vetch. And the noise—the undercover shuffling and snuffling. The torn cries of unseen birds or beasts uttered behind ten thousand leafy green hands raised up in alarm. "It's berserk, it's possessed," Rain said to Iskinaary.

"Don't talk to me about possessed," replied the Goose. "When we ditch the kiddo and head for the coast, this will soon seem like only a bad dream."

"We're finding the child a sanctuary first," said Rain, for the eighth time in as many hours.

"We should have gone with that guy and his uncle," said Cossy. At Rain's affronted expression the child continued, "I didn't know it would be like this. It's all—against us." She was right. In places the forest gnarled itself impenetrable. Wires, trellises, fans of stubborn growth.

"I'd like to get airborne and scope out the territory, but I'm afraid I'd lose you for good under such a dense canopy," said Iskinaary. "Not that losing one of you doesn't have a certain appeal."

"*Drop* it, Iskinaary. We'll hang together on the path, if we can keep to it," said Rain.

Mollified, the Goose ventured, in a false bright tone, "This isn't like any holiday promenade I can remember. Can you?" Rain got lost in thinking about it, lost in the woods in her mind. Her unidentified past stalking her like a predator. How could she identify future trouble if past peril was still a blank?

2

Nonetheless, she worked at it as she tramped on. Oh words. Fragments and vowels. Small glints and suggestions. As if her life were a picture puzzle that had fallen upside down on its face. She could get purchase only on a few interlocking bits at a time. She could turn them over. She could read them to remember.

She'd already recalled her father and her mother. Liir, a contemplative man who lived alone near an isolated lake in the outback of Oz. Candle, a Quadling woman from the south of the country, who'd left Liir for incompatibility. Rain could figure on no brothers or sisters, though.

The deeper past was coming clearest. Rain had lived an early childhood in hiding, hiding in plain view. Her natural green pallor cloaked by a magick so she could pass, she'd been tucked away into the household of Lady Glinda. Had the run of Mockbeggar Hall. In some ways she'd been little more than a scullery maid. Now, recovering from the concussion, she saw anew that Glinda's protection had been an act of mercy that lasted for years.

But for such a long time after that, Rain had lived as a criminal might live—stealing from one safe haven to the next rather than staying put to see the seasons become years, and the years decades. This couldn't be normal for a child?

She glanced sideways at Cossy to see how the girl was taking to the vagabond life so far. (Two days in.) Although now rescued from the weird practices of her situation on Maracoor Spot, Cossy had enjoyed there something denied Rain in her own childhood: constancy. So this business of not knowing what was to come next must be a great challenge for Cossy. While Rain herself had trained on the run to be on the run, even if she couldn't quite recall *from what.*

She took Cossy under her arm as often as she could—literally, draping her own arm over the girl's shoulders. Sometimes Cossy shoved it off. Other times she grabbed Rain's hand in both of her own as if she would never let it go. Once she began to nibble Rain's fingernails. Rain didn't let on how inept she felt at trying to comfort a child. The girl needed something Rain couldn't identify or supply. If Rain hadn't arrived on Cossy's island redoubt, the girl would be living out her circumscribed life as an unmarried bride, not fleeing from a conviction for juvenile murder. Rain had a lot to answer for, even if she'd intended none of this.

The track began to rise, if in no particular hurry. Rain and her companions sensed more than saw the tableland lifting beyond them. The third night out from the capital city, they found an abandoned woodcutter's lodge populated by mice. The stink was horrific. An air of mold, as if the whole earth were one rotten gravesite.

Waking in the middle of that night, Rain sat up. Iskinaary and the others—Tiotro, Faro, Finistero, and Thilma—were sleeping in heaps. Cossy resembled a lump of knitting. What a thin, wasted thing.

Rain arose. Out of habit she grabbed the broom on which she'd flown here from Oz. It had lost its talent of flight but it was a comfort to carry. She groped her way to the door and stepped out into a moonlight fragmented by overgrowth.

She paused, inhaling the ferrous and vegetable breath of the woods. After a while she saw that she was not alone. Across the clearing in front of the hut, half in shadows, a creature on four legs had paused, facing in her direction. It was perhaps, she thought, a wolf. When it stepped forward a yard or two out of the growth and into the clearing, she saw she was right. A grey wolf—or Wolf—made teal blue by some effect of moonlight and wet midnight.

"Are you the one I am looking for?" said the Wolf in a low voice—not quite a growl, but not especially affable, either.

"I don't know," said Rain, wondering if she was having a dream. "I doubt it. No one knows I'm here, really, so I don't know how you could be looking for me."

A blue Wolf and a green girl in the moonlight, talking to each other.

"I am newly arrived," said the creature. "At this moment, in this world, I am all but blind still. So I have to ask. Are you the green girl?"

"In this light, it's hard to say." She smiled at her own drollery.

"Do you have the amulet?" pressed the Wolf.

"I've got my broom. An old seashell, too, in my satchel. That's it. I don't go in for ornamentation otherwise."

"The amulet. You have the scent of it upon you."

"Sorry, but whatever scent you're picking up is due to a lack of decent sanitation. If you were a human person making such a comment, you'd be intolerably rude. However, as you're a creature relying on your nose, I suppose you don't mean to give offense." Rain was amused at her own poise. This Animal could fall upon her in an instant, rip out her throat, and slaughter all her companions. That she was so calm convinced her, for the moment anyway, of the dream nature of this interview. She waited, though she kept her broom tightly clutched in both hands.

The Wolf stepped forward again. Rain couldn't tell the sex.

"If you don't have the amulet, where is it?" asked the Wolf.

"I haven't any amulet and I don't have a clue. What's all this about then? Are you here to give me a secret message, a code, a curse? A job to do? A piece of advice?"

"Advice? Take care of yourself. You're in a treacherous situation. Trouble ahead."

"Oh, that," she said, nearly laughing. "Well, that's true for every living sprite and spirit that walks the holy ground, no? We're all in danger of losing our favored place. Thank you," she continued, "but it would be useful if you could be more specific."

The Wolf sniffed as a dog might. "Someone in your party is a danger to you."

"I've always hated omens," said Rain. "You might as well say 'Death waits for you.' Well, duh."

The Wolf didn't seem to take offense. "Look for me again. And watch your step. I'll consult with my delegation and I'll return."

"Advisors? You answer to some ghost-wolf council?" But perhaps that was taking insolence too far. The Wolf disappeared. It didn't bolt, just sidled a few feet and merged with the moonlight. "What should I call you?" she ventured to say. Her whisper was too low to be heard by anyone but herself. Anyway, she was the only one there.

So she'd thought her darkened memories were stalking her like a wolf, and it turned out a Wolf had been posing as darkened memories. This was worth only so-so in the consolation marketplace.

3

It was midmorning before Rain began to remember her midnight amble. Had she dreamed a blue Wolf? Before she could examine her reveries, the flying monkeys on the road ahead gave out a dreadful racket. Cossy and Rain plunged toward them even as the Goose warned them to hang back. "I forbid it!" he quawked. But at his age he couldn't run as fast as they, and the foliage prevented his liftoff. The others outpaced him.

The girls cleared a hump of ridge and started down the other side. The road curved around a dead tree trunk carved all over with forest faces. A demon badger, a crow king, a something-or-other with fangs growing where its eyes should be. But it wasn't indigenous art that had spooked the monkeys. Just beyond the stacked totems the monkeys were tearing at something thrashing on the ground.

She got close enough to catch a glimpse of the poor man between the clapping wings of the agitated simians. A toothless, middle-aged peasant. Being squeezed to death by a python. The monkeys had found a boulder and bashed the python's head in, but the dying serpent had only tightened its coils around its victim. Rain grabbed the serpent tail and screamed at the monkeys to lift the man up. When they did, she was able to unwind the first few loops, and the monkeys got the picture. They unrolled the victim out of his ropes and they cast the corpse of the python aside.

The man vomited. He was breathing shallowly but not yet conscious. The Goose caught up with them and quawked, "This was an attempted murder."

"Oh, I thought it was a picnic game," said Cossy. She was pale and hiding behind Rain.

"Look," said the Goose. He flipped the tip of his wing over the man's face. They saw that someone had taken a knife to the man's forehead and cut the shape of a crude S. Its edges were blackened with blood.

"A sign of the Skedes?" asked Rain. "What would they be doing inland? And so soon?"

The Goose hissed in contempt. "Or maybe it's S for *snake,* see? Someone was punishing this man and set him out here for the python to find."

Maybe so. His hands were tied behind his back.

They had no provisions to offer him, and in any case he was still out cold. Rain handed her nautilus shell to Thilma, who came back with a beaker of fresh water. When they tipped it into his mouth, the fellow began to choke and cough, and he came around. The monkeys were useless at knots, so Rain and Cossy worked at the cords around his wrists as he sputtered.

He wouldn't tell them who he was or why he had been set out as lunch for a local python. "They're all mad with fear, these forest people," he said. "And greedy? Won't share so much as an old tomato."

"It wasn't the Skedes?" asked Rain. "The invaders?"

"No, it was our own homegrown varmints, thank you. Begrudging a fellow citizen a little breakfast." He gulped some more water and only then seemed to take in the facts of Rain's green skin and her monkey consorts. "You're the invaders yourselves, by the look of it. Are you going to finish me off?"

"We're heading upland. We don't want any trouble. We can't stop you joining us but we're not going to hang around here till you decide."

"Stay clear of the settlements," he said. "I know this road. The chinless inbreds in Midasoor, up ahead, used to be tolerant of passersby. But everyone's ginned up for blood. They'll make monkey cutlets out of your pets by suppertime if they see you before you see them."

"You must have done more than steal a tomato," said the Goose.

"I don't answer to weird creatures from children's stories, it's creepy," replied the man, and he kicked out his legs, catching Cossy in the stomach. He was up and lopsiding into bracken before they could react. They let him go.

"Hope he doesn't meet the python's mother," said Iskinaary, insincerely.

The travelers chose to beat a berth around the village that had trussed a common thief for a python's snack. They spent the morning bushwhacking through bad-tempered vegetation. Some sort of nettle raised itchy welts on Cossy and Rain.

With all the crashing through underbrush, all the sweating and swearing, the fear of human mendacity grown stronger, it took a while before Rain again remembered about the blue visitation the night before. When she did, she wondered about her sanity and about the chemical architecture of the mystical world.

She couldn't tell if a dream could be an actual message from—as back in Oz some might say—the Unnamed God. Or whether dreams were disruptive, anarchic, and merely gaudy. Surrealism for the sake of shock.

Still, the young escapee clinging to her was more immediate than trying to plumb the niceties of the working universe. "Are we sisters now?" asked Cossy.

"I don't seem to have any other sister," said Rain. "So why not? For now. We're as good as sisters. Even bad sisters."

"Helia was bad," said Cossy. Helia was the oldest of the brides of Maracoor. Maybe Cossy was fastening on her own past to avoid the current terror of this woods.

"Ah, don't we all have some bad and good in us," replied Rain. Though this seemed like pablum, and old pablum at that. "What do you mean, she was bad?"

"Helia was the one who told me where to find the key to the holy Vessel. She told me that if someone unlocked the box and put some herbs next to the amulet, and then fed those herbs to someone, she wouldn't feel so great. Helia didn't tell me Mirka would *die*. Helia made me a murderer because she didn't want to do it herself."

"I wonder why Helia wanted Mirka so very dead, and all that?"

"Helia was scared of the Fist of Mara, but more scared of what Mirka might do if she got her hands on it. Mirka was hungry for it. Hard hungry. The Fist was the real king of the island, I now see."

The Fist of Mara. A strange dense item, the length of Cossy's forearm. Shaped a little like a hammer or a claw. Heavy as iron but dull as stone. It had been locked in the temple on Maracoor Spot until that fellow Lucikles had arrived with orders to remove Rain from the company of the brides of Maracoor. He'd removed her, yes, and the totem, too, as well as Cossy, accused of murder. He'd brought them to the mainland, Cossy and Rain, to stand separate trial for several crimes: Cossy for murder, Rain for seditious collusion against the troubled nation. From whose prison they'd escaped, and from whose officials they were presumably still on the run. While the Fist of Mara was now likely impounded in a vault guarded by gorillas.

"But," said Rain, as long as they had time to talk, "whatever do you think Mirka could have done with the Fist of Mara, anyway? Stuck on the outpost of Maracoor Spot?"

"I don't know. Hit someone with it?"

"People already have fists if they feel like punching people."

"This one is stronger. It's dangerous. For my whole life the Fist of Mara was just a stupid totem in a box, and now it's why I'm hiking through stupid woods with burdocks in my bum."

Oh. The totem. *That* amulet. The blue Wolf in her dream had come looking for it. The Wolf had thought Rain might have it. She shook her head to clear it some, and said, "Who needs a Fist of Mara when people can be so deadly on their own? But look, we've found a place to rejoin the main path. We've circled around that settlement of nasty thugs."

The road took on a steeper grade. They were making progress. Talking was harder. When it leveled out again, Cossy said, "So okay, tell me another story, I'm bored. Tell me a story about you."

Rain sighed. There'd always be outstanding payments due this child. But the recent past, like the distant childhood, came to the tongue in a narrative shape. In reciting it, she tiptoed around the subject of the Grimmerie. No one need know about that.

"Well, Iskinaary and I flew from a place called Oz. The flying monkeys followed but I didn't know about it. They were supposedly sent by my father to hunt for me and, I guess, rescue me if I was in trouble. When am I not in trouble? The monkeys never heard of an ocean before—few people in Oz ever heard of it, actually. The shoreline is back of beyond, and so the idea of an ocean was only myth. You call it the Sea of Mara, but on the Oz side of it, to the extent it has a name at all, and that's mostly to Geese, it's the Nonestic Sea."

To Cossy, having grown up on an island in the middle of an ocean, the idea of not believing in the sea seemed more bizarre than the idea of monkeys soaring over it. She rolled her eyes as Rain continued. "Tiotro and the others hoped to find us and usher us home, or to turn back when they could go no farther. But the same storm that dumped me on Maracoor Spot caught them, too, and pitched them to this weird unknown land. The monkeys want to go home. They want to take me with them."

The winged monkeys, eavesdropping to hear the parts about themselves, cheered at that bit. Enough with pythons and storms and these dank overgrown slopes.

"I'm with you lot," declared Iskinaary. "Home sweet home."

"We have company," said Rain, and indicated Cossy with a jerk of her thumb.

"As soon as you recover your ability to govern that broomstick, we're leaving," declared the Goose. "No discussion. You can't hold five of us hostage, Rain."

"We're going west while we can." Rain practiced being defiant. "For now. We have to find a place to settle Cossy safely before beginning to think about returning to Oz."

"I'm sticking with you," said Cossy. "I don't care if it's Oz or Skoz or the Island of Dead Fish."

"You'd hate Oz. It's a horrid place," said Rain.

"I'd fit right in. I'm horrid too," said Cossy. "A murderer. Don't forget!"

"You didn't know what you were doing," said Rain. "You didn't understand. Stop with that murderer stuff. You're starting to sound proud of it."

Alert to the possible creep of python, they feasted anyway, glad to be alive.

4

Again Rain woke up in the middle of the night. The air felt tired. Moonlight, unreliable in strength given scudding, furtive clouds. Cossy was alert too and standing, watching Rain with an inscrutable expression. The others were sleeping intensely. Whoever had been assigned the evening watch had nodded off.

There was no need to talk. In the dark all worries about moral status were retired. The two girls joined hands.

A few feet off waited the blue Wolf. Supremely patient, like a porter at the side of a railroad track, expecting the midnight local.

"There you are," said the Wolf. Tonight, Rain thought it more likely the Wolf was male, because the voice seemed lower. But perhaps he, if it was he, was keeping his voice down so as not to wake the others. "Let's go."

Rain didn't answer. She wasn't sure if Cossy could see the Wolf, and didn't want to frighten the child. But Cossy turned to Rain and said, "Well, are we going then?"

"I need my broom," said Rain. Force of habit. She also dropped the big seashell in her pocket. Touchstones of Oz, of home.

Cossy dragged Rain down the steps with her as the Wolf turned and paced into the forest. Every once in a while he looked back to make sure that the humans were following him.

No bite, no sting,
No anything,
No losing our way—

Cossy couldn't work out how to finish her spell. Rain offered, "Or losing our minds?" and Cossy stuck out her tongue.

As they followed the Wolf, it seemed that the Thalassic Wood began to organize itself. After a while Rain felt that the trees were shaping an ornamental alley in the heart of the wilderness. Their branches met overhead. The black night had a liquid quality, maybe that of squid-ink soup.

The Wolf lifted his neck and his ears pronged alert. His gait slowed. Rain and Cossy, still holding hands, stepped upon a carpet of cool dry moss. In the center of the clearing stood a stone monument—a much-overgrown mausoleum, thought Rain, or maybe a temple marking some long-forgotten sacred exposure. A graven figure in stone was picked out in shadows. An erect mermaid with bare breasts and the swiveled tail. Her head wasn't profiled like a face on a coin, but pointing at them.

"Lookit those legs," said Cossy.

Rain caught on. The ribs of segmented cane that emerged from the creature's waist radiated like the spokes of an umbrella. She didn't need her tail on land. She was presented as hoisted aloft the way the Bvasil in his chair-car had been.

The pause as the stone presence scrutinized them went on too long. Finally the Wolf said, "This is the appointed spot. I thought she might address you. It appears she won't. Or she can't. Or she has business elsewhere. I'll have to be her mouthpiece."

"She's made of stone," Cossy pointed out.

"That's the statue only. She's insubstantial fabric herself. But to the point. My name is Artoseus," said the Wolf. "Now that I've recognized you as the visiting green witch, tell me your name."

"Well, to be complete about it," said Rain, "it is Oziandra Rainary Ko Osqa'ami Thropp. But Rain suits me fine. And green I may be, but the witch part is too rich for me. I'm closer to the village idiot."

"And I'm Acaciana," said Cossy, "but Cossy suits *me* fine. Who is this lady? Is this the Great Mara?"

"It's not yours to interrogate the likes of us," growled Artoseus. "Her name is immaterial. It changes regularly, so if you called it out she might not even recognize it. No, she isn't the Great Mara, not in any way that you could understand. It's all right for you to be curious. You're young. You have to learn that you will never understand much in this life."

"She looks like an idea we once named the Ladyfish," said Rain. "Back home. Look, Master Dream Wolf, I've done what I set out to do—" No point trying to conceal her crime from a mythic figure, who seemed to know who she was anyway. "I got rid of a magic book of great power so it could never be used again. I sunk it for good. The Grimmerie, it was called. Then I was blown off course and landed wherever we are. It was messy happenstance. I don't know why you've been pacing me, but all this has got to stop. It's creepy."

"The best of our incomplete wisdom might help guide you," said Artoseus, "if you let it. You must keep on to the west. Across the tableland, beyond the alluvial wetlands. There's a forest deeper and trickier than this one. You need to seek the advice of an aged seer to find out what you should do about the totem. We can't advise you. We're shy of knowledge about the future. Only the eternal present concerns us."

"Right, you asked about an item—a totem, a charm of some sort?" said Rain. "Last time? Not my problem."

"Your arrival here gave aid and comfort to the foreigners looking for it. You are implicated. You've responsibility to help settle the matter."

"I'm hardly responsible for tying my own boots," said Rain. "You're mistaking me for someone with agency and power. Sure, I once could manage to fly on a broomstick, but that was as much the broomstick as it was me. It comes from honorable stock, as broomsticks go. Though it's lost its juice."

Artoseus looked peeved. The lowered brow, the curled lip. "The python was lying in wait for you, and that poor pickpocket distracted him. I've been fending off Skedes from the south and scabs from the half-light. You'd do better not to discount me."

"I didn't ask for an escort," said Rain. "But I suppose thank you anyway. But why me? You notice my skin color and you bring up that totem again. I seem to be a carnival of attractions for you. I'm feeling ganged up on."

Cossy said, "You mean the Fist of Mara? *I'm* the one who saw it."

The Wolf paid the child no mind. "Much in human affairs is too complicated for your sort to explain to yourselves. Still, you can appreciate the laws of consequence. When you released the great power of that book into the depths of the sea off of Maracoor Abiding, you unharnessed hidden powers and potentates that reside beneath the surface of things. It's how you can be talking to me. No, this isn't a dream. The creatures in which the ancients held stock never quite died off, just retired into the obscurity of half-light. The piskies, the bat-winged serpents, the hagwitches and wormwitches and centaurs and such. Few of these survivors have any agenda beyond conserving the life of this land. But they're stirred to the notice of humans by the release of potential that— you called it a Grimmerie?—that book brought to our shores. The very winds revolved in obstinate and contrary patterns, allowing a foreign army to approach and to invade."

"Hey, you're blaming me for the invasion? That's a step too far. I can't even make an omelet. I didn't go to university. I turned down the place they offered me. Hopeless."

"You didn't create the navy or the marching army or the totem that they seek—the Fist of Mara. No. True enough. But the change in the winds allowed them to sneak upon the capital city and to try to plunder it for the amulet, as it is called. They must not get it. The sacred conventicle that makes up the Great Mara's limbs and license is threatened. That's why I've deigned to bring you here tonight. Though I hadn't expected to do all the talking."

"I just want to go home to Oz," said Rain, not sure if this was true.

"You must get the Fist of Mara out of Maracoor first. If you can. I think you can. You owe us that much for having brought your troubles to these shores. And it will rescue us all if you are successful."

Rain's hopes sank. "We don't know where the Fist of Mara is, or really even what it is, and even if we did, where this awful thing needs to go?"

"That we can't tell you because we don't know either. But it doesn't belong here. It has never belonged here. Locate the one who might help. He's called the Oracle of Maracoor."

Rain pursed her lips. "You talk as if I am obligated. Well, I'm not. I'm done. I don't need an Oracle to tell me my business."

"He lives to the far western edge of our land, in a place called the Tower in the Clouds. A sort of hermitage, an outpost high in the Tenterix Range. The area known as the Walking Mountains. Our wisdom is of the ages and not always pertinent. But he is called the Oracle of Maracoor for a reason. He ought to be able to see what to do about the amulet. That's the magnet that has attracted the Skedes. It must go." Suddenly the Wolf sounded like a minor functionary in a government municipality, just realizing he was late for his elevenses.

A moment of pause. Then Rain said, "Since you're being a busybody, tell me. Whether I follow your suggestion or just go home, what am I to do with Cossy? There are, um, differences of opinion about this. I can't just leave her in the woods."

"You damn well better not," said Cossy.

"What is to happen to someone like her?" Rain was trying to choose her words carefully. "I'm asking about Cossy."

"You'll have help. Companions on the road. And guides are on their way. You'll need them. Your problems are more than human. You see, not all activated spirits of the mythologies are benign. The reckless and the desperate also assemble. About your companion—"

But then, like a quenched flame, Artoseus had disappeared. The night was buzzy with insects taking over the world. The wanderers would find their way back to the camp alone. When nearly there, Rain said, "No need to mention what you heard about the Grimmerie."

"I don't know what that is. Nobody explains anything. That Wolf had a lot of advice for you, but didn't give me the time of—night."

"I won't let anything happen to you," said Rain, on no other authority but hope.

5

She tried at dawn to clear the opinionated puppet from her mind. Dreaming about a blue Wolf, again! That her fears about her indistinct past should organize themselves into such a character out of some children's fable. It was worry on four legs, worry with hot breath, that was stalking her, nothing else.

But halfway through the morning, she was brought up short by overhearing Cossy retailing the midnight ramble to Iskinaary. So it wasn't a dream.

"The bossy Wolf, he said don't hang around on the plateau. Go away, go west. Rain has to help fix something that was all her fault in the first place. She can't go back to that Oz place yet."

"Is that so. A nightmare," said Iskinaary, with little enthusiasm. "Oh, Rain, there you are. Would you walk ahead with Cossy? I'm in no mood for fanciful tales—"

"I'm afraid she's telling the truth," said Rain. "I mean, about our stepping out in the middle of the night for a social call. We both went. Maybe that was so that we could prove to each other that it wasn't a dream. We got some instruction, Iskinaary, that you should hear."

He looked more and more annoyed. "This demi-monde should mind its own business. *We* decide what we're doing, Rain, and we choose when to leave for Oz. Not some charlatan sideshow spin-off of the spirit world. The winged monkeys came here to guide you home. As for me, I'm not eager to stay any longer than I need to, either. Another few months and I might be too old to make the trip all the way back across the ocean. Now, you listen to me and listen *hard*. I don't care if Lurline Lurline the Fairy Queen showed up and told you to fly to the moon. We have one destination, Rain, and it's home. No place like it. *Oz*. Keep that in mind."

They walked in the silence of disagreement. The monkeys had flown ahead to check out the route. "What if I don't remember?" asked Rain, at first belligerently, and then soberly. "Really, Iski-naary. What if I never remember how to fly?"

"We'll cross that ocean when we come to it," snapped the Goose. "Look, if you're being vouchsafed with visions of blue Wolves, you ought to be ready to fly again. Isn't it like riding a bicycle? Once you learn, you never forget?"

"What do you know about riding a bicycle?"

"Precious little. But I know something about flying." And the Goose allowed himself a self-regarding smirk.

Not long after that, Thilma returned. The three other monkeys weren't with her. "There are uh-ohs in the forest. The main path is safer right now. As far as Thilma can know."

"As far as Thilma can know," snorted Iskinaary, "doesn't inspire confidence."

But scarcely two miles on, in a stretch of forest flanked on both sides with high, open elms, the road veered around a standing boulder, and in the middle of the path just beyond the bend stood Artoseus again. In the daylight he looked porous. The green of the woods behind him stained his blue silhouette a shade of turquoise. Not his best look. An oversize plush toy more than a vision. He was planted crosswise along the path, as if studying something in the birch wood, but his head pivoted to watch them approach.

Iskinaary was a brave creature, but wolves are known occasionally to attack large fowl. "What a turn-up for the books. Living proof of your insomnia, Rain. Tell him to go away."

Artoseus said, "You need to divert. There are more dangers ahead than your airborne squad can easily detect."

"Thilma begs your pardon," said Thilma, keeping her own distance. "Thilma does her goodest." She flapped her wings, raising some dust and a little personal stink.

"Wolf-head, we'll take your recommendation under advisement." Iskinaary didn't like having his seniority questioned. "Move aside now, that's a good fellow."

"I'm not moving." With every utterance Artoseus's voice grew lower in tone and in volume; they nearly had to lean to hear him. "This isn't a suggestion."

"I do, as it happens, strenuously object." Iskinaary flared his wings and hissed. Artoseus snickered, which was, Rain thought, unforgivable. "We'd lose the airborne scouts, for one thing. They'd never find us in such dense forest."

"You can't scare me," said the Wolf, "but I have other business. I don't have time to argue. I'll chase you into the woods if I have to."

It was Cossy who brokered the matter. "I don't want to be chased," she declared, and walked staunchly into the ferns that garnished the spaces between the elms. Rain couldn't very well let the child disappear in the woods. And where Rain plunged, so plunged her rescue team.

Rain looked back, irritated that Artoseus hadn't made a better first impression. He was fading into the fretwork of landscape they had abandoned. The clear road behind them still looked blameless and inviting. "Good, he's gone," whispered Cossy. "Let's go back. I'm tired of tramping in the woods. The road will be faster."

"Got my vote," said Iskinaary, and they retraced their steps.

Hardly a mile on, though, as they were passing a quirky arrangement of standing stones, the threat that the Wolf had warned about made itself heard. A sudden and catastrophic sound they couldn't identify. It seemed part mineral and part animal—an explosion and a yowl, or a chorus of yowls. Among the sarsen stones, in a clearing of acid sunlight, something hustled to attention. A glinty scrape of claw, a sulfurous belch, a rubicund maw revealing three receding racks of choppers. The revelation was multiple, behind several stones at once—either a party of monsters or some decentralized spirit that hadn't finished assembling itself. Neither for the natural science nor the faith of it, the travelers didn't stay to watch it finishing its toilet. They took off through fields of fern as nakedly regular as a crocheted tablecloth, reaching the safety of knuckled vines and thorny hedge beyond. They didn't pause but plunged deeper into the wilderness. Cossy threw an arm around Rain's waist. "I wish I were home," she said in a small peeved voice, when she could catch her breath. "Don't leave me. Don't let me go."

Rain didn't dare point out to the Goose that the Wolf's warning had been sound. Iskinaary puffed up his breast feathers and kept out front, as if he'd intended this maneuver all along. But nobody knew where they were going, and they kept going nowhere much for several hours. Mercifully something of a meadow opened up, and the other flying monkeys flew down almost at once. "Well, there you are," said Thilma. "Keep up, fellows."

"Artoseus warned us," Rain said to the Goose as they bushwhacked upslope. "But we're still alive."

"Still alive to fret ourselves to death tomorrow?" asked Iskinaary. He looked fit to tie his own neck into a noose and hang himself.

As the afternoon sun lowered on their fourth day out from Maracoor Crown—or was it their fifth—their spirits began to sink, too. Artoseus hadn't appeared again. They could as easily be marching straight back into danger as around it.

Cossy sniffled repeatedly and Rain found her clinginess annoying, though she could hardly fault the child. Insolent one moment, sentimental the next—what an unnerving creature. A girl of knots and inadequacies, eyes hooded as with suspicion. Beneath the cherrywood gleam of her smooth bare legs and uncertain smile, who actually was hidden there, in one disguise or another? Would the child learn to trust the world, or anyone in it?

Every apprehension of individuality is a kind of spell, thought Rain. Can we break free from whom we're raised to think we must be? Can we brave it out? Cossy might be young, and on dangerous ground in terms of moral composure. Still, she'd proven herself strong, and determined. It would be Cossy's job to deal with her own revealed interior self, not Rain's.

And truth to tell, who knew about the outsides and the insides of any individual? In infancy Rain herself had been rendered pale of skin by a charm, allowing her a chance to grow up incognito. Unhunted and unharmed. Until Tip, her first beau Tip—but of him, nothing else yet. Not the how, or who, or why, or where. Just Tip. Alone of her recovered memories he kept slipping away, and she'd forget him, as if he wanted to be forgotten.

Iskinaary interrupted Rain's indulgence of dejection. "If we have to spend a night under the trees, let's at least find a spot where we can build a small fire against those larger creatures that might smell us out. We'll need a place open enough that we don't set the woods alight, but not too visible to airborne menace."

"What, like mosquitoes?" asked Cossy.

"Yes, exactly like mosquitoes. In fact, mosquitoes. Mosquitoes and vampires."

They gathered such kindling as they could find, most of it riddled with rot. Before they could spark a flame, a swirl of otherlight stirred in the distance just below treetop level. A sweep of color, a comet's tail, gold and orangey-blue, coursing back and forth. Moving too quickly, and too high, to be a handheld torch.

A lighted tailwind through the trees. A predatory beacon.

"Advance!" cried Thilma. Before the Goose and the girls could cry for them to stop, the four flying monkeys had begun the gallop that initiated their lift. They meant to get above the trees and look down on the phenomenon of winding colors and try to see what was causing it. Maybe intercept it and bring it down.

As the monkeys rose, the colors swooped deftly in, banking to avoid capture. More distinct now, an entity trailing blurs of light. Perhaps the monkeys' ascendance had attracted its notice, for the missile pivoted to come directly between the trunks of aspen and pennyfern trees. Toward where Iskinaary, Rain, and Cossy were grouped, standing frozen in caution and disbelief.

The airborne lantern slowed down as they drew nearer. The fizzle regulated itself into the form of—well, of what? A bird with a miniature human face, like a porcelain doll-face. Or a death mask. Slightly fixed, unnatural, not pleasant exactly, but neither did it seem adversarial.

"A vampire!" said Cossy.

"As if," answered the weird creature in a voice like a bronze nail on a sheet of tin.

The creature settled on a beech limb some feet up. "Other refugees are lost in the woods, I've seen plenty, but that one of them might also be a green girl is, shall we say, unlikely. *What* is your name?"

"I don't see why I should give it to you," said Rain. The winged monkeys came back to earth, landing a few yards behind the girls and the Goose. Craven things!

"Oh, spare me; I'm not the enemy. I'm Moey, for what that's worth. I've been looking for you to escort you out of these woods. There's trouble on and off the road, and no time to waste. That is, if you're Rain—"

Iskinaary decided he'd had enough, and he ventured forward till he was only six or seven feet off. "What's your business with us? State it please. All these procedures with you people, it's worse than taxes. We have our own timetable to keep to, and you're interrupting it."

"You're called to join the court of the Bvasil," said Moey.

"The Bvasil was murdered by his own people."

"He slipped away. He needs your help. I've been sent to bring you in. I was supposed to have a second but she's not kept up the pace, it seems."

"Not interested. The Bvasil's people condemned this child to prison," said the Goose, "and who knows what they would have recommended about Rain had she not escaped the chokey. The gallows for her, to atone for the invasion, I bet. Not pretty."

"This is more important. Come, we mustn't linger in the woods at night. I'm offering you safe passage for now, and glory tomorrow."

"We make our own glory," said the Goose. "On our own terms."

"We can be there before moonrise if we leave right now," said Moey. "You're closer than you realize. There's hot apple frumpkins."

The winged monkeys and Cossy all voted for hot apple frumpkins, so although Rain and Iskinaary remained dubious, they set out. The trees were spangled with the light of the flying creature, which hardly made the passage of the fugitive company more secret. But now perhaps speed was worth more than stealth.

As the moon rose, the band of refugees cleared the bowl of the Thalassic Wood at last. In the rising dark they crested the last incline, gasping for breath. The tableland opened before them like a memory of a happy childhood. Farmhouses with orange windows dotting the distances. A sweet domestic smell of cow manure. The sound of waterwheels creaking, of sheep sharing their good-nights. The tracks were clear of foot traffic at this hour. Those forces that might want to stop their progress were, for the time being, themselves stayed.

It was as close to coming home, Rain thought, as she might ever experience in Maracoor, though her home was Oz, and getting farther away with every westward-leading step.

"This is the gate," said Moey as she flew over it and settled upon the low roof of the farmhouse porch. She had the appearance of a folk-art hex. Droll and uncompromising.

A companion creature, inching out of the shadow of the chimney stack, said, "Took you long enough, Moey. Come, let's go tell the ragged congress you're back."

Moey said to Rain, "Knock on the door. A reckless bunch in there, but brave enough. They're expecting you. More or less. Surprise!"

THE COMPANY OF
THE SCARAB

1

Many years later, as he waited for the healers to settle hands upon him—or, if their prowess failed, to wrap him in a winding sheet for the funeral pyre—Lucikles found himself unmoored. Time toyed with timelessness, and at a moment's notice. Less alarmed than he might have expected to be, and with all his life on wide and immediate display, he drifted back to the day when the unwilling tatterdemalions of history assembled in his mother-in-law's farmhouse, convening the Company of the Scarab.

He remembered that morning as a vision preserved in amber—as if he too had become myth, and he could be viewed from all sides without blame or question. Or maybe this was just the vise-grip of death, pinching his perspective to a single instant. Back when everyone was still alive, was safe and whole. Potential in full bloom. And, whether by virtue of happenstance or design, a Minor Adjutant was in the center of the moment, for once.

The passage across the meadow. The sun is the everyday sun, yet under it the world is swollen with intensity. He can see himself below, walking, as if he's also hovering above himself with those gadfly harpies. Sandals laced up to his knees and a scuffed woolen tunic, a cape slung on against the morning chill. He looks a hayseed by any index.

Oena beside him, her helixing strands of char-black hair free of the usual combs. Her shoulders back, unbowed; her brow lifted as if, on this familiar soil of her childhood she need not watch where to place her feet.

They have, this once, latched hands, as in the olden days. Perhaps the last time?

The two harpies by contrast, are marginal creatures, swooping around the humans, trails of spangled light dissolving behind them. Mere alchemical reactivity of some sort, but arresting nonetheless.

Ever they remain like this, in Lucikles's mind, as he steps across the grass from the pond to the farmhouse. He is also aware of a presence he can't quite see, walking behind them a few feet. The sacred consort of the Great Mara of ancient faith, the one called Relexis Kee. Lucikles has only been granted a glimpse of the deity once, as all this was beginning—and he never will again, unless Relexis Kee waits for him on the other side of death's ebony gate.

Yet Lucikles is aware of the deity's presence on that morning of glory and catastrophe. The idealized structure of his naked form, adorned only with a collar of linked copper rounds dropping from neck to nipples. Walking behind the married couple the way a gentleman farmer paces his golden retrievers.

Yes, Relexis Kee: beneficent; but also distant, cool. The sense is of witness more than of aid or even succor. At the hour of Lucikles's death, now or at some future point, whatever testimony the god might offer will count.

2

After having met the harpies, Burden insisted it would be his decision, and his alone, how to proceed. Return to the city or keep moving on?—they'd take up the matter after supper. In the meantime, Tycheron and Leorix tried to repair the smashed gate, watching out for troublesome passersby in the bargain. The feathered torch-face calling herself Asparine played sentry along the roof beam, perfecting her wolfish yodeling. To distract the little girls, who were sulking at being dismissed by their chickies, Mia Zephana thought up gingerbread harpies.

Later, Oena and Lucikles strolled back toward the duck pond, wondering if the otherness there that they had both sensed would be still detectable. But the lip of ledge under which the harpies had emerged was no longer even visible. The usual grasses and shrub screened it. Perhaps if Lucikles went kicking through, he'd be able to find the fissure, the vaginal stone sleeve. However, when they saw Burden sitting on the Throne Tree, hugging a satchel on his lap, they diverted, skirting the sheep paddock instead.

They didn't knock shoulders companionably. They didn't muse over memories of how romance had been first snatched at right there, one night many years past. Now, only older, more labored, more alone than ever in their marriage, they walked two abreast, isolate and paired.

When dusk had fallen and a lamb stew ladled into bowls, Burden started in. "In other crises of my Bvasilate, I've relied on a privy council to argue the matter. Now I'm forced to my own mind. I've concluded that there's no going back until we can go back with an army. Nor can we stay here beyond tonight. We must light out at dawn. Whether we're ready or not. Find the Oracle we set out to find. We have to stay ahead of the forces closing in. Bloody Skedes."

"We've been happy to give you sanctuary," said Lucikles, "and we'll be sorry to see you go. Your visit, the honor of a lifetime."

"Don't say goodbye too fast," replied Burden. Before he could continue, the half-door filled with light like a menacing vagabond approaching with a torch. It took the seated humans a moment to work it out: Moey had returned and was perching on the edge of the lower door. Asparine had joined her.

"My chickies," said Star, but her heart wasn't in it.

"All the way from far away!" said Moey, a bit out of breath but pleased with herself.

"Lift the other latch, they're here," said Asparine, nodding to the door that fronted the road. Leorix leapt to oblige even as Lucikles and Oena told him to wait.

They came in, weary and filthy. Leorix fell back. He hadn't seen Rain and Cossy since last week, on the day of Cossy's hearing and sentencing. At the time, he'd expected never to meet them again. Acaciana, the convicted murderer-child. With Rain, the green girl from some other place whose name he forgot.

Then, that irritating Goose, stepping with muddy feet on the scrubbed flagstones of the kitchen hall. And behind him, looking like large mangy insects, dubious and vexed, four winged monkeys, one after the other.

"I thought our policy was going to be no more guests," remarked Mia Zephana.

"I didn't know about *bird-monkeys*," said Poena, and Star grinned as if they were new toys. Who needs harpies?

"It's all right," said the Goose, "they're with us. Don't look at me like that, so am I, *I'm* with us." After a pair of harpies, a talking Goose was only mildly bizarre.

"It's all right for you, but you don't handle the dishes," Mia Zephana muttered. "Well, good thing I made a double portion of supper. Draw up that extra bench. We'll make room. No," she insisted as Burden began to pontificate, "no, you. We serve travelers first. We talk later. That's how it works in High Chora."

"I don't do lamb," said the Goose. "Have you anything by way of barley, perhaps?"

"Look," said the one called Tycheron, "it's Pet, no less."

Rain stood at the door, unhappy to be here despite the aroma of supper. She saw before her, like pieces on a board game of competitive strategies, most of the dramatis personae of her time in Maracoor. Not the other brides, of course. But Lucikles, the Minor Adjutant, no less, who had pressed Rain and Cossy into custody. His adherence to duty had trip-wired this snare that had caught both girls. Though recognizing him, she didn't nod acknowledgment, but turned her face to the others.

There was his son. And here at the same table, that farmer-uncle and his nephew who had helped smuggle Rain and Cossy through the gates of Maracoor Crown. All together like a synod. She felt skeptical, paranoid; she was being played a pawn.

Hunching his shoulders against the improbability of it, Lucikles muttered that the big-bellied uncle was in fact the Bvasil of Maracoor, his superior. Oh, but how the gathering took on a sinister gleam then. Rain was dubious when the Minor Adjutant told her the Bvasil had stumbled upon his family's home by accident.

"I don't buy that," she said, now staring Lucikles in his scared eyes, now pivoting to the Bvasil. "You're in cahoots. You abducted me, charged me with aiding and abetting your country's enemies. You imprisoned me. For all I know you were ready to execute me. Now your harpy agent has lured me here. You expect me to sit down and break bread with you? Is this just another sort of wolf den?"

She'd have turned and broken ranks at once but for the sight of Cossy's sidling up to the kettle of stew, closing her eyes to breathe in the steamy fragrance. The girl was famished. And this was the closest to safety she'd known since leaving her island.

It was the quiet mother of the family who brokered the welcome. "You don't have to listen to them," she said to Rain, recognizing downright contempt. "But do take some supper. Stop with us tonight. You're right; there are wolves of all sorts abroad. Leave of your own free will tomorrow, if you must. No one will keep you. I won't let them. My name is Oena. This is my childhood home. You'll be all right here."

3

When seconds of stew had been lashed out, and thirds of ale had been quaffed and the mugs washed and dried, Lucikles brought forward the family icon. Ferona the Defender. It had traveled with them in the donkey cart as they fled the capital.

He lit a wick coiled in a shallow basin of quinseed oil. His mother-in-law sprinkled dust of lavender before Ferona. The group fell silent. Lucikles put match to a pinch of mint-weed and passed the pipe. Even the harpies were lowering their heads, if only out of respect for foolish human customs. So too were the flying monkeys. The Goose irritably rasped his webbed feet on the flagstones.

A strange consolation, Lucikles felt, to sit in stillness before an image in stone and mosaic. A saint who refused to come to life and have opinions. Such silence is faith's signal consolation. It beckons one's own complications forward, to be witnessed, forgiven, challenged. The saint's job: to help the petitioner face the wretched truth.

Rain held her tongue. Matters of devotion to foreign gods—too much to deal with. She wrestled with her anger. Artoseus had implied that the unspecified campaign to come would involve a team of disparate souls. What committee isn't? But this family man implicated in their current troubles? Was this some kind of theophantastic joke? She didn't owe anybody anything.

She tried to still her—what was it—horror? outrage?—tried to consider the reckless company. What a gallimaufry of types, taken together. Those weird truncated bird-women! Rain recognized the concept but had always thought it fanciful.

Cossy sat in Rain's lap and fingered Rain's tresses possessively. It bugged Rain but she let it go. She expected Cossy must be intrigued and threatened by the sight of Leorix. The boy and the girl had made friends on the ship sailing from Maracoor Spot to the mainland. Cossy must be awed by how the boy was nestled into this mysterious society called a family. A grandmother! . . . Two parents of different genders! . . . and two baby sisters! For Cossy, having grown up in a same-sex colony of unrelated females, it must seem as weird as having harpies bitching in the doorway. Here was something vaguely like a real home.

Lucikles, dawdling in his meditations and fussing over his pipe, found himself raked with an emotion he hadn't allowed himself to notice up until now. The arrival of the escaped prisoners had swiveled the pieces around in Lucikles's mind. He was, in the most basic sense, still vexed with himself over what had happened to the child bride. Sure, he believed that there was nothing he could have done differently. A Minor Adjutant had exactly the amount of agency the title implied—or less. But here she was. The girl had managed on her own. He'd abandoned Cossy to a jail cell; she'd wiggled away, straight to his own door. Uncanny.

So his behavior hadn't been honorable. But the Bvasil had threatened Lucikles if he messed up. The potentate had threatened to order one of Lucikles's own girls, the younger one, his little squat Star in her rosy-brown glory, to be seconded to the island colony for the rest of her life. To replace Cossy. There to live a life of forced sterilization in service to religious rites and to safeguarding the dangerous amulet, the Fist of Mara.

Lucikles gritted his teeth and drew on his pipe, as if force of will could opiate the tobacco. The mood on him was quiet, so quiet. It didn't make a hum any louder than the breath of a sleeping dog.

His faithful Cur was comatose in the light of the hearth, as if the entire hierarchical system of known entities wasn't on display around him. Ah Cur. He was still Cur, he was still only a dog. Lucky bastard.

Burden and Tycheron had begun to mumble together in the firelight. "Devotions are divine, but we don't have all night," intoned Mia Zephana. "Nations may rise and nations may fall, but the cock croweth in the morn. I'm yawning with my chin on my apron bib already. Let's hear what you lot have to say and then we can sleep on it."

"Fair enough," said Burden. "My loyal subjects, I will tell you what I know."

"I think you dropped your royal scepter in the royal river and a royal manatee made off with it," said Mia Zephana, "so you can drop that 'loyal subjects' business. If you've abdicated the throne, we're not your subjects. We may not even be all that loyal, depending on what you have to say. For that matter, how do we know you're not some charlatan actor putting one over on us?"

"Mamanoo!" said her daughter, laughing falsely, belying her terror.

Burden reached into the collar of his shirt and withdrew the ornamental device that the little girls had been playing with earlier. On its leather cord the heavy oval disc spun in the firelight. A jeweled scarab, its features of torqualine and waxy chalcedony picked out in a setting of blurred gold. One of the proofs of palace. The scarab a familiar emblem of empire—its flattened outline hammered a thousand thousand times over into coins of the realm. It blinked its authority and silenced even Mia Zephana.

"Hold your tongue, woman." Burden's voice had more edge in it than Lucikles had yet observed. "Hear me out. Time is short. The hearsay from that recent band of passersby pulls me up short. The Skedes aren't content with the treasury of Maracoor Crown.

Apparently they aren't abducting women or impressing slaves into service. Or not yet. Why not? The news that they're fanning out to search the countryside reinforces our chiefest fear. They've come to our country and made war against us for one thing only. The Fist of Mara. We evacuated it from the capital city, but they're coming for it. We can't let them find it."

"I'm all ears," said Mia Zephana. "What sort of animal is the Fist of Mara when it's at home eating crumpets and cream?"

The harpies inched closer together and pursed their lips in concentration.

"The amulet is an object of great power, the correct management of which is still unknown," said Burden. "Discovered in the north part of our country. Oh, years, years ago. When unearthed, it proved dangerous. Women became barren and a whole region more or less died out. The environs fell into abandon for several decades. A ruler long before me had the item smuggled off the mainland. In a special casket that seemed to neutralize some of its potency. It was hidden away on a far island for generations. But that unprecedented storm has stirred a change in the tides and allowed the Skedelanders from the deep south to sail unimpeded to our shores. Now we realize that, all this time, word of the holy totem had been bruited about in lands other than ours. After the Skedes made landfall, I had the Minor Adjutant, overseer to that quarter of the kingdom, collect the item before it could be stolen and used against us. I believe that the Skedes are after the amulet. It's why they're content merely to box up our forces in the capital. Why they're stealing this way even as I speak. They're hunting the most powerful weapon known to all of Peare."

"But why would they look in High Chora?" asked Leorix. Lucikles shot his son a look that said, as gently as possible, don't open your mouth once more, you, or I'll clock you one, but good.

"Because it's here," said Burden. "Tycheron and I removed it from the safehold where it was stored."

"What do you mean? Here?" asked Lucikles. Oena and Mia Zephana sat up straight on their bench, aghast.

"The girl smuggled it out of the city." Burden pointed at Rain. "She wore it around her waist, under her wrappings. As a fake babe in the womb. I hoped perhaps that she'd grow fond of it and keep it. I hoped this green-skinned aberration from abroad might be just the one to take our cursed inheritance away from us. Perhaps back to that mythical land she apparently claims she is from."

"What in hell are you saying?" shouted Lucikles, rising. His daughters started; he wasn't one to raise his voice.

"Don't be righteous. It's obvious and unbecoming. The Fist of Mara is in the satchel I was carrying when I arrived. I tucked it just inside the henhouse. I thought perhaps you wouldn't want it in the kitchen." His left hand flapped at Poena and Star.

"So that's what's kept the hens from laying," said Mia Zephana. "You rotter."

It was Rain's turn for offense. "But you gave it to me to carry—knowing what powers it has—you had me strap it around my *waist*?" she cried. "It wasn't even locked in its ironwood casket, just a poisonous lumpy heaviness—?"

Burden flicked his fingers as if at a mosquito. "Don't look so shocked. Think about it. You were under suspicion of collaborating with the enemy. You arrive on Maracoor Spot just as the Skedes are setting out to storm our coast? Coincidence? We didn't yet know. Your trial was interrupted by the invasion. And we had to flee."

"Are you going to put me to death now?" asked Rain. "Human sacrifice? Burned at the stake, perhaps? That's always a crowd-pleaser."

"When I offered you the Fist of Mara and you said no thanks, you proved your innocence," said Burden. "Argued your defense without knowing it. Case closed."

"I thought it was *pomegranates*."

"You knew it was no pomegranate," said Burden. "I could see that in your face. But if you'd been in league with the Skedelanders you'd have been keen to every weirdness in your weirdwoman path. Give me a break. You're implicated in all this, but I don't know how. You and the Skedes are entwined, even if you're not collaborators. In any case, these harpies named you as essential. The green stranger. So here you are. You already helped us shift the totem once. You'd better help evacuate the Fist of Mara from Maracoor Abiding, if we can locate the venerable sage who can tell us how."

"I owe no allegiance to Wolves or bvasils," said Rain. "I had one job before departing for my homeland, and tonight I've completed it. I've brought Cossy to a safe house where she can be protected." She turned to Lucikles. "I can see in your face that you recognize your hand in all this outrage against Cossy and me. You owe her protection now, since we both helped your supreme king and his lackey to escape the city by hustling out that despicable item under my burlap veil."

Lucikles flexed his hand open and shut, a gesture she couldn't read. But it seemed neither a nod in agreement nor a refusal of the obligation.

"Now you're talking, Rain," quawked the Goose. "We leave in the morning. Find some safe place for you to revive your broom skills. Then we light out for Oz."

"You'll guard Cossy here, and keep her like your own child. It's the least you can do," said Rain. She almost wagged a finger at Lucikles, but held herself from that, raising an eyebrow instead, which she hoped would seem more encouraging.

He suppressed a shudder. Rain could see that he didn't like Cossy one bit. The child was hardly a honeyed lump of innocence like his own two daughters there. But Rain thought it was his son's interest in Cossy that gave Lucikles the chills. Well, too bad.

"I get a say in this," interrupted Cossy. "I don't like it here. These stupid bird-ladies. I prefer the blue Wolf. Tell them what he said," she prompted Rain. "I can't remember. I was partly asleep. Something about a tower."

"The person who can give you some advice," said Rain to Burden and Tycheron, "is known as the Oracle of Maracoor. A hermit in the Walking Mountains."

"Are you making this up? We told you about him already," said Tycheron, and Rain now remembered this was true. "But we didn't know where he might be found. Only in the west. We thought High Chora? But you're saying he's beyond. In the Tenterix Range? How do you even know that?"

"Not important. But the district is called the Walking Mountains. You'll be looking for the Tower in the Clouds," said Rain. "Wherever that is. Good luck."

"If you're right, you've done us a service," said Burden, with lowered eyelids, judging Rain for probity. He glanced at the harpies. "You gloomy aberrations: do you have any secret chthonic knowledge to impart?"

Asparine said, "It will serve the soul of the land to remove this danger if it can be removed. We will help if we can be of use."

"You're so theatrical, Asparine, I love it," said Moey, sighing. "Me, I'd just love to do some sightseeing."

"Enough," said Burden. "We'll grab a few hours of sleep and set out before dawn." He palmed his pendant. "The ragtag Company of the Scarab, no less. Be calm, friends. Those invaders won't be able to climb the palisades in the dark. We can be grateful for the wolves on the high road. They'll slow the barbarians down. We'll go west, across High Chora, dropping down the plateau into the far-lands. A head start will help. Can you supply us with food for the journey?" he asked Mia Zephana.

"I assume you'll pay. This is a working farm," she replied.

"You'll keep Cossy here," said Rain of Lucikles, not as a question.

"She can travel with"—the Minor Adjutant didn't want to admit to *the Bvasil*—"the members of the court. Since she's the one who used the Fist for malice—she's the one with the taint. What with wolves about, and Skedes on the approach, she won't be safe here. Quite simply, and no right of petition about it, she must go."

Cossy blurted, "I'm not staying behind, Rain. I didn't get to be the first bride of Maracoor to leave the island in twelve thousand years only to wash up on a farm and see you fly off and have adventures."

"I don't care what happens to the child," said Burden, "it's not significant. But you're coming with us." He pointed at the Minor Adjutant.

"Oh you, you're famous for being out of your mind," said Lucikles.

"You're coming," said Burden to Lucikles. "This is a job of defending our nation. Tycheron is my chronicler, so you'll be my double. You're about my age and my size. You'll do."

Lucikles didn't have that belly, nothing like it, but only said, "You want me as a decoy—in case you're captured?"

"You're fast, too; I like that about you. Yes, we're close enough in stature. Now let's get some sleep."

"Your Magnificence," said Lucikles. "You can't expect a family man to leave his family at risk while foreign hordes approach. I refuse. I won't do it."

Burden cleaned out an ear canal with the pinky of his left hand. Just as a real farmer might. "Myself, and Tycheron and you. The monkeys for good luck. We can do without the unsavory green thing. She's told us where to look for the Oracle; her job is done. Whether we sleep or not, we leave in a few hours. Pack up a rucksack and hug your children. The quicker we go, the more likely we are to make it back."

"In that case," said Lucikles, for he knew how vindictive the Bvasil could be, if provoked, "I'll come on two conditions: that the winged monkeys stay behind to guard the farm. And that my children are left unmolested and free to live their lives forever outside of the reach of you and your court. *Forever*. And, yes; let Cossy join us. If she can keep up." He turned to Rain. "I'll find some other place to stow her that will be safer than this grange."

"You think I can trust you to do that, you who brought her to trial for *murder*?" spat Rain. "Remanded her to prison? I deny responsibility for the Skede invasion—" She suppressed mention of the Grimmerie to this scheming lot. "But I won't let you squirrel this child out of my sight just so you can abandon her to the first wolf pack you come across. You're not sound. You're an operator. Putting your nation and your family ahead of an orphan who has neither."

From his corner, young Leorix, in full agreement of this assessment, nodded his head. "I'll come with you too, to make sure no harm befalls you," he said, grabbing Cossy's hand and squeezing until she snatched it away, blushing with joy.

"I'll break your neck before that happens," growled Lucikles, saying to his boy what he didn't dare utter to his liege lord. "Up to the loft, all three of you. Leorix, Poena. *Star*! Away from those chickies. Scram." The girls left; the lad disobeyed, stayed put.

"Leorix is a brave kid," said Rain. "If he won't be allowed to go as a chaperone, I'll postpone my return to Oz. I'll accompany you only as far as I need until I see Cossy safely settled somewhere. She can't go back to Maracoor Spot and you won't let her stay here. If she goes on, so do I. Let the monkeys stay behind if they must. We'll collect them on the way home."

"Can the green menace stop her barracking?" asked Burden. "The matter is settled."

Iskinaary only now recovered his voice. Rain had never heard the Goose so angry. "You're hijacking *me*?" he hissed at her. "You were in prison and we show up to rescue you, and you're *what*? You're remanding the monkeys to some babysitting duty here and you're kidnapping me on this charade of a quest?"

"You can leave." Rain opened her palms to him. "I never asked you along. My father did. Go home to him if you must. Go back to Oz."

"If you were an egg of mine I'd leave you out for the water rats to get at."

"You needn't linger, Iskinaary. I'm dismissing you. With gratitude. You've done good work for me. Go tell my father I survived."

"He'd never speak to me again if I left you here. After all this! Besides, kiddo, what if I don't make it across the ocean on my own? If I die on a foreign strand, or three hundred miles out from such, I want someone to notice. Even a fool like you."

"On your own head, then," she said with a brutal clap of her hands. "Don't complain to me, Iskinaary. You're not under contract. You're a volunteer."

Burden sighed. "Can she at least argue her personal concerns outside, where all that noise might encourage a passing wolf to get her?"

So came about the Company of the Scarab. The journey to the west. Burden and Tycheron. Lucikles, a hostage obliged to serve as a royal decoy. Also the harpies. Rain and Cossy. Iskinaary would join them, quawking his protests. The others, including his son, would remain behind.

Leorix kicked copper pans and threw wooden spoons. "You've survived a wolf attack and beat it off," said Lucikles, aiming to placate the lad. "Mamanoo and your mother and sisters will need your strong arm."

"We don't need any help!" shrieked the girls from above, eavesdropping. Oena went to them.

"We'll be back as soon as luck allows," said his father. He'd broken his paternal pact with his son; there was hardly any more damage to be done. It didn't matter if he failed to embrace the boy before turning to the chore of packing. In any case, Leorix had swiveled away. He leaned against the chimney stack, streaking the stones with his tears.

Lucikles didn't indicate that he heard any of this, just sat down with Mia Zephana and Burden and began to work out logistics of a longer overland trip.

To clear her head, to get a break from the objections of the Goose, Rain stepped out in the dark. The land of High Chora around this farmhouse was swaddled; she didn't know ten feet beyond what she had noticed by daylight. So like her past—sleeved in velvet dark, an unsurrendered secret. She would have to wait yet, for other types of daylight.

Then Tycheron moved out of the shadows to join her. "I like this no better than you do, by the way," he said. "We're both of us hijacked here by these authorities."

"I thought you might be a wolf, you padded up so silently."

"No wolf," he said. "I'm in bare feet, Pet." He showed her a soft, gentleman's instep. "I'll save you from any wolf."

"I don't need saving," she said, but perhaps she meant she didn't deserve it. How could she be sure when she couldn't remember? An unremembered story is a secret.

PART·TWO

A STORY IS A SEED

1

They gathered in moonshadow by the bashed-up front gate. The little girls were still asleep. Leorix refused to come out to bid his father adieu. Everything stunk about this whole operation.

A gluey smear of clouds to the east. Apathetic stars above, no sympathy or warmth. The light wind that ushers in dawn hadn't yet begun to stir.

It fell to Mia Zephana to give the travelers a blessing: warm honeycake drizzled with cane sugar icing. "Come back safely, come back soon, come back all," she said, and loped toward the barn to surprise the animals by being earlier than usual.

Faro and Finistro, Thilma and Tiotro waved grubby fists at their companions. They'd put up no argument about staying, not after that nourishing stew. So much for rescuing *me,* thought Rain though, really, she didn't begrudge them.

Oena ducked her eyes and clutched herself with her arms, as if she'd become cold, cold forever. Lucikles couldn't address her. His feelings and hers, too high. "Hey, Cur," he said softly, but loud enough for his wife to hear. "Take care of everyone, okay? You're in charge. And remember me when I come home?" (If I come home.)

Burden had retrieved the leather satchel from the henhouse. Bloody bastard. The Fist of Mara, no less. Tycheron hauled other supplies in a pack upon his own back. Rain, Cossy, and Lucikles followed a bit behind. As they set out along the road, no one wanted to get too close to the Fist of Mara, at least at first.

Rain shivered in the farmhouse apron Mia Zephana had insisted she wear. She found that she was casting her eyes sideways in the morning mist—what was the opposite of gloaming?—expecting to see Artoseus, the blue Wolf. But no such luck. The only glimmer of magic was the ordinary kind—ducks making a roll call, a wind in the corn, a willow tree shaking its fronds silverly. Even Moey and Asparine, who as emblems of the mythic energy of Maracoor were proving a bit down-market, felt the isolation. "We're it," said Asparine, noticing Rain's glances slipping this way and that. "We're all you got."

"And we're not much," said Moey cheerily.

"Do you think there's any way you could, I don't know, dim your luminescence?" asked Iskinaary. "It lowers the tone. Besides, you'll attract attention to us. We'd rather pass by unnoticed. Three men, two harpies, a young green woman, a girl, and a talking Goose— we're hardly your normal parade of passersby as it is. And isn't the holiday glamor of your presentation tone a bit, um, affected? Pantomime almost. Not to be personal about it."

"You only need ask," replied Asparine. Through some agency of which the others could hardly guess, she softened her glow. What was left, while still harpy in shape and attitude, looked more like a normal barn owl. You'd have to glance upon it twice to notice the human face. "Come on, Moey, lower your wick."

"I hate this trip already," said Moey. "Are we there yet?"

As the sun lifted, and the fertile farmland of High Chora spilled before them, the harpies took to their scouting missions. They returned to report on makeshift encampments: city folk on the run from the invaders, shantytowning. But High Chora was tamer than the Thalassic Wood. Its roads and farm paths, shortcuts across orchards and alongside brooks, offered plenty of opportunities to sidestep trouble. The companions made good time.

Chatter was light. Lucikles was glad.

He took stock. He was trudging away from his family as if only slipping to a farm stall for onions and rutabagas. And why? Maybe because he owed something to Cossy, and even to Rain. But mostly because it was the only way he could figure how to protect his children.

Lucikles might never know if Cossy had done what she had been accused of, or, if so, how much awareness of wrongdoing she might have had in carrying out her crimes. She was, like Leorix and Poena and Star, still a child. Indeed, even Rain was a child, after a fashion. How old was the green girl? Eighteen? Twenty? It was hard to tell. She was a stranger in a foreign land, too. Stumping along with that ratty broom like a beloved comfort toy.

His feeling for the green girl was still a snarl. At first glimpse he'd taken her for a visitation of sacred grace—and she'd taken him for a fool. Still, she was young and a stranger abroad, and on her own. Tendentiously he told himself: a father on the road and far from home is still a father. Regardless of whose children are in trouble. And how vindictive they are. Oh, but she was a scourge. The skin color couldn't help.

Rain, meanwhile, though still skeptical about the coincidence that had drawn the Company of the Scarab together, felt a flush of remorse about having involved the Goose. "It's all my fault. I'm taking you farther away from Oz with every step," she said. "When you left Oz to follow me across the ocean you had no idea you'd be ensnared in a quest to keep going west, west west west, across yet another land."

"I'm already over it," he snapped. "You human thing, you only see geography in relation to your own life and being. The portable omphalos. So self-centered. Literally. While actually, wherever you are is at once west and east, and north and south, and far and near. I should think since you learned to fly on that broom you might've gained a little perspective. Those of us who fly just whisk on the margins of everyone's life. We aren't ever the center. We actually define the horizon. Can't you give it a break? Anyway, what do you want? You *want* me to turn around and waddle myself to the coast, and then start flapping back to Oz on a day-return ticket? I've dealt with this, sweetheart. Made my peace. Here we are, we're going somewhere else, and come what may, we're always on the edge of someplace yet farther off. I would have thought you'd have picked up on this by now."

To her hurt expression he added, "Come, I've been sharp. Never mind. You can't help being stupid. Flying for you isn't an instinct, it's a talent. You have to learn to use your talent. Before this adventure is done, you'll fly again, my girl. Don't drag your broom on the ground. It's in sorry enough shape as it is. Mind me now."

"I wonder how many girls my age have single-handedly been responsible for a foreign invasion?" she said, half to herself.

"Don't be smug. Depending on your definition of foreign invasion, I bet just about all of them."

2

But against her wishes, Rain found that the presence of the weaselly Lucikles brought back memories of her own more even-tempered father. She began to miss Liir, really for the first time since she'd left his humble home at Five Lakes in the eastern Vinkus. She had traveled in a state of walking catatonia, a blur of anomie, through the Thousand Year Grasslands of Oz, sheltering with nomadic clans. She'd hauled the Grimmerie with her much as, now, they were escorting the dangerous Fist of Mara toward some safer repository. She'd had no real aim or ambition until she'd stumbled upon the edge of the ocean, largely unknown to the cartographers and geographers of Oz.

She'd only intended to keep the book of magic out of the hands of anyone who could use it to abuse the world or its people. Why this moral urgency, she couldn't yet recall. The idealism of youth? Or had she been brutalized by its power in a personal way?

So much unknown in this secret world, even leaving amnesia to one side.

She didn't know if she'd ever reach any Tower in the Clouds, that rumored outpost somewhere in the Tenterix Range. Maybe there'd be a safe haven for Cossy between here and there. In any case, Rain was finding that she could now take in the world. Or, perhaps, put another way, perhaps the world was just a little bit more beautiful again. More, perhaps, like Oz. Was this mere homesickness? At last?

The low hills required little exertion to maneuver. Tracks tended to favor the curve way around a brow rather than the stiff mount. The villages, seen from a distance across fields and paddocks, looked prosperous enough. Snug, a bit smug, almost prettier than accident might be expected to allow.

Sometimes the companions could hear the sound of farmers at a pause, making music, or of children playing. So little sense of a world at war that Rain found it easy to ignore the panic that had stolen half their night's sleep from them. A nice place to live, High Chora. A home for Cossy here?

She glanced sideways at Cossy, who seemed indifferent to the varying views. Cossy was picking up stones. Rain caught her fore-arm and diverted the missile from striking one of the harpies—the nastier one. Asparine. "What do you think you're doing?" hissed Rain.

"You're so no fun. You ruined it," said Cossy. "I just wanted to see if she would light herself up if she got hit."

"You could hurt her. Did you ever think of that?"

Cossy shrugged. "Not really." Then she said, "Ow!"

Iskinaary bobbed beside her with a smirk. "Oh, I was trying to see if you would light up if I nipped you," he said.

"That's not fair, I never light up," she shouted.

"You're telling me. The life of the party, that's you all over."

Rain intervened. "Iskinaary, don't take your frustration out on a child. And, Cossy, get a grip. We don't go around striking out against one another just for the fun of it. You're just bored. Shall I tell you another story?"

"About the Oracle. What's an Oracle like?"

"I can't imagine."

"Imagine."

She tried. "Once there was an Oracle who lived in a high stone tower in the stony desert. Nothing around but scorpions and sand dragons. Every day he combed his long white beard and put on his high pointy purple velvet hat and his matching purple robe. Trimmed with ermine."

"What's ermine?"

"Trimmed with white fur. Every day in the desert wastes he told the future to the sand dragons. It was the same future every day, but they loved it, so they came back every day to hear it again."

"What was it?"

"Um. He told them they would all be kings of the desert after he died."

"So what happened then?"

Rain had walked herself into a corner. Storytelling wasn't her métier. "Well, one day they killed him, to see if he really could tell the future."

"Could he?"

"I don't know. The sand dragons all flew away to live in another story. The end."

"I like stories with murder in them," said Cossy at last, but it was clear she'd been struggling for a way to sound grateful. "Anyway, your story birthed a second one, so you can tell me the sand dragons' tale another day. I like that about stories."

"A story is a seed," agreed Rain.

3

The first day had been the easiest. The second was plodding, the third tedious, and the fourth rainy. Every day that they weren't set upon and killed blurred with the days before. They lost count of the number. As they ventured west, though, the frequency of villages and crossroad hamlets dropped, and the distance between farmsteads lengthened.

Lucikles had chosen the wrong shoes. Burden's capacious belly was itself a burden and slowed them down. Cossy was bored. Rain had run through any story she could think of to tell, and the ones she couldn't remember were driving her mad.

It was a relief one blustery dawn to crest a knoll halfway across a vast open meadow and to spy the start of the western downslope of High Chora. The drop looked even steeper than the approach from the coastal plain had been. A vast and indolent river, pewter in the morning sun, spread a swathe through iridescent grasslands. On the other side, forested hills lazed about.

They paused for lunch in the sunshine, about as relaxed as they'd been since their departure. The apples they'd lifted from an abandoned farmstand made a sort of one-note meal, but it was better than nothing. A sleepiness came upon the adults. They found a wooded dale and the adults settled into its shadows to take some rest. Cossy, bored, wandered away, probably to find toads to fling at the Goose. A nearby stream burbled. The girl came back without any wildflowers or toads. "We're surrounded," she hissed. They snapped to at once.

Cossy jerked her head. Across the stream, three men in light-weight armor and strange, coarse leggings moved slowly. Heads down, examining the far bank, as if for footprints. They hadn't yet spotted the travelers. Their mounts were tethered to the remains of an oak split by lightning.

Then Cossy pointed in the other direction. Farther away, four or five more men, equipped with spears, were thrashing in the bracken-wood above them, poking through underbrush.

The blue-black noon shade in which the travelers had spread out was, for the moment, dark enough camouflage. They didn't speak for fear that sounds would betray their whereabouts. They hardly dared move. But there was no escape route.

A finger to his lips—hush—Burden leaned toward Lucikles, who inclined his head forward. Burden settled the regal pendant over his shoulders. Ah, his last job as a Minor Adjutant. Lucikles tucked the scarab into his collar. If he was going to be mistaken as the Bvasil of Maracoor and assassinated, the Skedes would have to identify him first. He wouldn't badge himself for their convenience. With this investiture Lucikles would die as king of the nation. But Oena and Leorix and the girls would never know. An untold story is a secret.

The streamside group was moving away, but the spear-holders drew nearer. The operatives spoke a rough language, guttural and choking. They seemed ill-tempered, if one could guess by tone, but they were taking their time at their task and being thorough. It would be hand-to-hand combat momentarily. Against the Skedian weapons of war the companions could boast little. A paring knife with which they'd quartered the apples. Rain's desiccated broom, perhaps, might double as a staff of defense. The Fist of Mara, in its lumpiness, too heavy to wield as a cudgel.

In that his speaking voice still sounded like a goose if you didn't have the ear, Iskinaary risked breaking silence. "You silly creatures, do your party piece; it's your star turn," he quawked at Moey and Asparine. "Earn your keep!" The Skedes coming sideways down the slope looked around to locate the sound of an agitated fowl. Lucikles clenched his fists; Cossy shuddered and squeezed her eyes shut against the impact of an arrow or a lance. Rain threw her arms around the girl.

Asparine said, "All right then, we can take a hint." She and Moey launched in a diverting swoop toward the west, quickly banking in over the five soldiers on the hillside. The ostentation that the harpies had tamped down upon request flared up again—bronze-yellow, lapis, a hint of rose. Their hot color flushed across the hammered alloy of the Skedian helmets. One of the harpies keened, which may have meant to be a tantara of valor, but came out sounding like the battle cry of an airborne tea-kettle. That wolf howl Asparine had been practicing would have worked better, thought the Minor Adjutant. Too late now. In any case, the spectacle arrested the soldiers. Two of them fell to their knees in shock. A third raised a hand caged in a mailed glove of segmented silver. Protrusions like tiny ornamental halberds proved instead to be darts. Some coiled mechanism launched bright zinging missiles toward the harpies. They outmaneuvered the first several of them but Moey was struck by the last one, which had gone wide.

She fell in a graceless plummet as Asparine descended with talons outstretched for blood. Her lurid color hummed in the air; she circled the Skedes and struck, and struck hard. The stream-side contingent rallied to the side of their cohort, while the harpy's traveling companions took advantage of the distraction and bolted down the ravine and out of sight of the marauders.

The fugitives didn't dare speak until they achieved a blind of mountain bamboo several miles on. They'd lost the predators, left them behind. Lucikles said to Burden, "When will you take this pendant back?" The Bvasil didn't reply. An easy rain had begun to dance about, greening the green world.

"Are we going back to see if Moey is okay?" asked Cossy. No one answered.

4

The rain didn't slacken or intensify—for all the drama, it remained light. When the Company of the Scarab came upon a single hayrick, as if the field had gotten exhausted even yielding a pittance, they saw a creature beside it, some few feet away, observing them without menace. Artoseus, the blue Wolf, with Asparine in attendance. The shower had streaked the wolf's coat to translucence. His profile and silhouette were patched through with diagonal stitches of pasture and low mist.

"Thank Lurline you're here!" said Rain, the shock and fear drawing out of her a phrase of gratitude learned in a distant childhood, years and oceans away.

"I knew you'd show up," said Cossy. "Nobody believed in you. Nobody's sure what we're doing. You can bring us to wherever we're going next. That tower. Goody."

"No," said Artoseus. "I'm here to say goodbye and to wish you godspeed."

"Whatever that is," murmured Lucikles. "Speed us along as we spill out of the frying pan into the fire?" The Minor Adjutant was learning that regular terror had sapped his ability to be awed at mere spectacle.

Asparine perched on the haystack as near to Artoseus as she dared, pretending some sort of affiliation. Glory by proximity. "No, I'm not coming with you," said the Wolf. "You haven't yet got the measure of all this, have you. You're on your own. Such as you are." Artoseus looked mournfully at the Company—slack, disorganized, uncertain and unnerved. His wasn't a sneer, was it? No, a grimace of worry.

"But why don't you join us too?" said Cossy. "We could try to be nice."

The blue Wolf lowered his snout and glared levelly across the distance at Cossy and the other humans. "I've done what I could. I alerted the harpies to your whereabouts. I roped in Rain. I can tell you have the Fist of Mara among you now, so Rain still has a task ahead of her. But you haven't yet seen the reality of us. I believe you can't."

"You were the thing Oena and I sensed behind the weeds, then, the day we found the harpies?" asked Lucikles. "I ought to have trusted my instincts." For some reason these creatures blurting out of old legend made him irritated. Perhaps it was as simple as this, that they made the *minor* part of Minor Adjutant stand out in greater relief. His son having been attacked recently by wolves, Lucikles wasn't kindly disposed to this blue apparition. "You're coming to salute the Company of the Scarab now, at the edge of High Chora? Big of you. Thanks a heap."

"What you also haven't taken in is that while we ambassadors are both genuine and insubstantial, we are, at the heart, local. All the demi-urges are. I am the blue Wolf in the stories of the High Chora. Children who grow up here having seen me will haul off to other cities and tell stories of me. In that way I travel. But the essentiality of me is harbored here. In the stone and soil, the air and the cast of light, that make up the uplands. I have other work than tending to you. I remain here, and cannot leave."

"What's more important than saving the nation?" asked Burden.

"I have myth to make, old myth and new, before the millennium is out. I must get back to my task." The blue Wolf put his chin right down on the ground as if breathing the soil and grass into himself. His upslanting eyes looked tender, plangent, almost innocent. "We're not agents of much more than attitude," he said, as if relenting during a hard negotiation. "We don't change the world. Humans do. Now, I'll try what I can to scare your pursuers back to the coast. But some of them are bound to get through. Somehow the foreigners have determined a way to track the substance of the Fist of Mara. It must be issuing a silent siren song they've figured how to hear. As long as you have the thing with you, you'll remain in danger. They'll come after you like bees to a saucer of jam. Maybe not hordes, maybe not many of them at all. But beware. Even now they're closer than you think. I hope the Oracle of Maracoor can give you advice on how to handle it safely. Disposing of such a volatile item isn't as easy as it seems." He glanced at Rain and also at Iskinaary. "Look what *your* efforts provoked."

"Don't blame me, I was just along for the ride," said the Goose, but came waddling over to Rain's calves and stood with his head against her thigh, a gesture of tenderness beyond his usual practice. So Iskinaary knew about the disposal of the Grimmerie. Of course he did.

Rain remembered the Wolf's earlier caution. *Someone in your company is a threat to you.* She resented Artoseus for that, but had no way to prove him wrong.

"Listen to what the Oracle says," said Artoseus. "Take care of one another. And if any of you make it back this way, we'll be here, whether you can ever see us again or not. We're always here. You'll be able to feel us here."

"I can't even feel you now," said Cossy, in a slight sob, reaching out to pat the blue Wolf as if he were a dog. But her hand went through him like water, and perhaps because of her attempt, he disappeared.

"Let's keep on, then," said Burden stolidly. They made their way toward the cliff-edge.

"Asparine, is Moey coming back?" asked Cossy.

"Moey who?" replied the harpy.

5

By evening they hadn't yet found a way off the plateau. Having rejoined the Company of the Scarab, Asparine had become skittish and didn't want to leave. In missions of reconnaissance, Iskinaary flew southward along the escarpment but soon circled back. "This landmass is a natural fortress," he reported. "I suppose it explains why that lush river valley seems so unpeopled. At least from this height. If we can't get down, nobody can get up. Is that even Maracoor down there?"

"It is," said Tycheron. Almost the first time he'd volunteered an opinion. "On maps of this region the river is known as the Seethe. It begins in the Tenterix foothills to the north and flows south and west to some unknown destination."

"Wherever it debouches, we're not going to invent a staircase by complaining about its absence." The Goose took off again without a word, this time to the north. Lifting on thermals and angling into the light, disappearing from sight almost at once.

They decided to stay put until they had better intelligence on which way to turn. Since the tree cover was minimal, the travelers huddled out of the blustery damp in a roadside pocket that wind had notched in the hillside. Done with their meal of apples, they'd begun to grouse about the monotonous fare when a sound on the track above them turned their heads. It wasn't a groan from archaic demi-urges, nor did it sound like soldiers on horseback. More of a domestic sound. A farmer in a cart. They stirred to attention, ready for what peril or promise might be afforded next.

"Aha," said the driver, sounding triumphant. Cossy's head swiveled fastest. "The Goose told me where to look." Sitting on the seat, from sheer glee pounding his feet lightly on the toeboard, here came Leorix, perched behind the donkey pulling the family cart.

Leorix, of all the bloody . . . and Bob the donkey, so named because of the buckling movement her head so frequently made. Lucikles reached his son first, full of irritation and relief. He'd throttle the boy. "Why are *you* here? What's happened? What's doing? You were to stay put and help your mother defend the farm—I distinctly ordered you—"

"They didn't need me, did they. Mama and Mamanoo, they have it *under control.* Don't flap around. Everyone is fine. They're defending the farmstead from evacuees. Anyway, the news of the invaders fanning out across High Chora is exaggerated. They haven't chosen to come anywhere near us."

"It's *not* exaggerated. The harpies spotted small units going farmhouse to village and every cave and corner in between. And we've crossed paths with a contingent ourselves. How you avoided them, just dumb luck—you should be—"

"I'm not a half-wit. I went through meadows, taking down slat rails to drive the wagon through, and replacing them so only a keen eye could see I'd been there."

"But why? Why put yourself in harm's way? What's wrong?"

"The list is too long to run through." Leorix's cheer sounded almost nasty. "I stole away to make sure Cossy is okay. And I thought I'd replenish your supplies while I was at it."

His son didn't trust him to do right by the girl. And for good reason. Lucikles knew his commitment to justice for the child was unstable. If only she'd been charming. But the farther away from her island home, from which he alone had dragged her, the more feral she seemed. "What do you mean, stole away?"

"I didn't ask for permission to leave. I just sort of sneaked off a couple of nights ago. Taking the cart. Oh well. I thought you might need the provisions more than they did. I thought you might be *grateful*."

"But if they have to flee—"

"Mamanoo would never stoop to such a strategy. But they won't have to run, anyway. They have flying *monkeys* to guard them, Papa." He turned his shoulder to suggest flying monkeys were preferable to fathers. "How are you, Cossy?"

"Moey died," said the girl, "but we didn't get to see up close." She pouted at that.

"So you met up with Iskinaary?" interrupted Rain.

"I had made a good call of it on my own, but yeah, the Goose spotted me. He told me if I turned south and kept to the cliff-edge, I'd come across you. He was still flapping himself north, looking for a way off this high lump."

Cossy inched up to the edge of the wagon. The boy turned upon her an expression of open fondness that Lucikles found distasteful. So his son's first crush was a juvenile outcast. Leorix a fledgling adolescent and Cossy hardly in double-digits. Trouble. "Just because you got clawed by a wolf—" the father began, but stopped himself. "I'm glad you're here. The wagon will be helpful. Not to mention the food. How will you get back to the farmstead safely? Perhaps we can persuade Asparine to accompany you. We've seen her go on the attack, and she means business."

"Oh, I'm not going back," said Leorix.

The eternal battle of wills between father and son about to be rejoined—but a reorganization of oak trees downslope, subtle and stealthy, arrested them all. A landslide? Burden glanced at Asparine and said, "Some cousin of yours has an opinion on the landscape?"

Before the harpy could reply, a shoulder of land beyond the

grove of trees shuddered; some trees fell off the bluff. Something like an earthquake. Caves collapsing on themselves, and rearranging the surface of the world above. Lucikles reached for Leorix, who leaned toward Cossy. Even Asparine inched nearer.

A torso lifted out of the land—no other way to think of it— capped by a head and flanked by a pair of arms. A figure—male or female was hard to tell at first—rose in the setting sun. All eyes squinted into the brightness. The core of the body was like that of an ancient oak, ten feet in diameter maybe. When the humanoid form was fully upright, it was twice the height of the wasp-waist trees around it.

The gargantua turned to look down at the companions. It held out a finger the size of a loaf of bread. Without hesitation Asparine flew up, and perched, and it lifted her toward its imprecise head. It had an ear, or two; and something of a mouth; and even hair. It was a giant, no more and no less, a giant in human form. Even, now they were able to take it in, something of a dirt jacket with rough shale buttons the size of dinner plates. The garment fell from its massive shoulders and just about covered its personals. For which everyone was relieved.

It spoke in puffs of dust they couldn't interpret. Asparine replied in a voice too low to be heard. After a few moments she flew back down to the cart, which was suddenly the new base camp.

"If he spoke in your tongue he'd deafen you," reported Asparine. "His name is Yurkios. He's King Copperas, spirit of the copper water on this side of High Chora. He has come to help us if we want. But what he has done may not prove useful."

Burden cleared his throat. "Go ahead. Tell us everything, and I'll decide."

"*We'll* decide," said Rain. "You may be the Bvasil of Maracoor when you're at home. But you're not anymore, and I'm not a subject of yours anyway. So I get a voice."

Asparine said, "Yurkios composed himself out of the cliff-edge. He stirred himself to form and detached from along the edge of the bluff. Where he lifted himself up, he has left behind a steep downslope passage. He will lie back down again after we've passed, if we dare to try. We may not have any clear way home—this may be a solitary act he won't repeat. He can't say. But for now there's a descent of sorts; he has done our earthworks for us."

Obliquely Burden looked at Rain. "Well? Since you've declared yourself my equal?"

"I'm learning there's never a way home, only a way forward," said Rain. "So let's take it."

"I'm glad I didn't need to overrule you and put you in prison," said Burden, sounding like the Bvasil he was pretending not to be. "That's my decision, too. Tell this ground-fellow Yurkios to lead us there. We accept his offer."

"Leorix is going home," declared Lucikles. "Burden, declare it so."

"We could use the ride. I'm losing my strength," said Burden, flipping Lucikles off.

The giant stood with a kind of artisan's pride at the top of his work. A cliff-hugging ramp, just wide enough for the farm cart, angled to the valley floor at several pitches, some steeper and some more forgiving.

Asparine delivered Yurkios's message that he would descend with them if the science of ancient rules allowed it. Lucikles insisted Leorix descend from the cart and proceed on foot; he could lead the donkey by the bridle. The inconsistent angle of descent made Bob utter her complaints in ear-splitting, hawing editorial. But descend they did. Asparine flew in small hops—the wind rushing up the cliff-face was treacherous. For their part, the humans hugged the wall and tried not to look down. Yurkios strode ahead, investigating and revising his work.

They leveled out at the river plain just as the sun lost itself in the west. The moon wandered up the sky to see what was what. In slow curvets the water of the Great Seethe slicked by. The travelers pitched camp near the base of the palisade. Iskinaary spied them from on high and rejoined them, shaking his wings in disapproval, as if he'd hoped they'd reach a blank cliff and finally have to turn back. Yurkios sat with his massive spine against the fundament of High Chora. In the morning when they awoke, he was gone.

6

It didn't take them long to realize why the shores of this vast riverworld weren't thick with human settlements. The green that the travelers had seen from High Chora weren't meadows of a well-irrigated river valley, just sweetwater marsh grass. The ground underfoot: one step wet, the next dry, then splash again. It was hard to guess which way forward might be driest.

They weren't ten minutes in when Bob and the wagon became mired in the mud. Lucikles got his shoulder under the back axle as well as he could and nudged the vehicle forward about four inches. Working out of eyesight, he was spared the temptation to glare in disapproval at Leorix. His paternal feeling displaced itself from son to donkey. Bob having been driven all this way, only to be abandoned in this damp environment, to mildew into retirement and rot? Not if he could help it.

"Damn damn the damnedest damn," said Lucikles when he distended some tissue between muscle and bone. He couldn't stand straight once he extricated himself from beneath the wagon. His callused feet were torn up by the stony streambed.

"I told you so," said the Goose, having told them nothing of the sort.

The others had Bob from her harness and tried to prod her forward. Cossy was the pathfinder, as she least minded getting wet. She splashed this way and that, fecklessly, having fun. "We can't leave the cart behind," said Rain. "Who knows how it might come in handy on the other side. There could be quite the trip ahead through the Tenterix."

If only to prove Iskinaary's doomy predictions wrong, the taller humans—Rain included—managed to dislodge the cart's rear wheels. They hustled it along like a coffin among them. Bob kept glancing back hopefully, as if she figured it was her turn to get in the cart and have a ride.

Finally reaching the open river, there seemed no right place to ford it. Calmer where broad, the flood seemed a sea disguised as a river.

They chose a launching point and identified a possible landing opposite, somewhat downstream to account for the drag of current. "We'll take our chances," decided Burden. Rain nodded at Lucikles—her first moment of making common cause with him. It felt a kind of betrayal, but she had nobody else with whom to confer: though at loggerheads initially, they were now both responsible for Cossy's safety. She deplored the implied alliance but was stuck with it.

They unhitched Bob, who didn't balk at being led into the water. Their spirits lifted when Tycheron discovered that, at least starting out, the breadth of the river belied its danger. It began shallow.

The child begged to be allowed to ride in the floating cart, for the fun of it, but she was refused. If the vehicle slipped out of their grasp, she might be carried off around a bend of the river. Still, she was too short to wade safely. Water that came up to the forearms of the adults would cover her nostrils. So Lucikles hoisted her upon his shoulders and they set out. She grabbed the pendant's leather strands and pulled as if they were reins until he muttered that she was choking him. "Can't believe a girl growing up on an island never learned to swim."

Iskinaary called, "I can't fly at your emmet's pace. I'll make my way to the other side and wait for you." Asparine circled overhead as the company ventured farther out into the breadths, cheering their slow progress as best she could, given her default mode was High Acerbic.

The water deepened and hurried. With Cossy on his back, Lucikles took a misstep and went down. By the time he got his head back to light, the others had managed to detach Cossy from him. They'd latched her hands onto the rim of a cartwheel. She was sputtering and wailing. Bob went bobbing along, and the other humans could swim well enough, but the cart was beginning to veer. They couldn't guide the heavy thing with their shoulders. Inexorably they all began drifting downstream of their destination.

On the far side, the channel remained deep. They couldn't imagine how they'd scramble up the steeper banks. With his weighted satchel, Burden looked nigh to sinking beneath the glossy muscled water. That would be the end of the Fist of Mara, for good or ill. Remembering all that was said to have happened in her attempt to drown the Grimmerie, Rain tried to keep to Burden's side. Though she neither trusted nor liked him, his aims of protecting his people were sound. Why else go through all this? Her support was only moral, though. She couldn't keep him afloat by her mere company. He was a solid grown man, and his satchel weighed the world.

Above, the sky was stricken with a sere, inglorious blue, amoral in its beauty and blankness. The closer to shore, the louder and stronger rushed the flood.

None of the waterlogged contingent saw or heard the approach, behind them, of last night's savior. Then he was among them. At first they took him for a rising spirit of the water, a river dragon or some foul upright crocodile. Yurkios, King Copperas, up to his waist in the flood and naked above the waterline. He plowed through the battering current without acknowledging them. With one huge hand he reached for the laces and shaft of the cart, and with the other he picked up Bob and held her against his side as a child will hug a soft animal toy. He didn't look at the humans, who latched themselves to the edges of the cart. He dragged the whole assemblage and its human limpets to a sandstone bluff that he reduced to a powdery shallow. He dropped them there to make landfall on their own.

He never looked at them or explained his behavior. In his gargantuan nudity he fell face down upon the sand and died. There was no question about it. His substance withered to mud. A smelting stink caused most of the company to retch. Within minutes there was little left of him but some suggestion of a bone structure, a skull they could nearly have camped within. The big ribs resembled the hull of a wrecked ship. The travelers saluted the remains when they had recovered enough to struggle forward.

Rain guessed that Yurkios must have witnessed their plight from the tableland above and left his native environs. This essence of the High Chora, of the copper veins that must twine beneath the green mantel-land: he wasn't meant to leave his home. It was much as Artoseus had said. The blue Wolf had warned them. Rain tried to explain to Cossy. "The spirits of the land, though real, are . . . local players. They're the home team. Venturing abroad is fatal to them. King Copperas met his death for us, to help us on our way."

"Well, don't look at me, *I* didn't kill him," said Cossy. "Give me some credit."

Rain didn't reply. Would Yurkios be remembered in aeons to come as one of the demi-urges of the tableland, or would his legend crumble as his immortal body, improbably, had done? As all stories blew away eventually, one memory at a time, the way hers had done? Even Asparine hadn't mentioned Moey once.

7

hey'd floated downstream farther than they'd realized. The terrain they were investigating wasn't the one they'd seen from the promontories of High Chora. Iskinaary, who'd relocated himself to where they'd fetched ashore, had a worried look on his face.

The margin upon which Yurkios had deposited them was only the width of a cattle path. The sandy soil brought them immediately into a slope of pine forest. Trees, so tall that their tops were garlanded in mist, opened their canopies like a festival of umbrellas. The air was pungent with the resin of conifers, mercifully spare of flying insects. It seemed a kind of heaven looped in swags of green. Nothing like the Thalassic Wood: in fact, a haven.

They deserved a solid rest. After a short climb, they found a broody granite ledge beneath which they could all shelter, including the cart. All eight of them. Rain and Cossy. Lucikles and his son. Burden, Tycheron. Asparine, who'd gone taciturn; Iskinaary, who hadn't. Nine if you counted Bob.

Lucikles unwrapped his leggings. The instep of his left foot stung as if he'd stepped on glass. Ribbony with wet blood. When he wiped it dry, he saw a gash, and the hind part of a healthy brown insect twitching its rear feelers like a cockroach burrowing into a paper envelope. He was unable to pull it out but at least the thing froze at his fingertips. He palpitated the skin ahead of the parasite, hoping it might rethink its ambitions and back up. He set his foot to air on a rock. Let the others make camp.

Those farmhouse rations that Leorix had purloined—welcome even if devoured cold. A cooking fire might keep potential predators at bay but Skedelander teams might see it, descend the new ramp, and find out some easier way to breast the Seethe. So far, luckily, no sign on this side of any population, human, animal, chimerical. The spot they'd found made almost a grotto, which was nice: little wind, and the earth seemed warm enough. They squatted or sat cross-legged, except of course for Asparine, perched on a low branch, and for Bob, who on all fours had nodded off, perhaps resentful of the bath she'd been obliged to take.

Rain said, "Are we even still in Maracoor?"

They all looked at Burden. More and more quiet with every day—as if the chore of hauling the amulet took all his strength. The Bvasil, as they sometimes remembered he was, or had been, rolled his hand at Lucikles: *Tell them what you know.*

The Minor Adjutant snapped to the command as best he could. "The maps say so," he replied. "Though they go vague about it any distance beyond the Seethe."

"The Tenterix Range. A western wall to Maracoor. This section opposite High Chora is known as the Walking Mountains," said Tycheron.

Iskinaary quawked, "But is it a well-settled area? Lucikles, you must know about all that. You collect taxes and such, no?"

"My remit was only the eastern islands. Great Northern Isle and the Hyperastrich Archipelago. I'm not privy to reports from the west. I don't know much about this region. But Maracoor claims the range. It seems the mountains run deeper and farther west than maps have room to include."

"But of cities, settlements, industry?" asked the Goose. "Logging, mining? The usual work of mountain peoples? Give us something to work with here, man."

"Are you paying attention? You saw that the tableland is nearly impossible either to scale or to descend from. Trade with the

Walking Mountains isn't possible. It's an inland wilderness. If there are indigenous peoples, I don't know of them. Your Magnificence," said Lucikles, offering obeisance to Burden for the first time in a while, but only to get the answer to the question, "you'll have been better informed on these matters by those adjutants assigned to this region."

Burden roused himself a little. "The Bvasilate is huge and its management taxing. I don't remember much about the Tenterix Range. There are other populations to the north. About this stretch, we hear of arboreal dwellers, but they are a suspicious people. Nomadic nature. Keep to themselves. Those few explorers who ever claimed to have made it into the interior and made it back out again, well— They tell contradictory stories. Perhaps a bit of derangement sets in."

"If this district is so unchartered, we'll need a guide to tell us where to find this Tower in the Clouds," said Rain. "Unless Iskinaary or the harpy can locate it from on high."

Iskinaary said, "There's merit in your questions, all of you. Should there be a quirky neighborhood one-off, like that blue Wolf or another Copper King, we'd do well to get it on payroll. I have a bad feeling about these woods." He shivered his wings. "They're too quiet and—poised. Without a guide, we'll have to abandon the quest as impossible. Start home."

"Not going back. Not ever." Cossy thumped across the circle and sat down right next to Leorix, who neither blushed nor inched away, but reached out and held her hand.

"Oh, please, spare me," said Lucikles, and turned to the Goose. "So what, you have a bad feeling? I bet you have bad feelings about sunshine and birthday presents."

"When you all were crossing the Seethe," replied Iskinaary, "I took a detour west to scout out the terrain. I'm afraid that I could scarcely find my way back to the river."

Rain flinched. Even if she had tried to leave her suffering

younger self behind—to drown her, like the very Grimmerie, in the Nonestic Sea—that girl had survived, and was housed inside the modern Rain. Waiting and vengeful. Only Iskinaary knew that hidden girl. Her secrets were housed in his avian soul. Perhaps she should change her mind and question him while she could. He was an old Goose, after all.

"You earthbound folk can't tell from this elevation," continued the Goose. "The sky looks blue enough. The foothills are soft and appealing. But—at least today—a blanket of fog or mist distorts any geographical feature to the west. I couldn't fly high enough to get above it. Also, my singular talent of navigation by means celestial and barometric—it failed me. I don't say this lightly. Frankly, I was terrified. Like waking up blind, I imagine. Or paralyzed. I thought I'd lost you. Maybe tomorrow will dawn clear as glass. But to venture farther into the Walking Mountains as we find them now, wreathed in fog with little ability to ascertain north and south, would be—well, I don't want to say a suicide mission. But a foolhardy one."

"You've been working too hard," said Rain. "A good night's sleep will restore your sense of direction."

Leorix took his hand away from Cossy's and said bravely, "I'm all for making a go. We've come this far, and we're trying to save the nation. But I do ask one thing. No, I don't ask it, I insist."

"You did provide lunch," said Burden. "Very well. What is your command, O Minor Adjutant's Boy?"

Leorix said, "Don't make fun of me. I want to know what we're all risking our lives about. I've seen the casket—I was there when it was removed from Maracoor Spot—but not the amulet itself. The thing we're trying to land someplace else. Or at least find the Oracle who can tell us what is to be done."

"We're a Company, no?" replied Burden. "So you have a point, I suppose." He gestured to the satchel. It took both Lucikles and

Tycheron to lift it off the ground. Burden's hands trembled as he unbuckled the flaps and reached in.

The Bvasil must have ditched the strongbox that had held the Fist of Mara safe for so long, maybe centuries. Maybe the weirdness of this new world, this fever, had wrought changes upon the curious and dreadful item. They leaned forward.

The totem was wrapped in a cloth gone dark with grease and residue. Burden peeled away the towel the way someone might unfold the tired outer leaves of a cabbage. In the evening light filtered by green tree cover, the Fist of Mara sulked, if a mere thing could sulk. The item gave off a powerful emanation, though it wasn't odor, or light, or any sound a human ear could hear.

"There's not much to see," said Burden. "It's a bit of rock, or petrified wood. Or some other unknown substance. But the nasty influence. . . . Whoever holds it might find a way to wield great harm with it. Should the barbarians overwhelm us and capture this item, I can't answer for what would happen to the people of Maracoor. Friends, we've tried to be stewards of this thing. They may not be so cautious."

Friends. The word was lost on no one except maybe Bob, who was still asleep.

They sat glued in the presence of something neutral but not, it seemed, inert. "Wrap it up," said Rain at last, remembering how she'd been tricked into carrying it as they left Maracoor Crown. "I don't want to see it if I don't have to."

"Wait," said Cossy. She came a little closer on hands and knees. She had, after all, been one of the few ever to have looked upon it before. She'd used its power to kill her sister bride, Mirka. "I won't touch it, I'm not an idiot." But she put a finger on a corner of the filthy cloth in which the amulet had been carried. "I know this cloth. I saw old Helia, the senior bride, work at it during prayer hours on rainy nights. She was cross-stitching it—I recognize the edge here. I used to hand her her colors. I liked her patterns."

"So?" said Iskinaary, "I used to eat grubs when I was young and foolish like you, until my tastes changed."

"Helia made pictures," said Cossy. "Can we see what her picture is?"

Burden rolled the Fist of Mara onto the pine needles covering the ground. Taking the square of cloth by two corners, he lifted it and flapped it gently. Everyone turned their heads and squeezed their eyes closed so the castoff couldn't land in their faces.

The cross-stitched pattern was clear to see. There were several dozen hills or mountains. Upon a rise in the center, Helia had stitched the outline of a castellated tower standing on its own. At the bottom of the square cloth was a blue curve, perhaps marking the river they had just crossed. And at the top, in wobbly letters, the word *Walking.*

"How could she know we would need a map?" asked Cossy.

"Maybe it's a coincidence," suggested Lucikles. "That blue line could be the sea, not the Seethe. What ancient bride living her entire eight decades on an island doesn't dream of walking around some mountains? Perhaps this is nothing more than the escape wish of a shut-in. Don't start seeing omens out of mere panic."

8

That night, the mist crept closer. Rain woke, shivering, wishing for Artoseus, but saw only Tycheron. He was fussing with a flint and a small stack of kindling he'd collected. "I'm making a fire anyway," he whispered. "I think we're safe enough. Who could see any smoke rising in this fog?"

She shrugged and got up to help him. Everyone but Tycheron was out cold. Asparine made opinionated little whuffs with her pursed lips, sounding disapproving even in her sleep. Disaster was so exhausting.

He cut a nice figure in the shadows, but she tried to pivot back to somewhere else to that someone who lived in her heart like a small blue flame. A small hot tongue of light. An unanswerable need. Tarnish on the nerve of a tooth. Yes, she knew his name. She always knew it better at night.

The first love never dies and never comes back. One way or another, Tip had left her. She was hollowed out in memory and in soul. Had anyone in the history of human ardor experienced the like?

But then, no one ever experienced anyone else's life. That was the curse of individuality, and maybe the safety of it, too. The privacy of shame, of regret.

The curse of her own ignorance. The midnight hour made her dreamy and philosophical. It ought to be a moment for asking big questions, but even the stars were swallowed in featureless fog. "Who are you really?" she found herself saying to Tycheron.

"What do you mean?"

"So often people aren't who they seem to be. Burden is the famous Bvasil, the king or what-have-you of your country. Yet he
dresses like a corn-husk doll in a pantomime. Disguises! I myself
used to be a different skin color." At night her green pallor looked a
touch moon-milk. "So you keep to yourself and you don't say much.
Are you Burden's nephew, as he first told us? You don't seem like a
romantic type so I'm guessing you're not his paramour."

"I'm romantic enough, but not for him." Tycheron looked left
and right to make sure everyone was truly out cold. "I'm only a
functionary of the palace, Rain. I'm here to help him do what he
has to do, if I can. If something happens to him, and I survive,
I'm expected to bring news back to the capital city. I'm his public
relations counsel. A witness. Testifier to his efforts. Chronicler of
his historic legend once he becomes history, whenever that might
happen."

"A tall order for a young man."

"I'm a loyalist. I'm from good stock. The House of Opaleus.
We've been courtiers for four generations. A reputation for probity,
our line. I was brought up to serve the Bvasil in his court. That's
public knowledge. I am here to survive and to return with the tale
of his sacrifice for the nation, or his murder, or whatever may happen."

Rain said, "You serve him well, to come all this way. If he'd
drowned in the Seethe, you might have done so too."

"An honorable way to die." He slid a sideways glance at her and
grinned. He was suddenly sweet to look at. In the rising flames
in the small fire. She felt herself blush. "And you?" he said. "That
nosy blue Wolf seemed to imply you're obliged in all this. Or-
dained to carry the Fist of Mara out of Maracoor? Why are you
even here?"

"I was running away from—a failed romance," she ventured,

"and trying to do some good in the process. I dropped a volatile item in the ocean. I fear it unleashed all kinds of trouble upon your country." She hurried past the part she couldn't yet identify. "Do you have a someone back at home?"

He cocked an eyebrow. "I'm married to my work."

"You're too young to be married!"

"Nah, not really. Anyway, I don't mind. You're part of my work now. We're all bound in this effort together. So I'm married to you, Pet. How's that sound?"

It sounded, well. It sounded okay. For tonight. "Then you're married to that aggravating harpy and my bosom friend Iskinaary, too."

"We're out in the wilderness. I suppose conventions aren't as rigid here." He was joking. She hadn't heard a real joke for several years, it seemed. He moved near her and she was happy he did. It was just tonight, just in the earth-hugging clouds, and the firelight made his eyes brighter than they seemed by day. He leaned in to kiss her. She leaned in too.

"You're not married to *me*," hissed Iskinaary in the dark. "Youth is youth, but let's make sure that the mountains are the only things walking, not your lips. Cheap sentiment, bosh and balderdash. Cut it out. I have enough on my hands as it is. And I don't even have hands."

She pulled back, and Tycheron did too, but the grin that they shared at being caught out was somehow almost more exciting than the kiss. Which had been pretty sweet, tasting of river-water and fresh fog. But the buzz on the lips—like a kiss in a children's story of enchantments—inched like a slow fuse through Rain's lips and her jaw. It excited her tongue and moistened her eyes. A little less dark in that velvet sack of unknowing; a cord loosened, fresher air and ambient light.

She remembered him in the round, then, her erstwhile love.

Tip. A boy named Tip. Someone she had kissed, back in Oz, and not just incidentally like this Tycheron, but with purpose and ardor. Tip shook his head and lovely form out of her hidden past as clearly as Yurkios had made himself from insensate hillside. A boy about her age, with sandy hair and tentative eyes, loving her in her memory as much as she must have loved him.

And it had ended. He had left her. Somehow, how, death, some other love, she couldn't grasp that bit. The Grimmerie had been involved. A weapon, a curse. It had magicked him away. That was why she'd taken revenge on it, so it could do no harm to anyone else.

"Oh, no," she said to Tycheron.

"Oh yes." He leaned in again. She pushed him off as gently as she could, stung into the start of memory.

THE CARYATIDS

1

Dawn, a pall of nacreous whiteness before shadow eddied in. The moods of morning were unsettled, the travelers unsettled. They couldn't guess the accurate hour. They made their sloppy ablutions, shared what little to eat there was. Leorix and Cossy stomped the stuffing out of the embers with vengeance.

In such swaddling mists, neither Iskinaary nor Asparine wanted to launch in search of some obscure hilltop tower.

The Goose thought they might backtrack to the riverbank and see if the resinous air was clearer there, and check to make sure that the bounty hunters from Skedeland hadn't come upon King Copperas's ramp. The Company of the Scarab needed only to follow the slope back to the water's edge to see. But the downslope had disappeared. Hills rose all around. "We came straight up from the river to this granite brow," said Iskinaary. "One shot, no dips or reversals. What gives?"

Asparine said, "What granite brow?" and she wasn't kidding.

"The hills are pulling tricks on us." Lucikles tried not to sound as alarmed as he felt. "They're playing hide-and-seek." He wanted to call Leorix to his side, as if the earth might buckle and claim his son, but Leorix was proving too occupied with Cossy to attend to his father's claims of precedence. And she with him, more's the pity.

They fell still, to try to hear the sound of the river. It was gone. All they could make out was the ferny silence of the forest, the

occasional drop of a pinecone or the rustle of a rodent in the underbrush, the dew gathering and falling off the conifers.

"Really," said Asparine, "the nerve!"

Burden was miffed at the unreliable landscape. "Bloody unpro-
fessional. Still, what difference does it make? We were going to go
on. We'll go on. The map, if map it is and not just an old woman's
fancy, showed the tower to be on a hilltop in the middle of the
Walking Mountains. Any of these slopes might lead us there. We
have no choice. Let's go." His tone was false and cheerless.

Alone of them, Rain was calm. The Walking Mountains,
throwing up deception and mask, seemed the outward manifestation of her own interior confusion. How much more lost could
she be, after all? She hadn't known where she was going since she
left Oz.

The slopes were accommodating, made for a donkey and cart.
They let Bob decide which way she wanted to go, since all ways
were as one to them. Though Burden didn't ask for the privilege,
the others insisted that he ride. Hunched on the bench with his
heels on the toeboard, he kept the satchel laced to his back instead
of settling it down in the cart. He leaned forward with his head
in his arms like someone in distress. After the struggle through
the river, he seemed to have lost his momentum. Thinner in the
face and at the waist, already—his arms ropy and his expression
drawn. But a bvasil's brow, still fit for a crown? Perhaps.

Reluctantly, Lucikles had come to think that Burden had been
right to loop that emblem of the Bvasilate, that audacious jeweled
scarab, around his neck. Though he and Burden must be roughly
the same age, Burden looked ten years older than when they'd
begun. Should they be ambushed now, by anyone who'd even remotely known the Bvasil, they might be fooled. Burden's incoming
beard was white and his eyes had tightened in twists of skin. He
looked furtive and suspicious, even when he smiled. Perhaps this

is who he'd always been, and the pampered sybarite of court life had been an affectation.

The fog made it impossible to tell where upon a rising slope they might be—near a crest, edging a cliff. Sometimes Lucikles realized he hadn't taken in the moment they'd stopped climbing and begun again to descend. Also, anything that might qualify as a landmark seemed to change its shape the next time you looked over.

And yet, if they were well and truly lost, it was likely that any brigands chasing them would be just as befuddled. For the first time since leaving the farmstead of Mia Zephana on High Chora, the Company of the Scarab felt safe. Although the food that Leorix had supplied them wouldn't last forever.

They made lunch, they made a place to camp for supper. They slept and started over. And again. When she woke up each morning, Rain wondered if she'd awakened and talked to Tycheron again, but she apparently hadn't. This happened another day and night, and another. The only creatures they saw were rabbits, who would sit in cautious judgment as they passed, a look of something like criticism or apathy in their jellied, albino eyes. They didn't run away, though they might have if Asparine had lunged for them.

Rain was aware of Tycheron as one is aware of a weakness in a knee joint, wondering if the tissue will hold or buckle. She watched him from a canny distance. It didn't help that, now he'd begun to smile at her, he exhibited a certain male radiance. But she was rational too. If Artoseus's caution was accurate, ought she be wary of her newfound ease with Tycheron? Yet who else was she going to warm up to? Asparine was becoming quieter by the day. Iskinaary—for all his loyalty—he was really her father's familiar. True, he was seconded to her, and he seemed to love her, as much as a Goose can love a human. But so what?

"You've been sighing a lot since we crossed the river," noted

Lucikles. When had he fallen in step beside her? And how dare he? Ah, he dared because he was irritated at Cossy making close with his boy.

Still, she found she had to say something. "I'm regretting a life that never happened."

"Ah. There's a local word for that salty mood. Do you know it in your tongue? *Ephrarxis.* The state of nostalgia for something that has never been. The court appointment that went to someone else. The romance you never did consummate." He glanced at Rain curiously. "Something potential didn't work out, and yet you can't help but remember with longing what might have come to pass. In troubling specificity. Dreams trade in ephrarxis, I guess; but it's more of a waking illness. Sometimes a bad bout of it can make you change your life—for good, if you're strong. But the original need can never be slaked. That's its nature."

"That's a big definition for a small but nagging ailment."

"Any ailment that doesn't go away can't be called small." He pointed to his foot. He was limping a little.

Not to be tilting toward Tycheron was a momentary relief. "I fell in love with someone far away," said Rain, yielding, "and he fell in love with me. Then he was taken from me. A fierce book of magic, the fiercest, was somehow responsible. To wreck that volume's chances of ever ruining another life, I destroyed it. But then I guess maybe I brought trouble here, to a land I don't even know."

"Do you suffer ephrarxis for a Maracoorian childhood you never had?"

"Someone else might manage that. But I can't even remember my own childhood, so there's no point in trying to replace it with an imagined one."

"Are you replacing this someone with Tycheron?" At her expression he shrugged. "You seem to be enamored with him. The

Goose isn't the only one who wakes up in the middle of the night, you know."

"Is your attention to me a little unseemly?"

"Don't take it that way. We're adrift together, all of us. It's impossible not to notice what's going on. I know you rue the day I rowed into your life. Can't help that now."

Tip in her mind, turning, at the edge of a bluff somewhere, catching her gaze, smiling at her. And then, for all practical purposes, he had tumbled off, into nothingness. Was he even still alive? Was Tycheron, as Lucikles theorized, a pale substitute?

But why not? Under the circumstances this must be more than all right. Look at the courtier, in his slope-shouldered deference to Burden, his quiet conviviality with Bob, chucking her under the chin, as if she'd always been his special pet.

But the second kiss hadn't hovered in the air between Rain and Tycheron. A potential kiss, she remembered, was like an endangered butterfly. The only way to rescue that butterfly was to pin it gently between two pairs of human lips. Softly, softly. She couldn't detect a second kiss hovering between them. Maybe it was the weirdness of the woods.

"So is that bug still in your foot?" she asked the Minor Adjutant.

SINCE ONLY LUCIKLES and Leorix knew the same words and tunes, they sang to pass the time. Ditties and oddments from Leorix's childhood or from religious lessons in the agora, mostly.

The sacred text was solemn and the melody delivered in an obscure mode that reminded Rain, whose ear was foreign, of the pitches that donkeys use. Bob seemed to agree, for she swayed her head. The words were the same as devotional lyric everywhere. After each line had been sung it seemed to disappear into the air.

Under thy mercy thine subjects weep

After that credo, Rain stopped listening. If the mercy of the Great Mara made its subjects weep, this was a faith system Rain might do well to avoid.

But the children's song was more catchy.

When will we get there?
Never never never.
We're lost. We're lost.
We're lost we're lost we're lost.

How such a desperate message got coupled with a contagious jingle of a tune was beyond Rain's guess. Perhaps some desperate older sibling invented it to cheer up the younger ones as they wandered out of range of familiarity.

2

The next day—but how many days had it been really, they'd all lost count—the mist seemed less milky. Were they ascending more than they were descending? Maybe they'd break out of the collar of clouds and behold the peaks of the Tenterix Range at last. "Since the vapor looks to be thinning, how about somebody gets airborne to take our bearings?" asked Lucikles at breakfast, looking from one winged member of the Company to the other.

Iskinaary said, "When I'm ready to volunteer I'll let you know."

"Asparine?" asked the Minor Adjutant. But sitting on a dead branch as if she'd become an overnight victim of taxidermy, Asparine stared unblinkingly at Lucikles and didn't reply.

"No time to go sulky, you," said Burden. He wasn't looking up. The others caught on first. Little by little Asparine had lost her luminescence and her asperity—it had begun to happen when they'd left the tableland—and now she'd been reduced to an owl. Not even a handsome specimen—a bit astigmatic, and grey as sacking.

"Oh, look what you've done now; you've let yourself be bewitched!" cried Cossy, who'd never paid Asparine much attention. "What's to become of us?"

The owl didn't roll her eyes, but she seemed uninterested in pursuing the thought.

Before the others could devise some sort of experiment to see if Asparine continued to understand human speech, the light shifted. The mist hadn't cleared, but the atmospherics became glazed with a more amber light. A candle flame passing warmly through a glass of clouded ale. Perhaps it was merely hope having its taunting way with them.

"The day is brighter in that direction," said Lucikles, pointing. "Might as well follow it." He led, favoring his gashed foot. His visiting insect had disappeared by morning, though whether it had burrowed inside or departed intact was uncertain, and he didn't really want to know. Recovery was slow, the pain residual.

The tint of sunlight strengthened and beckoned. "It wants us somewhere," said Leorix, with the confidence of the young who believe that all the magic in the world is beneficial. Openly he was now walking hand in hand with Cossy.

Tycheron said to Rain, "If we're being led into a trap, I'm happy to be with you in these final moments."

"I feel the same, Tycheron." It was the first time she had spoken his name with any emphasis. His nod showed her that he noticed. Grateful for her intimacy or not, he really did think his life was endangered. Well, he was young to be going through all this. Not as young as Rain herself, she guessed, but she'd had more practice being endangered. "We've got this far," she said, but she had nothing to follow it up with. So what? We all get just this far right before we meet our ends.

For his part, Lucikles felt his eyes tingle and his hair stand on end. His chest surged with worries that had been postponed by the struggle of travel.

On the one hand, he recognized in how much danger his children all were, not to mention his marriage. Leorix, though just behind him with that kid, that Cossy, might never make it out of here alive. None of them could retrace steps that they hadn't been able to plot. Meanwhile, in High Chora, the little girls, his babies, his Star and his Poena: they were hunkered down in a part of the country swarming with barbarians hunting for the Bvasil. His Poena might grow up with only dim scraps of memory of her hapless father, who'd always meant well and leaned to the task without stinting, but hadn't been able to do what a father is there to do—to protect against attack, to keep the nursery free of pests. And Star, for her part, still so young. She'd forget what he looked and sounded like, were he never to return. As for Oena—well, things had been iffy there for a while. He didn't like to think about it. The thousand scars of marriage.

The members of the Company emerged onto the brow of a ridge banked like a burial barrow. To either side the trees nodded their heads, making a murmuring sound. The shroud of mist began to drop away as they climbed.

"And I'm back to being the Bvasil, then," said Burden, standing up and looking about him. "We've found the Tower in the Clouds, by the looks of it."

Ahead of them in bold sunlight rose a structure whose profile resembled a sculpture of chimneys or bottles grouped together, the highest of them in the center. Windows and a low door, and signs of normalcy about. Some laundry on a line, a goat tethered to a peg, ignoring their arrival. A table put out before the door, laid with white napery and set with plates and bowls, platters covered with ceramic or copper domes, and plenty of wine bottles and cups. The right number for all of them, including a bale of sweet hay for Bob and what looked like a bowl of fresh corpses of barn mice for Asparine.

"It could be a trap," said Lucikles. Well, he had to say that. He was the only father among them. No one paid him any attention. The chicken was delicious, he found; served with a tamarind glaze. And the fruits had no brown spots, and the jam pot was free of ants. They'd endured their spare rations all this time without complaint. If this is a magical repast, destined to be our final meal and turn us to stone, thought Lucikles, it's worth it. Ambrosia and nectar of the gods could hardly be much better.

Only when they'd finished the last of the blue-grape wine did they push back their benches and look around. "Did I drink too much?" said Leorix, belching. "I think the trees are people."

Rain said, "What is ever what it seems? We're all disguised somehow." But she saw what he meant. Some of the trees had followed them upslope. They had arranged themselves in a way that made them anthropomorphic—for lack of a better word. They stood in groups of four. Now that the mist had fully shifted away from the hilltop, Rain could see that the slender knobby trunks of the young trees were the legs of tree-creatures. "They're giraffe-trees," she said.

"What do you know, you're right," said Iskinaary. "I'd been having the feeling that we were being followed through the forest, but perhaps we were being followed *by* the forest. I feel humbled." He didn't look humbled, he looked outraged, as if he'd been spied on during a moment of personal hygiene or romance.

The nearest tree-thing contorted itself, some gesture like a genuflection or curtsey. "The Oracle of Maracoor is expecting you," it said. Its voice made one think of the music that leaves might make if so inclined.

The Bvasil adjusted his clothes. Simply by pushing it back off his brow, his straw hat took on the noble pitch of a diadem. "Your service, duly noted. The meal, very welcome indeed."

"That's not us, that's the handiwork of the house staff," said the creature. "We're the sheriffs of the forest."

"Wait," said Leorix. "Before you go in, Burden. We ought to know more. The Oracle can wait." He stood below the sentinel creature. "Who are you? Did you lead us here? Why?"

"Leorix, keep to your station," said his father. "You're taking license."

"The little human needs to question," came the reply. "So amusing. But why not. You live so fast, and learn so little, and pass on nearly nothing. You can be excused your temerity." The tree-creature rearranged the leaves about its face. Yes, it had a face, and Rain was right: it wasn't unlike a giraffe, though vaguely more humanoid. As the citizens of Maracoor didn't know the giraffe, they considered the tree's likeness to that of a camel. But it was more like itself than anything else.

"I am Peritir," it said. "I lead this delegation, which was dispatched to bring you here if we deemed you suitable. It seemed kinder not to uncloak ourselves until we arrived. We've been arranging the trip to be as brief as possible. It's taken some doing. I hope you're not too exhausted, or mystified."

Lucikles spoke next, as the Bvasil seemed to have lost the trick of being a manifestation of the Great Mara. "I'm surprised we're here this quickly. Or at all."

"We had shuffling to do," said the Peritir. "The Tower in the Clouds was quite some distance to the west. We moved as quickly as we could."

"Shuffle what?" asked Cossy. "The building?"

"The mountains," came the reply. "They are unstable, like clouds. It takes a lot of coordination to shift a destination forward. Usually we're engaged in moving something out of the way so it can't be found. This was a special project for us."

"The Walking Mountains," said Iskinaary. "That's a bit tricksy, don't you think?"

"You've come this far," said Peritir pointedly. "The Oracle waits."

"But the mists?" asked Tycheron.

"They're not separate from us," said Peritir. "They are our natural camouflage, as the dun coloring of the owl is hers."

Asparine hooted a couple of times, possibly to protest the loss of her internal holiday lighting system, thought Rain.

"And how do we qualify for the privilege of your escort?" asked Rain.

"You can still sing, despite everything," replied their emissary. "We enjoyed that."

"Oh, let me in," said the Bvasil, adjusting the straps of his knapsack. "We've come this far and been well fed. I'll face this Oracle and learn what I might."

"You can all go," said Peritir. "Except perhaps the donkey, who won't manage the stairs. So Bob will stand guard here. If she has no objection. Though, really, no guard is needed. No one could ever find you here without our complicity. And we're here to serve." He added, "Bring only what you must; it's a long climb." Burden handed to Tycheron the satchel with the Fist of Mara in it. Asparine perched on Bob's spine. She had no appetite for an audience with the Oracle.

3

The humans ducked their heads under a lintel into an atrium so high it felt like dusk. Iskinaary waddled in last, muttering, "We don't go in much for household furnishings, I see." A second, interior tower rose, as if it had been there first, and the flanking cylindrical areas added on, tapering into high empty spaces, like huge flasks or silos. Windows pierced the curtain walls at various heights. Shafts of green light evoked a forest in high summer. The structures looked fibrous, reticulated, as if tree bark grew on the walls. The Tower in the Clouds, maybe, was alive.

At ground level, though, the place was severe as a cave. The Goose was right; little here in the way of ornamentation. The Company started toward a staircase that wound, divided, rejoined itself around the interior tower structure. In some cases patches of moss adhered to stretches of wall. At the foot of the stairs solemnly waited a few figures.

"You made good time," said the stout one in a group of four.

"I believe," said Burden, "we had help." He nodded his head. This astonished Lucikles. He'd rarely known a bvasil to express gratitude except in certain temple rituals implying that he was grateful to be so wonderful.

The mistress of ceremonies acknowledged this but shrugged. She and her little party were like nothing the companions had ever met before. In this pretty gloom the hosts looked like humans made of wood—part natural growth, as when a broken twig or a snapped sapling approximates a human torso and legs and head—

and part hard-worked material, the carving of a master puppeteer. The effect was of a crude, nearly life-size set of ambulatory figures that hadn't yet been touched by the artisan's paintbrush. Instead, their features were marked by blushings of reds and greens against wood tones found in nature and in sawn planks. These individuals weren't statues, though. Their expressions were animated. The wooden folds of their clothes shifted with dry rustling or scraping or even clacking sounds. They were, Rain guessed, not cousin to the Wolf and the harpies and others who had blurted into her path since leaving Oz. These natives were more organic, less conjectural or mythic. Human forms of trees, she guessed.

She loved them at once. As if a diagnosis of ephrarxis had been false—she'd always known these people were here, and she wanted them to be; and now they were.

"She's a sharp one," said the squat chieftain, pointing at Rain and grinning a little through a smile both brown and ivory, not unpleasant. "I can see her working us out. It's always fun for us to watch, because we don't get the chance to astonish often. Yes, my dear, I'll put you out of your mental anguish. We're a different form of life though related to our cousins outside. I believe you met Peritir, and maybe his consorts, Liliacroia and Musxou? Only Peritir? Yes, we're all of a piece, though at different stages of growth. The rings I have on that young stropper, Peritir! Are you well nourished by what we supplied? Do you need to find a place to relieve yourselves in that sloppy animal way? The Oracle is waiting for you. He isn't going anywhere, so take your time. But he *is* eager."

"What's your name?" asked Leorix.

"I'm telling you again, don't be forward," shot his father.

"Oh, I don't mind," replied the talkative one. "It's the name thing, is it. I always forget. We only really bother with names if we're dealing with non-native species. You're not an invasive species, are you? That would be awkward. You can call me Mamanoo, why not."

"That's my mother-in-law's nickname," said Lucikles, as long as the conventions of ambassadorial protocol had been pulverized by his idiot son.

"Oh, is that where I got it? Sorry. I'm out of touch. I must have taken the easy road and gone rummaging through the surface material. I hope she wouldn't think it an insult, but anyway, I'll switch out. How about Tesasi? It's plain enough, in your tongue, and I'm plain enough. And these—oh, well, you won't be needing their names, I bet."

"I want a name," said the smallest of the other three, who was the arbor-people's number opposite of Cossy, by the sound of it.

"Pick your own," said Tesasi, "but let's get on with it, shall we? If there's nothing to hold us up?"

"I'll be Acornella, the fairy princess of the woods." She tossed a ducked-chin look at Cossy and rattled her tresses. Dominoes clicking in a chamois purse.

"You do just that," said Tesasi. "Now if we're ready?"

"Wait," said Lucikles. His training as Minor Adjutant was kicking in. "Before the Oracle of Maracoor receives us. Give us a little précis of what we're going to find. How does he even know to expect us?"

Tesasi paused with her wooden hands on her wooden hips, as if she'd just raised herself up from a kneeling position before a bucket of wooden laundry. "It's hard for me to guess what you might want to hear. We share our understandings without much language, you see. I get a little blocked when I come across one of your primitive kind. What precisely do you want to know?"

"The basics, for a start," insisted Lucikles. "Is the Oracle your king? How does he come by his power of soothsaying? Why do you serve him?"

"As if we'd bother having a king." Tesasi laughed, and her companions made oaky chuckles in their wooden throats. "No offense to the Bvasil, but that's too high-drama for us. No, my intrepid guests; he's not our king. He's not one of us. I daresay he must be one of you. He's been here for—rings and rings—what's the concept you use—yes, I think the idea is 'decades.' Where he comes by his awareness is uncertain. Not that *we* turn to him for counsel. We don't need it. But others do, and so they try to find him. If their cause is just, such as we can make out, we wander the mountains about so the Tower can be found. Otherwise we keep depositing nosy intruders or nasty characters back on the shores of the Seethe, where they eventually get the message, and float downstream to some other life that fate has apparently been intending for them all along."

"But our cause?"

"It appears to be worthy." Tesasi straightened herself up, a creaking of bones like the boards in an old house. "Now don't be alarmed. The Oracle is an ancient figure as you count life, though still a babe in nappies to us. He won't bite you. He'd like to meet you in common audience and then, depending, to consult with some of you privately. Mind, his energy level isn't high. Not at his human age. So let's be brisk about this, shall we? You have nothing to fear."

She turned to the littlest figure. "Ah, what was it? Acornella, Miss Fairy Princess? Would you dart ahead and let Zoar know that we will be up presently? That's a good little princess." The smallest wood-person marched up the steps with alacrity, leaving a fine dusting of sawdust with each footprint. It wasn't quite a scamper. She didn't propel off the ground as Cossy might have done. But something in the upward tilt of her chin gave her the look of a child—earnestness, eagerness. Pride at being trusted with a job. Tesasi smiled after her wryly. "She loves to be important, and she gets so little opportunity," she murmured to the Company. "Let's give her a moment on her own with the Oracle, shall we?"

"Who do you call yourselves?" asked Lucikles.

"We don't usually call ourselves anything. The Oracle—Zoar—calls us Caryatids. That name serves as good as our own generic name for ourselves, which anyway is unpronounceable in your tongue. If you mean is there a family name for the sequence before you"—she flexed a rough-hewn palm to indicate her two companions, who were only a little taller than she, and looked mute with embarrassment at having to be presented to guests—"you could just say we're the Towerkeepers. Tesasi Towerkeeper. How's that? It has a nice ring. What would you like to be called?" she asked those sentries on either side.

"Nothing," said one, and "Never," said the other.

"Nothing and Never, my partners today. About sums up their ambitions in life. Well, now, my friends. We'll follow the advice that the Oracle gives." She started to climb. Her calves like two slender butter churns clomping along. The stairs were shallow, perhaps to accommodate the abbreviated lift of the Towerkeepers' step.

"But by what name should we address the Oracle?" asked Lucikles. "Is there an honorific? Your Eminence? Something like that? You called him Zoar. Is he Kerr Zoar? Is he Kerr Towerkeeper?"

"Ask him yourself," called Tesasi over her shoulder. "I call him, 'you shabby old bag of bones,' but that might be a bit forward for you to begin with. Anyway, he's more your kind than mine. He'll give a better answer than I might do."

THE WINDS OF
CHANCE

1

The stairs began at the base of the interior tower, wound around it, then traced upon buttresses rising between the curtain walls and the stem. A casual aspect to the architecture, thought Rain—improvisatory as a spiderweb.

Eventually the flight passed into the heart of the core cylinder through a pointed, off-center doorway, like the profile of a crenate leaf. Here the staircase resolved into the spiral common to lighthouses and nautilus shells.

The visitors and their hosts climbed with care. Interior windows gave scant light. The Company of the Scarab leaned centrifugally, as the open space in the center dropped into a rank depth.

Their progress was slow because of Tesasi's shallow step. She took her time. Lucikles wasn't sorry. His foot was throbbing. Burden said, "I'd never have made it up all these stairs carrying my satchel. Tycheron, how are you managing?"

Tycheron didn't answer, but the sound of heavy wheezing clocked his efforts.

Their footing grew surer as the air grew lighter. They soon saw why. The tower had cleared the lower roofs of the dependences. It lifted above the highest treetops and those persistent mists.

Ordinary sunlight, with its green tinge rinsed out. A blue heaven, plain as milk. A few high clouds lazing. Everyday birds, too distant to identify, soaring on silent winds. And a crop of satiny periwinkle blossoms cresting upon the tops of the trees the way lily pads skim on pond water.

"So pretty," said Cossy, "flowers like the sun on the tips of waves, everywhere."

"Ah, yes," replied Tesasi, sounding suddenly grim, "but for naught, for naught, for naught."

Princess Acornella was standing inside a hatch at the top of the stairs, twisting her twiggy fingers together in impatience. The petitioners rose through the opening to reach the sanded plank floor of a chamber fitted into the cylinder space, snug as a cork in the neck of a bottle. "This is the waiting room," said the wooden child. "He's in the attic, one more flight. Under the roof. He'd like you to come up all at once, in case he dies before he has a chance to meet you one at a time. Not likely, but he's always saying things like that. I think you'll fit. Let's try."

The waiting room was kitted out something like a railroad station, though Rain was pretty sure that the folks of Maracoor didn't know what a railroad station was. Shabby curved benches built into the wall. A table on uneven legs holding a few ancient magazines. She glanced at one as she went past. If she was reading the curlicued script correctly, it said *Saint Nicholas Magazine*. The item was yellowed and the pages flaked away at the edge. But she had no time to investigate. Princess Acornella was saying, "Here, this way, come on!" and pointing them to the final flight. It began behind a curved bookcase and rose along the wall toward an even brighter space above.

"Hold on, Acornella. We're not needed upstairs," said Tesasi. "This is their audience, not ours. We'll wait here."

"I never get to do *anything*!" complained the tree child.

Rain, the last of the party, paused and turned on a low step and said to Tesasi, "Those blossoms, so luscious—why are you distressed about them?"

"Everything in its season," replied the Caryatid, "but the butterflies migrated early, two days before you arrived, and the blossoms only opened yesterday. Our pollen is embargoed this year. Missed its window of dispersal. Failed. Inert. I don't know what this means. Go on up, you'll miss being introduced."

"The Oracle doesn't want to see me," said Rain. "I'm only along for the chaperoning. Tell me more."

"Don't dawdle." Tesasi waved her on. "You've come so far. My burdens are my own."

Rain paused where she was. "I'm not on the Oracle's agenda, I'm just here on the stairs. I make my own appointments. What's troubling you?"

2

I t's my privilege to go first," said Burden.

Lucikles patted his chest where, under his tunic, the pendant still pressed. "Yes, but it's my duty," he said. Drawing a deep breath, he went to work. A Minor Adjutant in his most major moment, perhaps. Though who would know about it? Probably not Oena. At least, for all her grudgery, Rain would be a witness.

The final flight brought him to a plain circular room whose rough-hewn rafters converged at a high point, like a conical tent. A hooked rug on the floorboards declared HOME SWEET HOME in uncertain script. To one side, a flat wall of varnished chestnut divided the room into two unequal parts, the larger sleeping chamber and a smaller dressing room or water closet, probably. Against the interposed wall loomed a bed's headboard, a masterpiece of dead bramblework braided asymmetrically. As others of the company emerged behind Lucikles from the floor below, the vines rippled into lavender leaf from one side to the other. Shimmering, the growth paled to a dry marigold as Burden came up. Cossy murmured, "Oh my," and Leorix grabbed her hand. Lucikles suppressed a snort at the cheap emotions of the young. Upon Burden's shoulder Tycheron put a steadying palm. Iskinaary huffed, "Stage effects! A bit rich, for my money." The Goose looked behind him, saw Rain hesitating on the steps below with Tesasi, turned away, and let her be.

Lucikles readied himself for the diplomatic moment. This was his métier, after all. He watched for signs of whatever he could use to move toward the goal of the Company. He knew that he was, as some quarters might have put it sourly, an operator. So what. Someone has to be paying attention.

Rain had described to Cossy some kindly figure capped with a conical hat. Boasting half-spectacles low on his nose. From where had she gotten such a picture? Here lolled a sad case. Hardly a magician in opulent, fur-trimmed robes stitched over with cosmic shorthand.

Sagging against his headboard, the Oracle of Maracoor was propped up by a flotilla of dingy pillows. He was slighter around the rib cage than Cossy. His bony wrists, knobby nothings, stuck out from the sleeves of a snowy dressing gown. His hands arthritic and trembling. More washed-up pensioner than patrician mystic.

"Come here," he said to them, "spread out. Let me see you better. You're against the light just there, slide round. That's it." With that muskmelon head, he reminded the Minor Adjutant of a dusty toy exiled in some abandoned nursery. Bald but for a final surge of white ringlets wisping at his temples and creeping around at collar level. Either he'd been shaved for the occasion or his chin had given up on whiskers a long time ago. "So you arrive at last. I've been expecting you. Hail and how-de-do. They call me Zoar." An unoiled voice, as if he seldom spoke. Could that grimace be meant as a smile? Those irregular teeth poking from his gums, corn kernels dried to different hues.

"Kerr . . . Kerr Zoar? If you please. My name is Lucikles. I'm the Minor Adjutant of the House of Balances located in Maracoor Crown, with assignment to the Ephrarxis Isles and the Hyperastrich Archipelago. Emissary of the Court. I'm privileged to present you to His Magnificence, the Bvasil of Maracoor."

"Yes, yes, I've been briefed, though I tend to forget what I'm told. I thought there were more of you?"

"We lost one harpy on the way, and the other is outside. Also

the donkey." Lucikles hadn't noticed that Rain was lingering be-
lowdecks. "We've come on a matter of national sovereignty."

"You're being theatrical. I suppose. Hyperbolic. What's the fuss
about?"

For the first time sounding like the farmer he'd been imperson-
ating, Burden said, "You're called the damned Oracle of Maracoor.
You should know why we're here."

The bedridden ancient flinched. "Ouch. Oh, my. Well, yes.
There is that. A reputation is an annoyance, isn't it. Promoted
beyond one's capacities, perhaps. So much of what we call wisdom
is just the aftershock of survival."

"That's not enough to supply you with fortune-telling powers,"
said Burden. "Otherwise all ancient crones and cronies would be
oracles."

"Well, they really are, probably, but nobody listens to *them*,"
said Zoar. "A bit of dazzle in the presentation goes a long way, I've
always found. Okay, you're right; there's some aptitude involved.
An instinct. One picks up a few tricks. I used to read palms too
but my eyes are going. I have a certain pack of cards I'll show you."

The voice of Tesasi called from below. "They're not wearing you
out now, love, are they?"

"I've got a little coffee in the veins, old limb, I'm fine," Zoar
called back. He did seem to be gaining strength for the occasion.
"I was saying. You see, the Arborians know the world in a way that
humans and wizards and elves and Animals do not. Perhaps some
animals do, those who live in hives and colonies—but most of us
singular creatures are deafened and isolated by our singularity.
Peritir outside, and all the kin around on all these mountains—
they share a network of understanding that, should humans ever
learn it, could revise the nature of society! Spooky. I've never quite
grasped how—were these Arborians less ambulatory I'd have sus-
pected some communication system of the roots underground. Or

maybe it's an endless semaphoring by how leaves turn in the wind and sun." Boastfully, perhaps, the foliage in the headboard flashed a brilliant scarlet, then subsided to a greenish-lilac.

This old orator hasn't had an audience in years, guessed Lucikles. How he goes on.

"The work of an Oracle isn't to tell the future, though. An Oracle merely lays out the vagaries of the present. Let the supplicant make his or her own choices about how to proceed. This was so in ancient times and it is so now. Anything said cryptically enough becomes true sooner or later, if you wait long enough. But I don't *try* to be confounding. I try to tell what I know."

"You can read minds?"

"Ha! As if. No, the Arborians brought me information about you as you made your trek to me. It's part of the strategy, to require you to take some time. It's how I gather some background knowledge. Now I'm giving away trade secrets. I shall be banned from the society of tricksters for this, and have to send back my membership card." He smiled. He was making some sort of joke that they couldn't follow.

"Kerr Zoar," said Lucikles. "Do you even know what the Fist of Mara is?"

"Well," said the old gentleman, "I have heard of it, for sure. The Arborians have briefed me a little. I know that you believe it is deadly, and that you think it's being hunted by your enemies. You believe they're tracking it. Tell me all that you know of this foul item, before you take it out and show it to me."

The Bvasil nodded, and Tycheron stepped forward to relate the history of the amulet as best as they understood it. How it had been discovered. How it had brought barrenness to the women of the region. How it had been hidden for several hundred years on an island off the coast of Maracoor. How a small cult of women were enjoined to spend their lives in its presence, unmarried and, perforce, childless, in order to pray for the continuation of life on the mainland. Cossy, here, this girl, was one such child. She'd been brought off the island a while ago, the first bride of Maracoor to leave. Ever.

"The sacrificial lamb," said the Oracle. He seemed to notice Cossy for the first time. "Knee-high to a corn-stalk. What a concept. Come here, child."

Cossy hesitated, then thrust her chin out and brashed forward. Lucikles had to admire her grit.

"Go to the dressing room and get me my cards. They're in a fur-lined box on the shelf. Next to the razor and strop."

He waited, blinking at his guests with wordless patience. She returned with a parcel the size of a child's sandal. She set it in his hands, but he rested it on the coverlet before him and held out his arms to her. "I do so admire someone I can boss around," he said. Cossy submitted to a brittle hug. When released, she was flushed. Maybe the old guy was only playing for the crowd, but the child seemed pleased.

"And yes," continued Tycheron, "we've made our way from Maracoor Crown. Across High Chora. In the company of creatures from the mythic history of our race. We crossed the Seethe and found our way to the Tower in the Clouds. We're here to seek your advice about the Fist of Mara."

"Give me a moment. Presto zesto, abracazoo, Salve Regina, how do you do."

"You do magic?" asked Cossy. "So do I."

"Give me your best," he said, nearly twinkling at her.

"Well, my spells don't work yet, but they will when I get bigger."

"Neither do mine. Hopeless, always was. Stop apologizing and show me the goods."

Cossy cleared her throat and spoke.

Make me a warrior,
Braver, bolder,
But wait until
I'm a little older.

"That's just darling," said the Oracle, if a little flatly. "I love it, I really do. Now stand aside and let an old pro show you how it's done."

He took from the fur box a set of cards, worn at the edges and bleached by the sun. One side was printed with a pattern of irises upon an ecru field. The Oracle made a pig's breakfast of shuffling the cards. They flopped out of his hands all over the coverlet. Some fell on the floor. Cossy picked up the strays. "My party trick technique is a little rusty, but no matter. The cards are forgiving. Until they're not. Let me use the three you collected for me. Be a dolly and hand them to me face down. The grace of innocence. That'll improve the odds."

Innocence, ha, thought Lucikles. Maybe the shyster isn't as farseeing as he claims.

The Oracle laid the trio of cards Cossy had handed him, face down, upon his lap. Only then did he nod to Burden. "Set the vexing item here on the bed. No, I'm not worried about contamination. What more can be done to me? Some days I'd find myself grateful for a little toxic crumb in my lunch pail."

The Bvasil unfolded the cloth. The Fist of Mara seemed clenched, the calcified excrement of some malign creature. "It's a hammer," said the Oracle. His voice had gone gruff and low, suddenly no trace of the diverting patter of the confidence man. "A mallet. A gavel of some sort. An ugly article with bad-tempered inclinations. It wants something to strike. Where did it come from again?"

"When he starts asking the same questions," called Tesasi, "it's time to give him a nap."

"Leave me alone. You're not the boss of me," shrieked the Oracle. "But I need to think. All right, you lot; party's over. Get out. Divining is private work."

"Can I watch?" asked Cossy.

Gone the twinkling old gentleman. "A wizard never reveals his tricks. Scram."

"Pilgrims," called Tesasi, "I've a plate of biscuits and some lemonade set out for you down here. Come take your share and give him a moment. He'll be right as rain in just a few. When the spell comes on him, there's no point arguing."

Only as Lucikles came down to the floor below did he see that Rain was already there, having lingered with Tesasi. The others descended as ordered except Iskinaary, who settled upon a bedside stool. Ignoring the Goose, and showing little fear, the Oracle felt the Fist all over, a surgeon examining a tumor. Then with great effort he pushed the totem off his lap onto the coverlet. He straightened the three cards into a line and hovered his right hand about four inches above them, one at a time. His eyes were closed.

3

The others were murmuring about the Oracle, in hope and in doubt. "But what do you mean about the butterflies?" Rain was asking Tesasi.

At first the Caryatid wagged her hand vaguely, but at Rain's insistence she explained. "Our kind blooms for only about a week every year. Those flowers that look like blue lily pads on the surface of a green sea—that's our moment. We're in estrus, you might say. But our seed is heavy and doesn't blow in the breeze like, oh, pine pollen. Over the æons, we've evolved to rely on a symbiotic relationship with the local blue butterfly. In the normal course of things, when spring reaches its height, their cocoons split and they emerge. They rest a day or so, drying off. On the next sunny morning, they rise to alight upon the blossoms and feed on the pistils. The butterflies and the blossoms are subtly different shades of blue, so the act of mating, for that is what it is, in a sense, is the most beautiful day of the year. Then some secret signal for migration is given and the butterflies lift as a single thought and powder away, blue dots against the blue sky. As the butterflies migrate, they carry our pollen with them. These insects live only a week, but in that time they're able to move hundreds or even a thousand miles, and scatter our seed, and re-create our generations both here in the Tenterix Range and far away."

"So what went wrong?" asked Rain.

"This year the flowers were late to bloom. First time ever. The hatching butterflies alighted on the tightly furled blossoms, but after a day they couldn't wait any longer and departed. The pollen is ready this morning, but the butterflies have already emigrated. How far they'll even get without their first good meal, I can't say."

The others had begun to listen. "Why has this happened now?" asked Lucikles.

"I don't know," said Tesasi. "Was it that strange and stormy season? Or perhaps the arrival of the Fist of Mara has disturbed the order of things for us. The flowers timid, the butterflies skittish. And a generation of offspring wiped out, just like that. You described the unsettled fecundity in the human population of the region in which your totem was first discovered. It sounds like the same kind of thing."

Rain Rain go away; come again another day. She had inadvertently revoked the weather by dropping the Grimmerie in the sea. Whether the storm pattern that had washed her ashore in Maracoor Spot, and swept the Skedelanders northward on a surge tide, was the same thing that had delayed the annual blooming of the Arborian flowers, or whether it was the arrival of the Fist of Mara on the mainland—well, it amounted to the same thing. There seemed no end to the influence of a single action.

"A regrettable coincidence, I should hope," Lucikles was saying, without conviction. "Yet your family, the—the Caryatids, the Arborians?—brought us here anyway. A kindness."

"An uneasy moment," said Tesasi, "but all uneasy moments are cousins, no?"

"I'm so sorry," said Rain. She reached out to put her hand on Tesasi's cross-grained wrist. She surprised herself—it felt more forward than kissing Tycheron, than hugging Cossy. But before she could draw away, Tesasi covered Rain's hand with her own. Rain could feel something that wasn't blood but was still a pulse of life in the Caryatid's grip. The girl felt her eyes itch with sudden salt. Her sinuses thickened.

"Princess Acornella is going to show us where we can sleep," said Cossy importantly.

"Oh, they have rooms? I thought maybe they just planted themselves any old where," said Leorix, perhaps, thought Rain, touchy about Cossy's burgeoning friendship with the vineshoot child.

"Yes we have rooms, we're not *tumbleweed*," said Acornella, sticking out a hip. "Come along if you like. If not, don't."

The others weren't sure they wanted to make the trip all the way down to the ground floor, so they let the three young ones descend on their own. "Mind the railings," called Rain as Tesasi brought out a tray of ginger nuts and sweet early raspberries so small they had to be eaten with a spoon.

"She'll be all right," said Lucikles. "Remember how fast she gained her sea legs?"

"Rooms to spare, food for the visitors," said Burden. "You're almost too welcoming. I trust that boy is correct and you're not going to plant us in some grave for safekeeping."

"You shouldn't sound so surprised. Our kind has been giving hospitality to the world since before your kind was born. And back then, your first word was *tree*."

"I'd have thought it was 'mother,'" said Burden.

"As far back as I'm talking," replied their host, "there was only one word and it meant the same thing, tree, mother, world."

4

"Why are you looking at me like that?" snapped the Oracle.

"I've never seen fortunes told, or untold for that matter," replied the Goose. "I'd like to watch how it's done so I can tell my great-great-grand-goslings about it."

"I can't say I appreciate your tone. Then, I've never had much truck with talking Animals."

"I'm not sufficiently awed, I know. Rubs a lot of folks the wrong way. I mean no harm. Go on, turn a trick, show me your stuff. You let any professional secrets slip, I won't tell anyone. Geese don't gossip. How's it done then, these cards?"

The old fellow sighed. "You're going to wait me out, I see. As I can't take to my wings and fly away like you, I might as well get it over with. Okay. Watch. Any number of ways to do a reading, but the simplest one is to pick cards at random from this deck. No peeking at the pictures on the other side. You can arrange them three in a row, five in a row; in a pentagram, a circle of seven with an eighth and a roll of dice. Lots of variations. But you need your basic three, and I like the basic. Easier to control the cards, easier to read."

"The cards are, what, menus? Schedules? Bloodlines? I don't get it."

"Intimations of possibility. Shut up and pay attention. If you've got the touch, you can feel a minor vibration from the images hidden on the underside of the card. You can't identify what the cards are, mind. You can only sense which ones may be talking to you. Those are the ones you select to turn over and read."

"Like which bugs under the leaves are saying, 'Me, me, I'm full-on protein and will leave you with an aftertaste of autumn wheat.' I know what you mean. Talent, there's nothing like it. You either got it or you don't."

"So the soothsayer has to—"

"Remind me, what is 'sooth' exactly?"

"Be quiet. The soothsayer has to hold a conundrum in his mind. The cards respond to the thrum of his agitated cogitation. Today it's the question of what to do with this foul detritus on my bed. I respect the concerns in my mind—everything that is known about the object, and unknown—and allow the pack of cards to reveal something the universe has to show me about the possibilities that lie ahead. Of course I have to interpret the symbols. It's like translating poetry from an obsolete language. It's neither verifiable nor precise. But it's effective."

"Go on, show me already."

"Well, these ones came to my hand randomly, from that vexatious child, but sometimes the random universe is smarter, randomly, than I am." The Oracle's mottled hand hovered, trembled over the three cards, and then he selected the card on the left and turned it over. "THE SOWER," he murmured. He showed it to the Goose. Emerging from clouds like bunched theater drapes, a great hand was extended in a gesture of dispersal. Below, on an entirely different scale, a small faceless peasant scattered seed into turned earth.

With squinched eyes, the old man tried again and turned over the card on the right. "THE CUP OF BLOOD. *Really?* Is this about sowing dissent? The jolly metaphor, no good can come of this? Or more literal, a portion of, say, aneurysm? Either way, it bodes bad, bad. This is a total rout, isn't it. Come on, hinny, three's the charm." He held both cards over the middle one, as if their presence might alter the hidden image. Then he set them aside and flipped up the last card. It proved to be an image of a hot-air balloon. The caption read THE ASCENT. "Well, that just takes the cake," mumbled the Oracle. "Almost insulting."

"How would you translate this particular poem?" asked Iskinaary.

"Best two out of three," mumbled the Oracle. He shuffled and tried again with another set of three cards, and then a set of five. He didn't interpret the findings, but grew more and more agitated. Finally, stroking his chin, he said, "The consistency is confounding. Call them back from the waiting room. It's worse than I guessed."

5

houldn't one of us go check on the children?" asked Lucikles.

"They'll be fine," said Tesasi. "We wouldn't let anything harm them. I'll climb up with you. Come, my dear," she said to Rain, and took her by the hand. "It's time."

"Really," said Rain, "there's no need," but Tesasi was persuasive.

They rose again into the glare of the highest room. Iskinaary was waiting there, and quawked, "He's said his sooth, and we're not out of the woods yet. In several manners of speaking," he added, nodding at Tesasi with more respect than he generally managed to show.

The Oracle was less serene than the first time they'd met him. He fussed, he griped, he squinted into the light and gestured at Rain. He asked the Caryatid, "What's happened to the little island girl, old limb?"

"She's downstairs at play," replied Tesasi, "with the lad and my tender sapling."

"But who's this one then? A new arrival? Move over, I can't see you against the window like that." He waved his hand impatiently. Rain obliged. "Well, well," continued the Oracle. "So it comes to this. I might have known. I mean, given my reputation. But where is Galinda?" He was talking to Rain; his voice had changed again; a wobble to it, a tentative or even whining quality.

"Your worthiness," said Lucikles, wondering if the old man had outlived his own mind, "we know of no such thing or creature called that."

"I know about her," said Rain, astounded. So this *was* an Oracle at the height of his second sight, proving it the first instant of their acquaintance. She'd been dubious. "Glinda, Lady Chuffrey, née Upland. Why do you ask for her? How do you know about her?"

"We need to discuss the Fist of Mara," Lucikles reminded them all, but the Oracle of Maracoor was talking back to Rain as if protocols were to be ripped to bits and stewed for supper.

Though his chin trembled and his hands picked at each other, his voice recovered its vigor and became a little testy. "You used to pal around together, you and Galinda. I'd have thought if you were making another foolhardy excursion, you'd have dragged her along too. You always were a bit headstrong that way."

"Lady Glinda?" said Rain again. "What does she have to do with this?"

Burden said, "Has the Fist of Mara confused your thinking? Stop this gossipy nonsense so we can focus on the matter at hand. It's our national security at risk."

"Wait your turn, sonny boy," said Zoar. "You get to my age, there's nothing left but patience. Patience on a monument, they used to say. Where I come from, we have all kinds of talent for rushing slapdash fixes. We call it progress. But I'm slower in my dotage, so I need to take my time. As you took yours," he said, inching his head back to look at Rain. "I thought you'd turn up to scold me years ago. What've you been doing with yourself?"

Rain cast a sidelong look at the men she'd traveled with. She shrugged, trying to work it out. She spoke tentatively, aiming for something that was true, "I've been looking for something lost, but I didn't think it was you."

"Your heart's desire? More of that? You want my advice and a wooden nickel? You can have them both, and spend them both wisely," he said. "But aren't you here to hector me about something or other? Rarely knew the Wicked Witch of the West to take anyone else's advice," he cast in an aside to the others, winking.

"Stow it, Rain," snapped Iskinaary. "He thinks you're Elphaba."

They all froze, though the Maracoorians didn't know what *Elphaba* meant.

"I'm—I'm not Elphaba," she stammered.

"And I'm not the Wizard of Oz," he replied. "Not anymore. What else you got for me?"

Light-headed, weak-kneed, she subsided. Tycheron caught her around the waist. Lucikles and Tesasi pulled forward a bench and Rain was lowered upon it. She leaned her chin upon the wretched old broom as if she were the one near ninety years old. Everyone but Iskinaary was clueless. "You *know* each other?" asked Lucikles at last.

"Yes," said Zoar.

"No," said Rain. "No. I'm not Elphaba Thropp."

The old man seemed bewildered, a bad look for someone doing trade as an oracle. "But no one else is like Elphaba. You must be her." His voice faltering, more question than conviction. "She has no second."

"I'm Elphaba's granddaughter. The child of her son, Liir."

"You're her *granddaughter?*" he said. Staring at Rain, and blinking. A runnel of moisture formed in the inner corners of both eyes, a meldrop on his nose. "The granddaughter of Elphaba Thropp." He used his sleeve messily. "Even Dickens wouldn't have dared it. And he dared a lot."

"Are you getting overexcited?" asked Tesasi. "Don't do that."

"I believe," said Zoar, "according to relatively late-breaking intelligence, that I may be your great-grandfather."

"Whatever part of this is frail or delusional, can we push it to one side and get to the matter of the Fist of Mara?" asked Lucikles. Though he had no fondness for Rain, he didn't like seeing her upset. Her verdancy was paling. She looked ill.

"You're here under sufferance, Extremely Minor Adjutant. Don't forget it." Kerr Zoar arranged his hands one on top of the other upon the blanket edge, showing preternatural calm under the circumstances. "I admit I'm as startled as this girl is. But I have limited endurance these days. I've done some initial readings for you and I shall need to rest before long. It takes a lot out of me. But let's clear up the confusions before I turn to your needs. I'm old as sin, or maybe older, but I haven't lost my marbles, so don't patronize me. Or you can go wait outside with Bob." As an aside to Rain, he said, "I don't suppose you brought any flying monkeys with you? My, I would love to lay my sentimental old eyes on one of them."

Rain knew precious little about the provenance of her grandmother, Elphaba Thropp. The Wicked Witch of the West. Her campaigns against the Wizard of Oz and her agency in the Matter of Dorothy—how long ago was all that? A quarter century or so? More?

By the time Rain had left her father, Liir—Elphaba's only child—to wander away with the Grimmerie, to discover an accidental ocean and fly over it on a flitch of her grandmother's broom, Elphaba Thropp had become a two-dimensional cartoon from the past. Even Liir, about forty now, didn't mention his mother often. It was generally conceded that Liir's father had been Fiyero, a prince of the Arjikis—but *Elphaba's* family? *Her* father? The famous old Wizard of Oz? Hadn't Elphaba's father been a minister plying his trade in the outback somewhere? Where did the Wizard of Oz come into it?

And he had left, the onetime Wizard of Oz—he had absconded from the Palace of the Wizard, as it had been called back then. After the vanquishing of Elphaba by that Dorothy Gale, the Wizard of Oz had disappeared. He'd launched himself in the basket of the same hot-air balloon in which he was said to have arrived decades earlier. He'd whisked off for parts unknown. Presumed to have gone back to his own land.

But maybe not.

He saw the puzzle in her expression. He had to. Maybe he recognized it from his own face in the mirror, if he truly were an ancestor of hers.

"I'm sorry," he said to her. "I don't usually get muddled in my thinking. Of course you couldn't be Elphaba. She'd be long in the tooth by now and cackling away like some demented Rhode Island Red. It's just—just—well, you look so like her. You have her nose."

"I'd have thought it was my skin tone," she replied, a bit brashly.

"Whatever. There you are. Shall we become formally introduced, as long as we're meeting for the first time?"

"Rain Thropp," she said. "Oziandra Rainary Ko Osqa'ami Thropp, if you want the legal turn of affairs."

"Pleased to make your acquaintance. Oscar Zoroaster Diggs, born in one of the territories of the United States, if I'm not dreaming up all that childhood. At your service."

"They call you Zoar?"

"A diminutive of Zoroaster, invented by the Caryatids. I never put the kybosh on it. I may have been menacing once, but I'm just an old hunting dog by the fireplace now." His eyes were gleaming, not only from sentiment. He was still sharp, she could see that.

Lucikles tried again. "This is all very well—"

"*Wait*," replied the Oracle, and his voice had more thunder in it than they expected. "It's her turn. Tell me, Rain, how you came to be here, and I'll tell you how I came to be here. Then we'll discuss the troubling matter of the amulet. So it's *your* charge to evacuate it. Now I get it. If I'm reading the cards clearly. But you, you: tell me all."

"Very well," she replied. "It isn't hard to tell. I left Oz under a punishing moment."

"Punishing for Oz or for you?" he asked.

"Both. I took from Oz the book known as the Grimmerie—"

His eyes lit up with lust. He was wicked with greed at the sound of it.

"—and I flew across the Nonestic Sea, as the Goose called it. The ocean that so few in Oz have ever heard of. Since it begins so far away from the margins of habitable Oz. In the middle of the trackless water I dropped the Grimmerie."

His face fell and he began to cry. "You were bringing it to your great-grandfather, who sought it his whole life—his whole cursed life—the great ineffable masterpiece of charms—and you *dropped* it?"

"Not by accident," she clarified.

"Oh, you *are* Elphaba's granddaughter," he gasped, "you wretch, you clumsy cow."

"I didn't lose it from you, but from the world."

"Well, that explains a lot," he said some moments later, when he could master his emotions. "I should have my reputation as an oracle impounded and sold at county auction. I didn't see *you* coming. You have some native power yourself, I'd warrant. Like your grandmother. You slipped in past the sentinels, unlike these bozos you're traveling with."

"I can have you arrested," began Burden, but Iskinaary nipped the Bvasil's leg. So he fell silent again.

"It's your turn," Rain said to Zoar.

"Hold on, I'm just piecing this together now," he replied. "So it was the *Grimmerie* and the force of its impact that called up the weather and disrupted the mechanisms of spirit in the Maracoor mainland? Of course. I should have known. Good finale, anyway. But if that was your aim, you've achieved it. Why are you looking for the Oracle of Maracoor if you've already got your heart's desire?"

"I wasn't looking for you. And losing the Grimmerie wasn't my heart's desire," said Rain, as much to herself as to him. "It was my attempt to cope."

"Selfish," he said, sighing. He was still. They thought he might have fallen asleep with his eyes opened. Or perhaps died of grief. But eventually he cleared his throat and said, "Oh, all right. I did promise. I'll be quick. I left the Emerald City in Oz those years ago—I'm bad at counting years now. I was in late middle age, as we call it where I come from. I hoped that perhaps I might return to where I was born, that other land that no one here really believes in, and die there. Not die happily, mind—for I failed in my quest for the Grimmerie, which was why I'd come to Oz in the first place."

He began to shuffle the three cards in his lap. When his knee trembled under his blankets, the stack of remaining cards started to slide off the bed. Rain reached and caught the top one in mid-flight and stayed the others. She handed it to Zoar.

He glared at it. "Don't you just hate the significant world sometimes?" His tone was bitter. Rain caught a glimpse of the image—a divided human with two faces and two halves, male and female sides conjoined in a single figure. Her heart split in two with memory.

"Please," said Lucikles, "meaning no disrespect—the Fist of Mara . . ."

"And all those years inventing a life in Oz, and being honored and then awarded with power. And consolidating it. And building up the tattered kingdom of the Ozmas into something better."

"Kingdom of Ozmas?" Rain's voice, cold fire in a blizzard of steel snowflakes. Having come all this way to escape the tragedy of her romance, she bit the inside of her lip and tasted blood.

"Oh, okay. Queendom. If you must. Back in the day. Anyway, I got busy uniting the separate populations of that vast land through the system of roadworks, and of coordinated taxes. And whatnot. Government was a kick. I was good at it."

"But the Ozmas."

Zoar tapped the runaway card. "Oh, yes, the former royal line. Are they still remembered? The last one was a mere child. Easy enough to tidy away without stooping to murder. I suppose they're all ancient history now."

The gloaming of her apprehension lifted into punishing moon-struck clarity. Tip, Tip. He hadn't left her so much as been stolen from her. By the Grimmerie. "Go on," said Rain. A false, bright interest. She even worked up a smile. This very man had bribed the old sorceress, Mombey, to conceal Ozma into the form of an ageless and unsuspecting boy. The wonderful Tip, against whom Rain had dashed herself in love, and he her. Until a spell in the Grimmerie had charmed the male husk of Tip off the person again so the female Ozma could be restored. Forever regal, forever un-available to Rain.

"Go on, how did you get here?" she pushed, ice all the way through even though the sunlight on her shoulders was strength-ening. Tip. Tip. Melted away.

She leaned forward in her mind to understand as she backed away from them all. Unwittingly to have carried this love to an-other continent, to another world. To have fled from him—from her—and from herself. The words being spoken in the Tower in the Clouds now sounded flat. Scattershot and incidental. She was already dead. Perhaps she had died in that plummet into the ocean, perhaps that had been her ambition, and all this—this

Maracoor—was merely some posthumous nightmare she needed to endure before finally withering away, smoke uncoiling from a dry husk.

She'd adored Tip, but there had not really ever been a Tip. Only an Ozma in hiding.

In hiding like us all, in our hopes not to be either slain by beautiful fictions or slaughtered by truth.

"The winds of chance that blew me into Oz came from the east," he said, "and the winds that escorted me away from Oz came from the east, too. There seems no returning to my homeland, not until I die, and probably not then, either—I'm not sanguine about my prospects for life eternal. I haven't exactly been a model citizen, hey hey. The afterlife, if there is one, will take note. No, my hot-air balloon, in good shape though the rattan basket needed some reinforcing, carried me west across the Thousand Year Grasslands. I must have lost consciousness somewhere over the ocean—you called it the Nonestic Sea? Never heard that name. Back then, no one knew it was there. When I saw it I thought it might be the Indian Ocean, somehow. But my food had run out. I must have collapsed of malnutrition. When my flight finally came to ground atop this particular peak in the Tenterix Range, as I learned it was named, I called it quits. I'd survived one more exhausting voyage and I didn't have another go in me. Frankly I wasn't ever sure this wasn't yet a third universe, since no one here had ever heard of Oz."

"You established this outpost," said Lucikles. "That took some arranging?"

"The original tower was here, I don't know why. Perhaps the Walking Mountains hadn't always moved around so much. The outbuildings and dependences, if you will, have grown up organically since I arrived. Initially my bedroom was on the ground floor but it has lifted over the years. As I don't have the strength for stairs anymore, I can't comment on the management of the estate. It's quite a comedown from the Emerald City, isn't it? But I'm at that age. I did my work. I tidied up Oz good and proper. I earned what I have. I'm at peace. I deserve it." He wiped his hands together with a dry whisper, as if dispensing dust. "I don't know, old limb, why you failed to give me some notice about this one."

"Oh," replied the Caryatid, "since she's kin, I thought you'd have sensed it yourself. Being the Oracle of Maracoor. There's nothing like family, is there?" she said to Rain.

Someone in your company is a threat to you. The notion came to Rain blue and cold as the Wolf who had delivered the warning. Suddenly, his riddling about it and his reluctance to say more made sense. He'd meant Rain was a danger to herself. If he'd been more direct, she might have abandoned the mission, quit the Company.

She'd changed places with Cossy. She'd learned to tolerate the thought of assault. If not of this old reprobate, then of herself. The high window beckoned. She could no longer fly, but she could fall.

She fell forward in a lunge more paroxysm than battery. Her hands raked the air. The Oracle reared back in alarm, raising his fingers to screen his wattled neck and his sunken chin.

At the last moment her broom betrayed her, tripping her. "You—you deserve peace? You deserve *anything*?" she sobbed as the others crowded her away from him. The Oracle blinked with baleful temerity.

"You will now retire to the waiting room," said Burden. He didn't repeat the command. She wanted to get away from the old fiend. My great-grandfather. The Oracle of Maracoor.

And get away from herself. It was what she'd been trying to do since leaving Oz. Amnesia had nearly done the trick, but she'd accidentally recovered. She pivoted and all but fell down the steep flight to the floor below.

"What's her problem, she's a menace!" rasped the Oracle behind her. "She's got the devil in her just like her grandmother. She's the one who should be locked up here."

Tesasi turned but couldn't hope to follow as quickly.

6

As if back at his administrative post, Lucikles stood with shoulders squared and thrown back, an imaginary cloak of the court falling behind him. Upright despite his troubled foot. Military bearing. Tycheron looked desperate for hard cider. And by now Burden appeared only a few years younger than this old Zoar.

"Don't mind her, she's high-strung," said the Minor Adjutant. "Now the niceties have been cleared away, tell us about your reading."

"Get lost," said the Oracle of Maracoor. "All of you. Goose included. I've been thrown off my game by that harridan. I have to reconsider what the cards have said, and what this monstrous piece needs in order for us to avoid catastrophe."

They left the old man to his fretting, abandoning the Fist of Mara upon HOME SWEET HOME. They wound down the spiral and across the struts of the tower. The light grew thicker as, through the greenery, the sun shifted toward dusk. More time had passed than they'd credited.

"He'll be wiser in the morning," said Tesasi. "Aren't we all? I'll show you the washrooms—yes, we have washrooms, we're not inconsiderate of our pilgrims! We've laid some supper out on the table in front. Then, if you've been sleeping rough for weeks, you'll enjoy being tucked in tight."

The meal was as fine as the first one, but Rain didn't join them. The companions ate in silence. They'd yielded the pursuit of their quest to an old reprobate in a soiled dressing gown. They lived by his mortal schedule now and not their own.

Leorix seemed torn between wanting to scamper with Cossy and Princess Acornella and needing to sit and nod thoughtfully with the grown-ups. How hard it is to be young, thought Lucikles; how much like him I still am. Not knowing whither I go from here, or whether return to Oena and my old life is even possible.

Burden without his burden seemed slightly lost. Tycheron hove to his side and selected delicacies for his plate, but the Bvasil only picked at his food.

Asparine kept her distance. She had jettisoned the last vestige of half-light mystique and become mere owl—if still an owl with a certain degree of hauteur. When a haunting hoot threaded through the limbs of the Arborians, Asparine replied in a plaint that might have meant "Goodbye." Or not. In any case, she flapped off into the dusk.

Iskinaary kept close by a terse and silent Rain when Tesasi brought them to their rooms. Never and Nothing, if those were really their names, stood on either side of a doorway cut into a tumulus of some sort. Still, their expressions, if wooden, were warm.

"They look like sentinels," said Lucikles. "Are they going to guard us from leaving in the middle of the night?"

"No need, you wouldn't get anywhere," said Tesasi. "But my, you're suspicious. I suppose after what you've been through, it's understandable. No, my brethren have been busy setting up while you were in audience with Zoar. We hope you'll be comfortable here and will enjoy the rest of your life."

"I don't especially like the sound of that," said Lucikles.

Tesasi reddened like forsythia wands in springtime. "Oh, my; I just heard myself. You'll forgive me. I mean *enjoy an unusually good sleep.* We Arborians don't speak in double meanings so I forget to parse your language for likely misapprehensions. It's a question of translation. Here we are."

The carved doorway had opened to five stone steps that broad-
ened and curved as they descended into a large chamber with separate, well-appointed nooks dug out between the central roots of a
grove of trees. While the space was largely underground, it proved
clean and dry and was fitted out with hooded windows in spandrel
spaces near the timbered ceiling. They were open for light and for
air, and the sound of evening nightingales ushered in a sense of
calm. Beds were outfitted with clean unwrinkled sheets and cover-
lets of obscure but pleasing design. A small central fire in a floor
pit crackled. It smelled of applewood. To one side, a table was laid
with a cordial bottle and some glasses and a tray of gummy sweets
rolled in dust of hazelnuts. "I hope this satisfies," said Tesasi.

"It's terrific, no complaints." Burden threw himself on the nearest bed and turned his back to them.

"It's been a long trip." Tycheron shrugged an apology for his
liege.

"I fear it will be longer still," said Tesasi. "I'll bid you good morrow when a good morrow comes." She withdrew. The solemnity
was ritualistic and the visitors were all cowed, and found their separate beds and repaired to them alone. When someone came to
her in the dark Rain was alarmed but almost hopeful, too, that
it might be Tycheron, since it couldn't ever again be Tip. Tip the
golden falsehood, Tip the never-really-was. It hadn't been his fault.
Her fault. Anyone's fault except that of the false wizard, the lame
soothsayer.

But here was only Cossy in the dark, which was perhaps luckier.
The child crawled in with Rain and huddled under her arm as if
for a final time.

Rain didn't think she would sleep but in fact she was almost
there when Cossy murmured, "I wonder what he's thinking of, all
alone and way up there in the air?"

ASCENT

1

The boy had grown up in windswept land, a place made mean-spirited and severe by drought. Scoured with grit in August, hail the size of peppercorns by October. After only two generations its acres were nearly farmed out. The territory had been promising to his forebears but it was a liability now, a prison without need of walls. Seneca, Kansas—little more than a post on the Pony Express—was seventy minutes away. The rumor of a Missouri River. The Atchison, Topeka, and Santa Fe hardly even a myth. Such bitter fruit. Out of reach and so barely imaginable. Whatever might a railroad even *look* like?

His mother was a hard woman. Her people were Scots and hailed from Aberdeen in the Dakota Territory. She was a steady worker and denied herself pleasures. While she was driven by Scripture to weep for the needy and suffering, she failed for undiagnosable reason to care warmly for her own children.

His father, born in Limerick Town, Ireland, genial but stupid, too easily duped. Early on in the boy's life the father had sold half of the family acres to pay off losses in some deal involving a trade of cattle that went bad—perhaps the cattle had all committed suicide just before conveyance. The boy never learned the details.

In any case, the family's circumstances remained a source of vexation. Poverty shamed the father and glorified the mother in her righteous fury. Poverty made the children hungry.

Children. There were four. (Had been six. Or seven. Yellow fever, infant seizures. The usual. The firstborn had a slow head and he had walked into the strut of a turning windmill and that was that.) The remaining offspring were oldest Frank; then himself; and the younger two, Tobias and Clementina. They'd slept four to the single pallet in a room, to the left at the top of the stairs, until Frank threatened his father with a poker one morning and disappeared by nightfall. Word eventually came he had made it as far as Fort John on the Laramie, out in Wyoming country. Lakota land. That was the last of Frank as far as anyone knew.

The younger two, Toby and Clementina Diggs—now that was a story farmers and cowfolk talked about until the day the boy left for good. Probably for years after, too. One Sabbath in July, the boy was supposed to be paying those scamps mind while his mother prayed for their sins and her own. But he sneaked the bairns out the kitchen door, shushing their giggling. They grabbed their poles and lines and scarpered to the anemic stream that bordered the smaller buckwheat pasture. An afternoon spent in lollygagging, hooking no fish but oh yes catching sun. Come supper and the mother wasn't blind; she had her wits about her, and knew what was what. The hot sun had painted their faces guilty, red as Eve's apple.

Besmirching the Sabbath with recreational pleasures, would they? She ordered the father to hammer the doors of their room and lock the younger children in so they wouldn't escape. She sent him and the boy to get the minister. The father to pitch the request and the son to make sure the father didn't divert into a saloon. The preacher just might come with his holy book and shout some salvation through the door until the wicked children repented. She could do nothing with them if they hadn't obeyed her already that day. As for the boy: "Just you wait," she'd said. "I'll deal with you. I've got to do some praying on it first. These little children can be rescued. I'm not sure about you. Mortal stain, it's contagious. You stay off track from them until we get discernment from the minister. You'll find soon enough whatever mischief you've been fishing for."

While his father and he were out on the open road, they didn't talk. His father was no match for the mother. He didn't condone fishing on the Sabbath, but he wasn't going to break a federal treaty over the matter.

The preacher wasn't free to come that evening as there was a casket to sit with, Ole Miz Harkins originally of Glasgow, don't you know, having fallen off her porch and broke her hip, or broken her hip and then tumbled off the porch. But it didn't matter which way because she was dead by the time they found her. The minister had to offer the obsequies. Graveyard words tomorrow morning, and then the compensatory sherry in a sitting room with drawn drapes. He'd hustle over after that. Noon would be time enough. The matter could wait. Let them fret the matter overnight, good for their stinking little souls. (Bless their hearts.)

On the way back, the father chewing stems of sweetgrass and the boy so wicked that he forgot it was the Sabbath and he was whistling at the stars—they realized all too gradually that the glow on the horizon wasn't a distant grassfire, that not infrequent summertime affliction, but something closer to home. It was, to be sure, their home. It was busy burning to the ground. The mother had been unable to open the door to the children's bedchamber because the hammer that might have clawed up the nailheads had been thoughtlessly carried to town in the jacket of her husband's Sunday meeting frock coat. She had died of smoke inhalation, it seemed. Her body was found at what was left of the base of the flight of stairs, untroubled by char though covered in ash. Tobias and Clementina—well, their lone surviving sibling hadn't been put to the ordeal of inspecting their corpses. They were gone.

That his mother may have set the fire herself didn't occur to the boy for decades.

As soon as his father found a suitable widow to remarry, the boy had left the area. Snip, snap, and that was that. More or less orphaned by circumstance, he'd gone east. He'd tried to study at an agricultural college in the Ohio Valley, but got distracted, first, by the professor's fetching and pliable wife. Then by sniffing at the incense of spiritualism, which had only grown denser and more intoxicating, in different guises, following the Southern Secession and the War of Northern Aggression. Some of it seemed obvious chicanery, which appealed to him. Perhaps he might take up a career as a fortune-teller? He hadn't predicted what would come of his tempting his younger brother and sister to fish of a bright Sunday afternoon. But look what happened. Soothsaying would be a good skill to learn.

Also, a son of poverty, he warmed to the idea of exploiting someone else's fear of the future. Advantages abounding. Cash to be had in this trade. Work for the Irish wasn't always easy to find if you had never again in this life dared to pick up a hammer.

His cleverness at chicanery, surprising him as it did, caused him to turn over cards he hadn't anticipated for himself. The sideshow sizzle of hucksterism evolved, for him, into a taste for something less false. The attraction of real power. Hypnotism; necromancy; spells, should they prove to be something more than mere stories. This led him to fold his career (an hour or two before he was to have been tarred and feathered for bedding a Pennsylvania state senator's nubile daughter) and to light out as his brother Frank had done. To Camden, New Jersey; to the Brooklyn docks; and then by steamer to the continent.

There his searches for the secret history of sorcery began in earnest with an unauthorized midnight stroll through a vault in the Vatican. This led him to a certain well-appointed library in a remote Hapsburg palace in the Carpathians, where he argued the Prague Absolute with a heretic nun while rifling through tomes.

More hints. A disestablished monastery on a Hebridean peninsula turned up an ancient text in Pictish/proto-Saxon. Sleight-of-hand stuff. And he assembled clues to the presence of the rumored book he was seeking. The Arthurian tome of Gramarye. And his fingers were gloved in the glue of avarice; he financed his travels by pocketing the occasional bibelot and selling it on.

Once or twice he located in himself a genuine twinge of instinct for soothsaying, could he learn to master the technique. But he hadn't wanted to summon up the spirits of Tobias and Clementina, even if they were available, for fear his mother might be standing behind them with her ghoulish thumbs pinching their shoulders, keeping them in her grasp for all eternity. He didn't expect to bring them back. He granted them their permanence among the dead. What's done is done. *He* hadn't hammered nails in the doorframe or lit a match to the kindling.

He didn't anticipate anything like an Oz. There really was little precedent for it as far as he was aware. Spiritualism hadn't mapped out such neighborhoods. When Darwin puttered about upon his *Beagle,* a novice unearthing otherness, it was nonetheless earthly otherness. The discovery of Uranus last century was a knock on the noggin, pushing against the exterior margins; his own generation's colonial investigations into the Congo and the Andes burrowed toward the interior. All that was heady but somehow still *here.* An idea of an Oz—another realm of existence—would have seemed to the boy a mere nursery tale, the dish running off with the saucy spoon and all that. Or maybe an offshoot of the pious geography of Heaven and Purgatory, which the gullible Polish Catholic kids, from a few towns over, had been able to describe in lascivious, feathery detail.

No, from his blistered youth he could have figured no magical continent, apparently existing in its own private hemisphere or upon some other-struck globe. For all his trust in the power of incantation and chimærica, he hadn't possessed the know-how to conjure up a separate world called Peare. Therefore, charting his hunt for Merlin's grimoire, the fabled Grimmerie, his arriving in Oz, by dint of some catastrophic annealing of tragic luck and magic, was entirely unforeseen.

Unforeseen but not fully unwelcome. He had, after all, escaped. It was as simple as that. He had fled to a world where his childhood had not happened. He knew in a more forthright way what anyone who survives puberty is forced to learn. Childhood is a country to which there is no return.

2

Just before dawn in the Walking Mountains. A freshness stirs in the underbrush. Over the kettle pond rings the croak of bullfrog. Rushes bend in the moving air. They touch their dry tips to their wet reflections, pull back. The fox inches toward the nest of the peahen, contemplating eggs for breakfast. Everything alive gets up to no good or gets down to business; everything still remains still.

Iskinaary observed the creaking machinery of the wild world and wished, not for the first time, that he hadn't been born with the gift of speech or reflection. For him, the preferred death wouldn't be a winging into darkness and flying forever toward no possible dawn, but a renewed contract with the world, this time free of babble.

He sighed. Even to pose himself such alternatives, which only happened in the mornings before humans around him began to bumble against one another, was a trick of his able and unable mind. He was stuck in his circumstances no less than any other living item in the world. Mollified, resigned, he nipped some visiting mite from his nether regions, and then he turned to waddle down the steps into the Arborian hostelry, whose doors were flung open to the weak sun. The woody people were laying out fruits and cheeses and some kind of pastry. Where did they get all these provisions?

"Time to get up," he quawked to the mounds made by his slumbering companions. "Today's the day we get some answers. I'm skipping breakfast and heading up to beard the old reprobate before he has his wits assembled. Wake up, sleepyheads, have you abandoned our strategy of pointless milling about?" He left them as they were, dead to the world. Bob brayed her salute, however, and Iskinaary condescended to return best wishes with a nod. He exchanged a few words with Tesasi, who was pouring juice, before marching up to the Tower in the Clouds.

The stairs were made shallow for access by the Caryatids; Iskinaary still needed to use his wings for balance. It took a while to reach the top level. The old man was out of bed, standing on his own. His nightshirt was a little stained and when he saw the Goose he pulled a light throw from the bed and drew it over his shoulders. "I haven't announced for an audience yet," he said. "You catch me in dishabille. At some disadvantage. I have no advice for you at this hour."

"I don't want your advice. The whole idea of a heart's desire stinks—so grasping. But I do ask a favor. For my limited part in bringing your great-granddaughter to your bedside, you owe me something." He leaned forward and said, "That is, if you have any power of sorcery at all."

"I didn't ask for a family reunion. So I owe you nothing."

"You've never given much, have you?" replied Iskinaary. "You're a taker. But for an old sinner you've still got some tricks up your sleeve. You recognized the broom your great-granddaughter, like some charwoman, hauled up all these stairs. It's not quite Elphaba's broom, but a generation down-brush, let's say. As Rain is to you. The thing got drowned in the salty-salt sea, and has lost its gift of flight. You might know something about this. Anything you can do to revive it?"

"I doubt you could make it worth my while. And why do you care anyway?"

"I won't leave her alone in this foggy backwater, and I can't return to Oz until she can fly again. We're stuck." The Goose came as close to giving a grin as he could manage. "Stuck here, I mean. With you. We wouldn't make very good neighbors, I have to say."

Zoar rubbed his bristly chin. "How do you even come into this?"

"Me? I'm nothing. I'm a Goose, a creature more addle-pated than I like to admit. I'm the familiar of your grandson, a man in his young middle age. Liir Ko, sometimes known as Liir Thropp. Poor fool. He tends in a different direction from the one you took in your life—not to dominate, but to duck away and be still, and leave the world as it is. I love him and so I love his only child, Rainary. I'll get her safely back to Oz, if I can. You might help. You've been a wretched soul upon this earth."

"The scorn of barnyard foul. Oh, it scorches." The Oracle spit in his washbowl.

"Others may kowtow but I won't. I can't. Do this much for someone else. It won't undo the damage you did, slapping people in chains, putting people to death, smothering communities and hounding them. Tearing lives into tatters. Going up against the Wicked Witch of the West. That treachery is history. But you've learned a few tricks in your day. I bet you can do this one thing. Which, if not a making of amends, is at least a transposition into another register. Before you die. Whether you wanted to or not, you've brutalized your own kin. Rain is shattered."

"She may be my kin, but she gives me the creeps. Reeks of a sullen kind of entitlement, like no one has ever suffered but her. I owe her nothing. What has she done for me? Everyone has to pay for what they get, and she has nothing to offer."

The Goose snapped at the Oracle's ankle. "I can do this all day and I can draw blood. Just like you, I have no conscience to speak of."

"I have so few active nerve endings in my feet that I'm not even bothered. Ow. All right, Goose. If I can manage anything like what you ask, it will be only so Rain can take the totem away from here. ASCENT. It's in the cards. Bring it to Oz if she likes, I don't care. It's her duty, no less than that. Meanwhile, get the Great Panjandrum himself back up here so we can discuss strategy. It's a horrific item he's hauling about. The sooner Rain evacuates it from Maracoor, the better."

The Goose kept his own counsel and merely replied, "I don't know what's taking them so long. I'm not going to do those stairs again so soon, and there's no runway for me to get a liftoff out your window. We'll wait. Do you want to play cards?"

3

You took your sweet time," said Iskinaary when Burden appeared in the doorway.

"We slept like rocks. All that good food. The others are just coming around. I couldn't wait though."

The Oracle said to Iskinaary, "You're dismissed," but the Goose didn't budge.

"Insurrection at every turn." The Oracle sighed. "Now look, you, Mr. Bvasil sir. I've given this matter what attention I am able to summon. My process involves—well, never mind. Tell me again how the item came into your hands."

The Bvasil repeated the story of the origins of the amulet, the effect it had upon fertility. The Oracle listened like a bored schoolchild. His hands touched the pack of cards but turned none face up.

"It's time to let me know what your reading reveals," said Burden, more gently than before.

The Oracle pulled himself to the edge of his bed. He cupped his knees with his hands. "I can't tell you how your totem comes so powerful into the world. But I agree it's a dreadful thing. What I might have done with it had I come across it in my prime! Ah well. Water under the bridge. Now listen. In the land where I come from—no, not Oz, a land even farther away than that—scholars study the skies. No sane man can follow their rhetoric, but their scrutiny turns up interesting notions. One such idea is this: that from time to time, flotsam from the stars or some exploded comet or suchlike flings its way through the dark empyrean wastes to breast the world's clouds and to crash upon the earth. Of what material these items are made it's impossible yet to determine. It may forever be a mystery. But the attributes of the Fist of Mara are unlike those of any substance discovered hitherto in your world or in mine. So this suggests to me it originates from a mysterious place, outside of what is otherwise known. Extra-terrestrial, that's the concept."

"So the Great Mara threw this upon the earth to confound us."

"Yeah, more or less. Why not. Does it matter which agency delivered it here? The damn thing isn't of our place, not yours, not mine. It's trouble. It levels a dread toxicity upon this susceptible world. You've been right to keep it sequestered."

"That wasn't my idea," admitted the Bvasil. "I inherited the situation."

"Could it be broken up itself, with a stronger hammer, who knows but that its fragments wouldn't poison the whole world? Could it be sunk in the sea, as Rain did the Grimmerie—don't get me started—it might murder all life therein. The sea is a powerful sister to the gods and holds back no message they want to spread."

Iskinaary hadn't an eyebrow to raise, but he looked as if he wished he had. He had little truck with the whims of deity. The Oracle took note and lowered the tone of his rhetoric.

"I'm trying to say," he continued, "there's no place for it here. It has to be expelled. I confirm your instinct about the need to nullify it somehow, but I can't tell you how. I can only say that returning to the capital with it is a mistake. Those who seek it will get it. The trouble you imagine being unleashed is genuine. The tarot cards have told me it should be evacuated by air. If I revive Rain's broom as the Goose requested of me, she can slip it out of the country."

Burden lifted his chin. "That doesn't seem just. I tricked her into carrying it once. I don't want to do it again. Can't I send Ty-cheron or that Minor Adjutant away with it, then?"

"By air? They won't manage a broom, I bet. It takes a powerful witch."

Iskinaary said, "One of the cards you just read had a hot-air balloon on it. No?"

The Oracle of Maracoor looked slantwise at the Goose. "I fly too," said Iskinaary, "and so did you. You just told us. The balloon. Rain's not the only one with flight in her."

Burden stepped up. "If you have a balloon on the premises, tell me. I'm the Bvasil of Maracoor. It's not in my power or in my nature to sidestep this responsibility. That's why I've come this far and why, I'm guessing, I'm only halfway to where I'm going."

"Rain's behavior put your nation in mortal danger. It's her fate to export this monstrous item!"

"She's a child. I'm the king. You don't negotiate with the king."

Zoar stroked his chin. He wasn't used to being second-guessed. He didn't speak for a quarter hour. Then: "Now look. I suppose I can supply the means if not the maps. You're right. I have a hot-air balloon somewhere around here. It was damaged upon landing and for several decades it's been stored in tatters somewhere on the premises. You'd have to dig it out. Repair the rips in the fabric. I imagine the basket would need a bit of restitching, too. The Caryatids are good at that kind of thing. You could inflate the old show-horse by igniting the air in her heart once again, and soar away from Maracoor. Taking the Fist of Mara with you. I give up. I believe," he concluded, gasping from the effort of a long speech, and perhaps the grief of giving up, after all these years, his means of a quick getaway, "I believe you'll do the job you need to do, to save your nation. That's why you are Bvasil, and why you absconded the throne in the first place. Not to save yourself but to save your country."

Burden nodded as if unsurprised. Carrying the Fist of Mara for all this time, the Bvasil of Maracoor had become married to it, in a way he'd never been married to the Bvasilina.

"You're not the omniscient sage you pretend to be," interposed the Goose. "You're a broken puppet. Ancient and gone to seed. So why would you help out by giving up your balloon?"

"I don't want that Fist around here any more than anyone else does. Get rid of it, take it away. I'm no saint, but that thing is of another order entirely. Where I come from mothers used to call ill-behaved children 'limbs of Satan.' That amulet you have on your hands is just such an item, as far as I'm concerned."

"Don't get the reference but I recognize your tone," said Burden.

"You're all a menace. I'm done with you lot. I suppose I'd better do kissy-kissy with that green witch if I want you all to clear out," said the Oracle said to the Goose. "I wasn't such a straight dealer with her grandmother. Not that I understood our relationship at the time. I can do better now. Send the young rebel up here again. Make sure she has her broom. Might as well send the overseer, too. Oh, and Mr. Bvasil, take that thing with you. It is *such* a fist. It *so* wants to punch someone. I may deserve to be assaulted, but I'm too much of an old sinner to offer myself up for the punishment."

"You're considering my request," said the Goose, a little surprised, but pleased.

"You all bring down the tone of the neighborhood. I don't owe anybody anything, but I'd prefer to go back to my dotage in peace. I've earned it. Leave me alone. Scram, Goose."

EMERGING FROM THE SNUGGERY, Lucikles found that the greenish light of yesterday seemed cleaner now. The trees having withdrawn, like a falling tide, a sunlit, grassy rise had emerged from mists. The breeze upon it felt sweet and keen, the mountain horizons reliably static. Despite the dubious résumé of the Oracle, to judge by Rain's reaction to him, this place nonetheless had an aspect of the sacred.

Could holy mountains really heal the wretched, he wondered. Be it so.

After all, this tower had been grown by forces of organic life, forces that had found in the location something to solemnize. Maybe this hilltop was the original omphalos of Maracoor, after all.

Rain was perched on a small outcropping of rock, where the mists nearly lapped at her feet. Knees drawn up to her chin, she looked blankly outward. Her seashell was set to one side of her, the withered broom to the other. Emblems of a broken history.

Shoulder to shoulder like fellow travelers looking seaward, Lucikles said, "You're not as alone as you feel" just as Cossy darted up and put her arms around Rain from behind. Cossy the damaged, of all people. Lucikles flinched, struggling not to betray his surprise.

"My eyes," replied the green girl, "they burn." She wiped them with the back of her hand.

Though Lucikles would make nearly any effort in a time of need, he knew he couldn't be the father to the whole world. His own son still would hardly speak to him. But here was Rain, the child at hand. And no parent or grandparent of her own to comfort her. So he patted Rain on the back of the head and said, "There, there."

Those words of no meaning would have to do. He had nothing to convey beyond—I see you there, I am with you there. There there.

Rain didn't respond. She'd traveled this far under some misapprehension that she could make things better. All she'd done was come even more sharply face-to-face with the regret she'd known in Oz, the misery she'd hoped to flee. For losing the Grimmerie, she could say it now, had been little more than an excuse to get out of there. Away from the reality of Tip being a falsehood, a dis-guise, not available—as good as dead.

And this damnable, well-meaning civil servant next to her kept saying, "There, there," as if to push her back into her unresolvable conundrum.

"He wants to see you again, Rain," said Burden, approaching with the totem. "He has his little wisdoms, after all. You too, Lu-cikles."

"If you're going to set that thing down," said Tesasi, wiping her hands on her wooden apron, "put it on a different rock, not near us and not on the grass. Please." She pointed to a farther outcropping.

Lucikles took off his sock and examined his foot again. It was bleeding, shallowly, as if it would never heal. Tesasi leaned over stiffly to have a look at it. "You've been visited by a burrowing beetle. A scarab or some kind of leech, perhaps," she said. "That's risky. You'll have to live with the blood."

He thought back to the Brides of Maracoor scoring their feet ev-ery morning for the good of the nation. Same thing, maybe. "The stairs will take me longer, I'm hobbling so. I'll start up. Rain, are you coming?" Rain shrugged at the Minor Adjutant as Cossy ran off to find Princess Acornella.

The Caryatid and the green girl were alone in the light. Tesasi said, "You're worried about the little girl."

"She'd had a lumpy life. You may not know that she was con-victed of the crime of murder. Young as she is." Rain said, "There's so much blame I won't accept—I didn't invent the power of the Grimmerie or the danger of the Fist of Mara. But my arrival on Cossy's isolated island put her in danger, even if I didn't mean it. She has no family, no home to go home to."

"Whatever happened to you to make you feel you have to solve her life for her?"

"Maybe because I can't solve my own. She's a menace, Tesasi."

"You're so young and, well, green. Listen, sapling: she can't murder us."

Rain lifted her chin. "Every living creature can be killed. Every hope can be slaughtered."

Tesasi folded her arms across her oaken bosom. "You know precious little about it."

"Are you saying you're immortal? Like the Great Mara, like all these pesky clandestine spirits of Maracoor?"

"I think spirits materialize when humans need inspiration. While we Caryatids, in either of our forms—and there are others you don't know about—we share our life force perpetually. So we're not deities, no, I admit it. But we're not quite mortal either because we're not—sliced so thin—as all of you, and as the rabbits and dogs and birds and worms and suchlike. Such trouble in individualizing everything. How you manage it is as a holy mystery to me."

She reached out. Rain set her own warm hand in Tesasi's dry one as the Caryatid went on. "The Oracle might tell you that we're your ancestors, that humans descended from us. Maybe he's just being polite, or maybe he's right. I don't read magic cards myself. But Arborian life, my dear: we're the real immortality. If we're truly your antecedents, we didn't do a decent job passing on much of what we know. My, how you all suffer being split so, when you don't need to. You're broken up mostly because you *feel* so broken up. I don't know how to heal that, except you should spend some more time with the trees." She nearly smiled. "You'd fit right in."

"I haven't had an adult woman to talk to in a long time," Rain said, very low.

"I'm only womanly in appearance," Tesasi said. "Though happy to oblige. Now before we finish up, as long as you're feeling vulnerable, do you want to tell me about this Tip?"

Rain told the story aloud, testing it for its ridiculous reality.

With her sanded thumb, Tesasi wiped tears away, both Rain's and her own—which were more like sap. When the green girl had finished, Tesasi said, "I have no comfort to offer except to tell you that Peritir and I, we're the same thing in different form. Lucikles and Leorix are the same in different form. Your Tip and your Ozma—it's just window dressing. Clear away the dead foliage in your thinking and locate the unfurling bud. Come now, say goodbye to your great-grandfather so you can get on with your life. It's waiting for you."

"It's all because of that—that *ancestor*—that I suffer so," said Rain.

"Perhaps," said Tesasi. "Though, as you tell it, had our Oracle not hired a sorceress to enchant the young Ozma into the form of your lad Tip, Ozma would have grown up and died decades before you were even born. You'd be here, but—you'd have a different suffering to outgrow."

Not to have known Tip at all—a new kind of unbearable.

"You don't need to say thanks to Zoar," recommended Tesasi. "But perhaps you can retire your complaint, at least over the matter of your lover? However it may seem to you, the Oracle isn't immortal."

They stood and walked to the Tower, holding hands. "And when you get back to Oz," said the Caryatid, "plant a little garden and think of me. I won't come visit, even in your dreams. But that doesn't mean I'm not holding you in my heart."

"Everything I plant dies," said Rain.

"Now you're being maudlin, which is age appropriate but becomes tiresome fast. Of course you can put in a garden and make it grow. A witch's garden, if you like, with lots of lovely weeds. I can see," she added, "you have a green thumb. And another to spare."

4

When she emerged into the Oracle's chamber the second time, the sun was directly overhead. No slanted oblongs of yellow light to stamp the floorboards. Iskinaary, stout bird, stood by, unflinching as an iron garden ornament. Lucikles stared out the window, his back to her. Giving her both privacy and, maybe, protection. Rain moved forward cautiously, watching the ancient sage labor with the effort of breathing. His eyes were open but glazed. She reached out to feel his forehead.

She didn't know what her expression might be saying, but he seemed both tender and alert, as if he might at any minute transform into a cockatrice and sting them both to death.

"Oh, there you are again, green as a bad penny," he said, almost nastily. "Just who I wanted to see. Shall I read the cards for you? Tell you your future? We could do the Celtic Cross layout—that usually gives good value for money."

"I need nothing from you, and I have nothing to say to you," stated Rain. Now, she saw the headboard as a dead garden—it had autumned over since her first audience. And the Oracle a feckless ghost caught in its bracken, little more than that. "And I see you for what you are—useless, a parasite in this world."

"I'm offended. I know what I know. There's a saying in my native world—*Más sabe el diablo por viejo que por diablo*. The devil knows more because he's old than because he's the devil. Yeah, I come by a little wisdom merely by not yet having died. Regardless of my aptitudes at charms or my petty morals."

"I don't know your tricky foreign tongues. I have nothing to give you and I want nothing from you. But you called me to this audience, so what do you have for me? Hurry it up."

"You'll never make a nurse, no bedside manner," said Zoar. He slid the cards into their box and put them aside. "Back in the day, I craved my own heart's desire. It was thwarted. Elphaba was partly to blame. But while I ruled Oz, I was known for trying to give any petitioners granted an audience a chance at their heart's desires. A sort of party game for me. Long since given up on *that* gig. Sure, I can read a little future, predict the punch line of a joke—but mostly what I have now is human knowledge. While my brain still works, I have two worlds to hold in my head. It's by contrasting them that I come upon any wisdom, any right to advise. No, I can't console you. Consolation was never my bailiwick. But I've watched how things work in my own world and in yours. That's all I have to go on to clarify what I see of your circumstances."

"You don't see anything," she said. "You don't see that it was you who bribed or paid old Mombey to charm Ozma into a boy whom I fell in love with. I've now remembered it all. His name was Tip. He didn't know he was Ozma and he fell in love with me. You got rid of the princess regent of Oz so you could ascend to her throne, and you ruled like a despot. That was old news by the time I came along, but the rancor lingers like the odor of spoiled milk. You betrayed your own daughter and, whether you knew it or not, you set your descendant up to lose the only love she's yet had. I wouldn't take your advice if you ladled it out upon a silver platter in a sauce of gold."

"Rain," said Lucikles, without turning to look at her, "mercy on the old man."

"Your heart's desire," replied Zoar, "is hidden in the subterranean passages of your own anger. I can't spelunk in those fetid depths. Who could. You do have your grandmother's zeal, though.

You may even have her power. All I can say to you is that your future—this is my telling, pay attention—your future is committed to the task of finding out. You have to dig up your buried heart and acknowledge it. To train yourself in magic and to master it. That's your future, that's what I see for you. Whether you embrace this at all, because it is me who is saying it—well, more fool you if you don't. Don't confuse the message with the messenger."

"You're saying precisely nothing," said Rain. "I emigrated from Oz with the sole intention of losing magic from my life. I flung the Grimmerie away from me. I'd rather a smaller life, with a limited range, like the one my father has chosen. But even in this, I did damage, if my plunging the Grimmerie into the waters off Maracoor helped reawaken the spirits of this benighted place. Helped unspool the wind systems, and hurried the invaders from the south up north."

The Oracle reached over and began to lay out cards for himself, a simple line of three. He turned up the first one. "Death riding a wolf. The caption says THE PENALTY. Fun. I always get that one, and I never seem to die. The second was that split figure, male and female with two faces. EITHER/OR. The last was THE GREEN MAN.

"You want to try your hand at interpretation?" asked the Oracle. "I'll tell you that The Green Man is an ancient symbol of eternal life in certain pagan circles. The vegetable impulse. Maybe it means you. What do you make of it all?"

"I don't do party tricks. I'm not social like that."

"Snippy, aren't we. Virtue. Prudence. Thrift. Three cents return on the dollar. Old Dominion to win, Tarbelly to place." He tossed the cards aside. "Who cares. Listen to me, hinny. Did you ever think that some of this current mayhem was waiting to happen? As history, patiently, tends to do? Okay, maybe your action channeled a change in tides and winds. But it also seems clear the Grimmerie didn't create the local deities—it only made them apparent. They were already lingering around waiting to be noticed. Maybe they wouldn't have come forward without your intervention. But you didn't invent them. You didn't conjure up that foreign navy. The Skedes are a real people, not an army of ghosts."

"Legitimizing my mistakes after the fact. Justification. Something I bet you've always been good at, no?"

Cossy came thumping upstairs. "I want to go to the brook with Princess Acornella and have races with leaf boats. Mine is going to be called *Fist of Helia*. All right?"

"Wait your turn," said Lucikles, and stayed the girl with a chop of his hand. She pouted but held her tongue.

"*Listen* to me," the Oracle said to Rain. "Without the arrival of an invading navy, would the Fist of Mara ever have been evacuated from the nation's treasury? No. But now it's set to leave this land. When there's no more chance of finding it here, the invaders will, I predict, withdraw. Having caused relatively little upset when all is said and done. I hope. Perhaps there'll be new trade opportunities, or, oh, a certain fellowship among nations will emerge. Mark my words, babies will be born, half Maracoorian and half Skedian. The world gets on with itself. And as a result of your brave if foolhardy behavior, the Fist of Mara will be evacuated from the land. No one may quite appreciate you for it, but you are a liberator. You'll notice that all the dryads and briskies and their weird kin could only advise; they couldn't lift a finger to do anything useful."

"The giant did, and he lost his—his being—over it."

"How the young like to argue. Is that so? Well, maybe so. But it's rare. Sounds more like a garden-variety landslide to me. Human history requires human agency, and you've been an agent in the history of Maracoor. Now go back, go back to Oz, and be an agent in your own life."

"I can't go back," she said.

"Oh, but you can," he said. "You've always had the power to do so, if you only knew." He winked at her. "Hand me your broom. No, I won't break it over my knee, I haven't the strength in my hands. Or my knee."

Rain wouldn't even do that, but Cossy took the thing and walked it forward.

The Oracle of Maracoor lifted the broom over his head. The browned leaves of the headboard rustled as if in a wind. While a few leaves dropped onto the pillows, and one upon his own head, the others flicked into life. A wave of green, the natural peasant green of the world, coursed around him. Was the broom reviving the illustrative headboard, or the other way around? The Oracle held the broomstick against the leaves. It didn't look much different, but the last of the salt saturation from the Nonestic Sea seemed to evaporate off it in an ashy puff, and Rain guessed—and she was right—that the broomstick was revived.

He held it out to her. "Pax?"

Still she wouldn't take it.

"See, haven't entirely lost my old strength," he said.

Tesasi lumbered into the room and made a sign that clearly meant *audience over*.

"What is the charm upon your bed, that you live in it so long?" asked Iskinaary.

"It's mere life," said the Oracle, yawning. "The Caryatids trimmed their own hair to weave me this fretwork of life while I am imprisoned in a tower in the clouds. Some of their wilding knowledge comes to me through it. Magic is less technical than you suppose. It's just life, life brought to the boil. That's the Oracle of Maracoor speaking, and now the transmission is concluded. I need the water closet and I need some privacy. I'm spent. Family reunions are fun and all that, but there's a limit."

He started to get out of bed and paused. "I think the Caryatids put me here the way my parents put my own grandfather into the poor farm run by the Methodists. I mean to say that there's no escaping this room, my lofty prison tower. I've left earth for good, though I'm not yet launched into theosophical orbit. My bed is my grave, and my grave is woven with life. Isn't that how it's supposed to be?"

The headboard was now flecked with white flowers, something like lilies, that dropped golden pollen upon his pillowcases and his bald pate. A look of sanctity belying his history of selfish ambition. "Well, we don't get to ask for how we're going to die, do we?" he said, defensively. "Here, Rain; take this broom and do with it what you will. I'm done with you. I have nothing more to propose. No apologies, no requests. But I've given flight back to you."

As Tesasi began to help him from the bed, he held out the broom to Rain, not meeting her eyes. "While there is still a home to go to. Go back to Oz."

"Here's your broom, what's your hurry?" said Rain in a monotone. "Nice."

"What about me?" asked Cossy. "Am I to go to Oz too?"

"No," said Iskinaary. "The broom carries only one rider, and she's Rain."

"Well, where's the story I walk into and shut the door and it's my story, then?" asked the girl. She sounded more curious than alarmed. "Now can I go to the brook with the Princess?"

"You think I care?" said the Oracle. "I know that Acornella can't drown. So on your own nickel, sweetheart. Knock yourself out."

"Nobody's the boss of me," said Cossy, anticipating Lucikles's objections. "Once upon a time I had my own story. The end."

On his feet, the old scoundrel was, oh, such a short person. Not taller than Cossy. His shoulders curved with scoliosis, and his legs were bloated, bolsters of royal purple. "One thing more, Rain," he said over his shoulder. "You may find, after all, that the Nonestic

Sea rejects the Grimmerie, the way a mare can refuse to recognize her own foal. On your way home, keep your eyes alert for it. I'd be surprised an angry teenage girl could subdue it so easily. No, I won't ask you to bring it here. Though if you wanted to—"

"It's time," said Tesasi, "for you to stop talking. You're not an Oracle, you're an incontinent old fellow nearly late for the useful seat. Come along."

Rain said, "I want to say goodbye to my great-grandfather. Would you give us a few moments alone?"

5

When the others had left, and it was only Rain and the Oracle, she rounded on him. "You've revived my broom," she said. "How do I know you haven't charmed it to drop me off the next time I manage to get it aloft?"

"Oh, what a good idea." His sneer was partly stagey. "Sadly, I don't have that kind of skill. But I like the way you think."

"If you want to get out of here," she said, advancing upon him, "here you go." She held out the broom. "The maiden voyage of the rehabilitated. You belong together."

He backed away, clutching the footboard of his bed. "Well. I didn't see *that* coming."

"Some fortune-teller. Can you picture me taking the Fist of Mara and clobbering you with it? You deserve it. Or I could follow the recipe that Cossy used to poison her fellow bride, and serve you up a doom sandwich. You have no right to a peaceful retirement after the hell you've rained down upon the world."

"Look who's talking; I guess it runs in the family." But he backed up farther, finding strength in his fear, and he ended up with his hips against the ledge of the open window. "I don't go any farther. You're going to push me out the window?"

"You don't want to fall even now? Use the broom. I dare you." She thrust it at him. "Go on. Climb onboard, in your nightshirt and your sleeping socks. Nobody cares if you tumble to your death. Test out the old thing."

"This is abject abuse. No one is here to fetch—"

"Fetch it yourself. I'm giving you the means."

"Stop! Stop." His pale eyebrows were arched in primary shock, like that of a baby discovering thunder for the first time. "Give over. Let me be. I've already recovered your broom for you, what else could you want of me?"

"I'd prefer revenge." She was only inches from him, and when she leaned down their chins nearly met. She could topple his old hips out the window by slotting her broom behind his quaking shins and pulling upward. "It would do me good to choose the damage I do, for once, instead of just to survive the mayhem I wreak by happenstance." But she hesitated. "So you won't take my invitation to fly? After all this time, all this hankering after secret power, and when it's presented you, you choke on the offer? Very well." She backed up a step and looked him over. "Tell you what. You and the Caryatids give Cossy a home here, where she can grow up without being hunted by the law or punished for being young, and I'll call us even."

"Cossy? That horrid little vulpine child?"

"I'll take that as a yes?"

"She won't want to live here."

"She can be the daughter you never bothered about," said Rain. "Here's your chance to make amends. She's never had a father. Too late for you to learn? Well, too bad. Do a bad job and perhaps in turn she'll do you in. She's had practice."

"I'll read you a fortune you'll wish I hadn't," he ventured, stammeringly.

Rain was almost at the top of the stairs, her broom over her shoulder, and she turned and said, "*Pollus intensis, ar vexum vexatum,*" and pointed her broom at him as if it were a rifle.

"All right!" he shrieked.

She almost grinned going downstairs. She could be as big a fraud as he was. The words she'd uttered were gibberish, invented to alarm. Still, upon her shoulder, the broom quivered with a life it hadn't demonstrated since before she'd come to her senses on the harbor sands of Maracoor Spot.

Lucikles, Tesasi, and Iskinaary were loitering in the room below. She didn't know how much they'd heard. She didn't care either way. "Go on up. Or not. No concern of mine."

OUTSIDE THE TOWER IN THE CLOUDS, Rain and the Goose found Tycheron with several Caryatids she'd not yet encountered. They were working over a huge flop of fabric laid out on a circle of lawn. It had once been a vivid item, whatever it was, but now the colors were faded. Stripes of black and red were faded in places into mortuary greys and pinks. "What are you up to?" she asked, if only to clear her head from the interview she'd just abandoned.

"This colossal bubble. A long rip in one side," said Tycheron shortly. "Trying to patch it." His warm eyes avoided hers, kept to his task. "Sew it up, strengthen it, varnish it."

"And what is all this for?"

"Moving on," said Tycheron, wielding a curving needle made from some kind of thorn. The implement was threaded with a lacquered kind of twine that the Caryatids must have supplied him. As he worked, he didn't glance at her. His face was rigid, the look of a soldier called into battle, determined to answer the call stoically. She recognized the expression from a mirror, once upon a time.

High above them, Lucikles waited till the Oracle returned from his ablutions. When he padded back, he didn't return to the bed but made it to the windowsill, and looked out over the kingdom of his prison.

"This has all been an ordeal for me," said the Oracle to the Minor Adjutant, "even though I've given only common advice to

the Bvasil and to that green girl. They could've thought of it themselves if they'd tried harder. For you, I have something else."

"I didn't come here seeking enlightenment," Lucikles reminded
him. "I'm a functionary of the court. Bullied into service. Little
more than that."

"Nonetheless. You'll have heard? The Bvasil will continue on in
the balloon I've supplied him. It's impossible for me to remember
how to manufacture the hot gasses with which I used to fly the old
girl, back in the day. But the Caryatids can summon up something
that will do in a pinch. They're talented, you know. They could
rule the earth if they wanted, but they have no ambition in that
direction. They're a startlingly content species. A lesson to us all
that I fear we have no hope of learning. Ah well."

"If there's nothing else . . . ?" said Lucikles.

"I'll read you your future." He looked about. "Tesasi must have
put the cards back in the dressing room. Or I did. The memory of
the current moment goes but the curses of childhood, oh, young
man, they never leave you. Now listen. You've been the chief of this
expedition, whether it's been acknowledged or not. So I give you
the marching orders, my man. Burden will continue on alone. Only
he can learn where and how to dispense with the Fist of Mara. If
it's to be learned at all. Maybe other people somewhere else might
know how to neutralize the element, even put it to some good use.
For now, it must be evacuated. And soon. When it's safely gone,
the invaders will follow suit. Whatever obscure skill they have to
track the totem in Maracoor, they'll use it to learn that the item
is disappeared from here. They'll withdraw. This will save your
country."

"It's not my country," said Lucikles, but of course, it was, it was.

"For the others. Rain and the Goose will return to Oz if they
can. You will escort Tycheron back to Maracoor Crown."

"He's not going to continue as the Bvasil's companion and aide-
de-camp?"

"The Bvasil is on his own. It's a lonely way he flies now. I know it well. No, Tycheron is the testifier. He'll return to the court and announce the news of the country's delivery. He'll take the pendant scarab from you and produce it in the throne room. He'll testify to the abdication of the Bvasil. Poor fellow may be hated throughout history for this, but that's neither here nor there. Or maybe Tycheron may be hailed as the new Bvasil. These things happen sometimes."

Lucikles couldn't help himself, and muttered, "So much for soothsaying."

"What they will do with the old Bvasilina," continued the old man, unperturbed, "I can't imagine. Perhaps she'll mount an army of her own and contest the elevation, which eventually would be fun to hear about from the next visitor seeking the Oracle of Maracoor. Or declare herself divine—it's been known to happen. Who can argue with the divine? But I digress. Tycheron is protesting all this but the Bvasil understands the need to go alone. You must help him achieve it. As for the others, the little one will stay with me."

"I heard about that from downstairs," replied Lucikles. "So did Tesasi, who was nodding along at the plan. If Cossy is safely sorted out, I can go home with some honor. A small portion of it. My being along was part of her rescue after all. But I'd be at fault if I didn't tell you that she was convicted of murder."

"Frankly, some days I would welcome a little murder," replied the Oracle mildly. "To get this very old isn't easy. But maybe having someone young around the place will be rewarding. Doesn't she seem at home? The truth now."

Yes. Yes, she did. Lucikles had an inkling why. The Tower in the Clouds stood on a hill above the featureless surges of forest on every side. It was an island, like Maracoor Spot, a green speck in a sea. Lapped by the changing tides of mist. Here she would play, and no one would make her slice her feet to ribbons for daily bleeding. She might never locate a boy to love, but back on Maracoor Spot, that wouldn't have happened anyway.

And Lucikles's own son, poor Leorix, could be safely ushered away, to find his first true romance with someone who wasn't an unwitting accomplice to murder.

"I don't believe I can trust you," said Lucikles, "but the Caryatids strike me as worthy folk. And Tesasi says they'll be sympathetic to the notion."

"They do what I tell them," said the Oracle with magisterial detachment.

The Minor Adjutant said, "At least here Cossy will be out of reach of Borr Apoxiades and those other arbiters of the law. If you and the Caryatids are agreed, I won't stand in your way. It's not mine to decide, anyway."

"And so," said the Oracle of Maracoor, the former Wizard of Oz, at last. "Who's left? Not the mightiest among us, the Bvasil, or the weakest, that funny misguided child. Not the green girl, nascent in her powers and unsure of them. All your companions can guess what comes next. That's what an Oracle does, he supposes the future. I hint at possibilities, sidestep forecasts. I only suggest. I've read what I could for them, said what I might, with cards or no. But you? You're the last one. So here goes. Most of us flee home to escape how we seem to be becoming. Some of us never stop fleeing. But in this world, hearth-tenders are urgent agents, too. Go home and tend your hearth. If you can. Do a better job than I ever did."

6

When Leorix learned that they were leaving Cossy behind, he turned on Lucikles like a wild thing, growling, "You'd put her at risk again, just like you did by hauling her off of her island and dragging her to court?"

"She wants to stay," said Lucikles, "and we have no other safe harbor to promise her."

"I'll keep her safe."

"Don't be a fool. It's not your place and you haven't the slightest—"

Leorix barreled into his father and knocked him sideways, and Lucikles landed a punch to the side of his son's head—deadly intent in the moment of red alarm. They went at it on the grass, rolling over the banner. Leorix pummeled his father's side where the left kidney and the spleen would feel it for days. Lucikles just barely stopped himself from kneeing his son between the legs. Cossy was paying little attention, running a race with Princess Acornella around the base of the Tower. Tycheron kept to his task with the balloon repair, and Rain and Tesasi had wandered into the edge of the woods. Iskinaary brought the matter to an end with a series of brave and judicious nips upon tender portions of both their anatomies.

They sat up at last and looked in different directions, gasping and nursing their pains.

Well, that was a long time coming, thought Lucikles. Still, I held my own against the rising generation.

Beat the old bastard at last, and I'll do it again, thought Leorix. "I'll come back and rescue her, I swear," he said when he could speak.

Lucikles allowed his son to have the last word. It was his due. Better a boy should become a man than a wolf.

7

The margin of the woods, a threshold between secrecy and openness. Fringed with fern below, nearly turquoise above, where sunlight fell through the scooped blue flowers of the younger trees.

Rain said, "I'd like to do something for you, to thank you for taking on Cossy."

"We don't do debts and favors," said Tesasi. "That's not our way."

"Will you let me try?" She explained her proposal.

Tesasi seemed taken by surprise. "Are you ready? Why risk life and limb on our behalf?"

"Well," replied the green girl, "because it seems to me that you're the actual Oracle of Maracoor. Aren't you."

She leaned forward and kissed the solid sandalwood cheek. Then she backed up to where the woods petered out. She felt for the seashell in her satchel and she steadied the trembling broom in her hand. She looped up her skirts and mounted the broom, drawing up the shaft until her rear end was steadied against the top of the brush. The broom trembled like a skittish filly, but steadied as Rain urged it forward. It hovered above the close-cropped grass, rose by delirious inches at a time.

She felt like a single breeze let loose from a storm, a solo voice liberated from a raging choir.

Iskinaary looked up at the movement in his peripheral vision— almost all his vision was peripheral—and he quawked, "That's my girl!"

Tycheron fell on his hands and knees upon the folds of balloon, picked up the fabric and buried his face in it. A green girl was one thing; flying on a broom was quite another.

Cossy screamed, "My turn next!"

Rain's vertigo was mild and she was glad she'd skipped breakfast. She looped about the tower, and spied the Oracle at the top window. She couldn't judge his expression. She didn't care what he thought. With a sense of doom and hope, she circled the trees around the mount, which seemed to be reaching their branches higher to her. Against their soft cerulean blooms she dragged the brush of her besom, sweeping clouds of pollen into the air. Banking and circling back, the pollen made an ivory cloud above the trees, a different consistency and color than the mists in which the Arborians waded.

Taking out the seashell, she held it like a flour scoop. Back and forth she flew, collecting the seed and shaking it for safekeeping into the deepest recesses of the shell, and going back for more.

If the Caryatids could care for an abandoned human child, Rain would preserve the possibility of life for the next generation of Arborians. If she could. Scatter it where she might. A story is a seed, but a seed is a story, too.

8

They stayed a few days longer, to make sure that Cossy wouldn't change her mind about their leaving her behind. Also the repair of the balloon was more laborious than it had first seemed. Nothing and Never directed the operations, but human fingers were better suited to detail work.

On the afternoon the Company chose to begin their return journey, a tidal surge of royal saffron burned in the western sky. It seemed as good an omen as any. It was damn sweet to look at in any case.

While the balloon began to inflate, Cossy and Princess Acornella joined hands and swung them. "We'll start out now," said Lucikles to Burden. "The Caryatids will be ready to launch you in the morning, they say. You're in good hands with them."

"I've been in good hands all along," said the Bvasil. He clasped Lucikles's arms warmly. But Lucikles wouldn't embrace him, for the Fist of Mara was still upon Burden's back. That close would be too close.

Leorix tried to wrap Cossy in a hug, but she pulled away. "Come and see me next year," she said to him with little depth of feeling. The boy merely answered, "Wouldn't that be nice!" Unnoticed, Lucikles scraped a tear or two from the pockets deepening under his eyes. Not at the pain of parting, but to see how much nearer Leorix had come to those blandishments and falsehoods that mark the adult status. The beginning of the end.

Of Asparine nothing more was known. Cossy had supposed

that as an owl she might have flown back to High Chora and found Moey had returned there to recover, and they'd become harpies again. It was a sweet thought for a child to have, and the others let her keep it. The giant, King Copperas, had died on leaving the fervent magic of his homeland. Asparine, being a less magnificent specimen of the spirit world, had probably lit out to join owl society. She'd make a dyspeptic owl. And probably fit right in.

To Lucikles, Tesasi said, "Get that administrative scarab out of your foot before it crawls up your leg and gnaws a hole in your heart. If you have access to a healer, use it." Turning to Rain, she said, "I don't know how you'll route yourself home, by foot at first I assume, and then perhaps by ship or by air, but if your journey takes you through Maracoor Spot, give my best to Mother of Olive. We go way back. And you might think of pausing at Ithira Strand. They've had some sort of plague there, I believe. Some of the seed cast upon those soils might be a blessing to them."

"What if it doesn't take?"

"It's not your job to decide which crop grows, just to give it a chance. You've done me a power of good, my girl. But you have to make your own way now."

Peritir took the lead, swinging a bright blaze in a glass lantern. Down the slope they wound, a dissipated group. Lucikles and his moody son, Rain and the Goose, and Tycheron, who led Bob by the bridle. They'd have to pitch camp one night, Tesasi had told them, but the next morning it wouldn't take long to reach the banks of the Seethe. The Walking Mountains could deliver them there almost overnight. The arduous passage inland had been a test; there was nothing to test now.

Once at the edge of the Seethe, Peritir and his crew would carry the travelers in their arms. The humans could hug onto the tree limbs and ride drily to the other side, where they'd learn whether or not the giant's ramp was still negotiable. Going home would feel faster than coming out. It so often does.

They slept in their private cocoons of relief, grief, and worry. Not too long after the break of day, the troupe arrived at the great river. Everyone had forgotten that Bob would have no inclination to climb into a tree. She bucked and resisted being tugged toward the Arborian arms. In the end, they left her and the farm wagon behind. Peritir could lead her back to the Tower and she might come in service there, or enjoy an early retirement cropping the sweet grass that surrounded the Tower.

With their guests in their arms, the tree people waded hip-deep into the flood, and the companions turned to watch the Tenterix Range shift and sheathe itself in mists once again. Leorix thought he caught a dot of red-black floating above the mist. The hot-air balloon? Rain and Lucikles agreed. Tycheron wouldn't pivot to look. Iskinaary said they were all nuts.

The ramp that Yurkios, King Copperas, had sledged out of the cliff-side on the far shore stood out in mauve morning shadow. After delivering them to solid ground at its base, Peritir made a deep bow on behalf of his kin, but only said, "We'll wait until you reach the summit safely before we turn back."

The trudge upslope took all day because Lucikles's foot leaked constantly. They had to keep stopping. Rain and Tycheron ignored each other with cutting precision once she had said, "No one can pet rain." Leorix singsonged, "When will we get there, never never never," just to be annoying. It was nearly dusk when they arrived at the headland of High Chora. Then, appearing so suddenly that the ragtag remains of the Company of the Scarab all but choked in alarm, stood Artoseus.

"Well done," said the blue Wolf. "You survived yourselves. So far." To the human males, he said, "You go take up your lives." To Rain, he growled, "I sent you to the Oracle believing you were the one to evacuate the Fist of Mara. You confound me."

"I don't take instruction easily," said Rain. "Iskinaary could have told you that. Want to try again?"

"Go home to your life, then, and become the obstinate witch you are ready to be."

"What about me?" asked Iskinaary, but Artoseus didn't bother to give him instructions. The Wolf winked out unceremoniously. "Good," snapped the Goose. "If there's one thing I can do without, it's bossy gods."

The Witch of Maracoor, why not. With her revived broom, her familiar. In her pocket, a seashell containing new life. Maybe she'd been made infertile by a brief encounter with the Fist of Mara, but she carried seed still. Also something she'd filched along the way. A small box covered in fur, containing a wicked pack of cards with potential for cartomancie, if she could figure out how it was done.

"Home?" she said to Iskinaary. "Do we dare?" The Goose didn't bother to nod; his opinion was evident. To Lucikles she added, "Have we done the right thing for Cossy, do you think?"

"A parent doesn't know, and never can. But we've tried." He flashed a wan smile at her. She nearly returned it. Together they looked west one last time. They could still make out Peritir and his clan, the ambassadors of the Oracle of Maracoor. The Arborians had begun to wade through sluggish currents.

Beyond them, staring east—but who knew where the Tower was, precisely, and what could now be seen from its top room?—Cossy and the Oracle of Maracoor stood together at the stone window-ledge. The old man had dropped his palsied hand upon the girl's shoulder. She put her own hand upon his. As much safety as either could count on, for the moment.

BY LATE AFTERNOON, Rain had begun to outpace the men, the boy, and the Goose. Her broom was over her shoulder, so that wasn't it. At first, she thought the valediction of Tesasi must be speeding her heels. Tesasi's blessing had been—that quality so unfamiliar in Rain's life—downright motherly. But Rain shook this notion out of her head as sentimental sap. It seemed more as if she was being spirited along by some lower-echelon fragments of spirit, maybe those acerbic and congenial harpies. The unseen wings of Moey and Asparine, perhaps, on one side of her and the other.

Blessings come in too many flavors to name, she decided, so who cares? Still, she felt less alone even while distancing herself. With whatever anonymous encouragement, she strode toward the indifferent horizon. However blistered or iron-cold it might turn out to be, she no longer wanted to sidestep whatever future might be on offer.

FINI

Volume Three of Another Day will be called
The Witch of Maracoor.